The
Country Village
Allotment

Cathy Lake is a women's fiction writer who lives with her family and three dogs in beautiful South Wales. She writes uplifting stories about strong women, family, friendship, love, community and overcoming obstacles.

Also by Cathy Lake:

The Country Village Winter Wedding
The Country Village Summer Fête
The Country Village Christmas Show

The Country Village Allotment

CATHY LAKE

ZAFFRE

First published in the UK in 2023 by
ZAFFRE
An imprint of Bonnier Books UK
4th Floor, Victoria House, Bloomsbury Square, London, England, WC1B 4DA
Owned by Bonnier Books
Sveavägen 56, Stockholm, Sweden

A CIP catalogue record for this book is
available from the British Library.

ISBN: 978-1-83877-606-0

Also available as an ebook and an audiobook

3 5 7 9 10 8 6 4 2

Typeset by IDSUK (Data Connection) Ltd
Printed and bound in Great Britain by Clays Ltd, Elcograf S.p.A.

Zaffre is an imprint of Bonnier Books UK
www.bonnierbooks.co.uk

To Yvonne, Valerie and Julie, thanks for the inspiration.
Wishing you many years of friendship and happy
times at the allotment.

Chapter 1

Heart racing, palms clammy, Liz Carter leaned against the closed door of the reprographics room. She scanned the space, leaning slightly to check behind the largest photocopier, but there was no one else around.

She was alone.

Thank goodness!

She sucked in a shaky breath and winced at the sharp scent of toner and the strangely savoury smell of warm paper that made her stomach churn. How Polly, the elderly reprographics woman, could stand to be in here all day was beyond Liz's comprehension. Just a few minutes in the small, hot room was enough to give her a headache. But, for now, she needed to be alone and it was the closest place to the head teacher's office she could run to before anyone else, be it member of staff or pupil, saw the tears streaming down her face or the steam pouring out of her ears.

Liz stepped away from the door and paced the length of the room, which wasn't very far considering it was small and most of it was taken up by machines that constantly clunked and whirred, but she needed to move so she could think. She'd just screamed in the face of Mr Brownlow, head teacher. And that was Mr Brownlow, BA, MSc, NPQH, to be precise. Screamed rather loudly, in fact, after he'd said something that she hadn't wanted to hear, and then slammed out of his room and darted into the reprographics room.

Was that a sackable offence? *Maybe.* Was it wrong? *Perhaps.* Would he understand if she explained why she was so worked up? It depended if Mr Brownlow's reaction to finding out that her fiancé was having an affair with his personal trainer – also their neighbour – stretched to compassion and empathy. He might be expected to feel some sympathy if she did explain. Although, of course, she didn't *want* to tell anyone what had happened because it would make it seem . . . real.

Gah!

Bloody Rhodri Langley and his decision to get fit and toned for their July wedding and subsequent honeymoon!

Bloody Pete Jenkins and his insanely large pecs, toned abs and vacancy for a new client.

If only Rhodri hadn't decided to employ Pete's services – with his special extras, it seemed – then none of this would have happened.

Would it not?

Liz raked her hands through her hair, realising that it felt quite greasy. When had she last washed it? *Saturday morning.* She should have washed it last night after her run but shampooing and conditioning her long, wavy ginger hair had been

2

the last thing on her mind. She usually ran for about an hour, listening to podcasts on her earphones about how to plan the perfect wedding and what foods to eat in order to conceive quickly, but yesterday, twenty minutes into her run, she'd got an agonising cramp in her left calf that lasted for all of ten minutes so she'd returned home early.

And found them . . .

A foul taste filled her mouth and she retched as the image of Rhodri and Pete filled her mind. She'd let herself into the home she shared with Rhodri, got herself a glass of water and two ibuprofen from the kitchen, then limped up the stairs, intent on running a bath and soaking the offending limb. But as she'd reached the top of the stairs, she'd heard a strange noise. Fear had gripped her as she'd wondered whether Rhodri was being attacked or if he'd fallen and hurt himself, and she'd hobbled to their bedroom doorway.

She gasped now as she had then, recalling how the glass of water had fallen from her hand and bounced on the plush cream carpet, its contents spilling over the thick pile and sitting there for a few seconds before slowly soaking in.

There had been nothing wrong with Rhodri. Oh no, far from it – he had been, it seemed, having a great time. For a weird moment she'd thought they were wrestling, that Pete had come round for an impromptu workout session, but then her mind had caught up and she'd realised what was actually happening. And she had to be honest, Rhodri had never, ever been so enthusiastic during lovemaking with her.

Liz had stood there, mouth open, heart beating so hard it felt as if it would burst from her chest. Then, as if in slow motion, Rhodri had looked up and his expression had changed from one of ecstasy to horror.

While the men had scrabbled to extricate themselves from each other, Liz had turned and limped down the stairs, shock wrapping itself around her like an icy blanket that made her limbs heavy and her thoughts foggy. She'd sunk onto the white two-seater loveseat with its flared arms, tufted back and nail-head trim, her whole body trembling, and then everything had gone blank.

She'd woken early this morning on the loveseat, neck stiff, injured leg still sore, in her running gear. Confusion had made her brain hazy and she'd wondered if it had all been a bad dream. She'd plodded upstairs, showered quickly and brushed her teeth, then dressed in the first things she grabbed from her wardrobe, gone outside to her car then driven to school. She hadn't seen Rhodri, didn't know if he'd left last night or early this morning, but his car hadn't been there so he'd left at some point.

Questions burned inside her on the drive to work but so did the urge to suppress everything and forget it had ever happened. It would be so much easier if she could just unsee it all . . .

Now, as she stared at the inspirational quotes someone had Blu-Tacked to the reprographics room wall, she began to question everything. Hadn't she sensed that something was wrong over recent weeks as their wedding got closer? In less than five months they were due to say their vows in the garden of a fancy local hotel while the warm breeze toyed with Liz's lace veil and guests gazed admiringly at her designer backless dress, dewy skin and sapphire satin Manolo Blahnik slingback pumps. She was meant to have the Wedding of the Year, to be admired by all of their guests, then to jet off to honeymoon in St Lucia. They'd booked two weeks at a luxury resort situated on an old coconut plantation on the northwest coastline, surrounded by palm trees and beautiful gardens. Liz had envisioned lying on couple-sized daybeds, positioned on the shimmering white sand of the beach, while the sheer fabric curtains fluttered in the balmy air. Her plan had been to post numerous photos to Instagram so everyone who saw them would be in awe of how wonderful her life was.

How wonderful her life was *not*!

As the reality of what had happened grew on her, Liz sank to the floor in front of the largest photocopier and clutched at her chest. Now it was all gone . . . because Rhodri had betrayed her. The credit card debt she'd amassed, making only minimum payments each month, no longer seemed worth it. The months of surviving on salad leaves and fresh air to look trim in a bikini had been pointless. The hours she'd spent pounding the local pavements listening to podcasts and indulging in daydreams of how she'd announce her pregnancy three months after returning from honeymoon, along with flashing a grainy scan photo, had been a waste.

Without Rhodri, there would be no wedding, no marriage and no babies. Her dream life was disintegrating and it was all his fault.

Wasn't it?

The thought that this was it and there was no going back was far too much to bear.

Her eyes rose again to the quotes on the wall, the Blu-Tack visible through the thin white paper. She scanned them all but her gaze kept returning to the middle one.

IN THE END, WE ONLY REGRET THE CHANCES WE *DIDN'T* TAKE

She said the words out loud, trying to understand them. 'But I *was* taking a chance. A chance on love.'

At the back of her mind, a small voice whispered, 'What about the chances you didn't take in the rest of your thirty-five years? The things you gave up for Rhodri? In pursuit of the perfect life that only exists in fairy tales . . .'

She waved the voice away. It was far too irritating to listen to, especially now.

Something touched her shoulder and she gasped but turned to find a sheet of paper had drifted from the full output tray. Something inside her snapped. Standing up, she reached for the rest of the warm sheets, pulled them from the tray, then threw them up in the air as fury boiled in her veins.

'That sodding Geography department!'

She growled as she stamped on the papers that had fallen to the floor, picking some up and tearing them to shreds then flinging them like misshapen confetti. Clearly, Geography had been hogging the machines again, which explained why it was taking so long to get photocopying done.

Turning, her gaze landed on the wonky tray of the smallest photocopier. Whenever the tray held more than a few sheets of paper, it fell off and had to be manoeuvred back on, which was a complete waste of time as it always fell off again. *Always!* Why keep trying to fix something that was so broken?

She swung her leg back and kicked the tray, experiencing a rush of joy as it flew off and smashed against the wall. She tried to ignore the instant throb in her toes that were encased in a black leather ankle boot that seemed to offer little protection. The times she'd imagined kicking the tray off but held back for fear of causing damage or being seen as a loose cannon were numerous, but Liz always maintained her self-control, had always been calm and composed in front of others. Appearances were important to her and essential in order to create the perfect life.

But today, quite frankly, Liz had had enough!

Zelda Grey shuffled through the hallway of her large Victorian house, avoiding the piles of books, plastic storage boxes and black bags of clothes and fabric, and entered the kitchen where she spent most of her time these days. Snuggled between the scullery and the study, the kitchen was warm and cosy and, on a chilly February day like today, sitting in her old armchair near the Aga was the best place to be.

She placed the copper-bottomed kettle on the stove plate then dropped a teabag into her Queen Elizabeth II coronation mug, hearing her mother's tut of disapproval as she did every time she made tea this way. Even though her mother had been dead for eighteen years, Ethel Grey's presence in the house, and in Zelda's memory, was strong. She had been a stickler for loose-leaf tea served in a bone-china cup and saucer, and had never taken to teabags or mugs – not even coronation mugs. Therefore, using teabags and a mug was still, Zelda mused, a small act of rebellion on her part, as if, even though her mother lay with Zelda's father in the graveyard of Little Bramble church, Zelda still felt the need to prove her independence.

Tea made, she added a splash of milk then picked up her mug and placed it on the small table at the side of her chair. It was dark in the kitchen this morning, despite it being gone ten. Late last night a terrible storm had set in; the rain had pelted the windows, making them rattle in their frames, while the wind had howled down the chimney and the sky was still grey, as if it had billions of tears left to shed.

Zelda sighed as she sat down and pulled the crocheted blanket off the back of her chair, settling it around her shoulders. She'd been out to check on the goats and chickens earlier, fed them all, then trudged back up to the house, leaving her battered yellow wellies by the back door. That was the thing with having animals: you couldn't leave them to fend for themselves; you *had* to go out in all weathers, which was bad enough when you were young, but at eighty-two, it felt much harder. At her age, she thought, the ideal pet was a cat, not three goats and ten chickens.

A cat . . .

From the corner of her eye, she saw the flick of a ginger tail as she often did, even when Flint wasn't on her mind. He'd been her companion for almost seventeen years. She'd adopted him from a woman in the village whose cat had a litter and Flint had been the scraggy runt. Zelda had brought him home and bathed him, wrapped him in a fluffy towel and cuddled him day and night, feeding him canned tuna and tiny pieces of roast chicken, nurturing him as though he was her own baby until he'd grown in strength and size. Flint had become her faithful sidekick, followed her everywhere, had even slept in her bed. It was another thing her mother would have frowned about. The old woman hadn't liked animals indoors, had said they belonged in the shed, the stable or the coop, and refused to entertain the idea of getting a dog or a cat. So it was only after she'd passed away that Zelda had been free to adopt a cat. Her mother had controlled her life in so many ways and only after she was gone could Zelda finally start to do things how she liked, despite the fact that she'd been an adult for decades before her mother was laid to rest.

Pressing a hand to her chest, she coughed in an attempt to clear away the grief that made it hurt to breathe. She missed that damned cat so much. Even when he'd lost his teeth, his vision had grown poor and his breath had become stinky, she'd still adored him. He might have been old but he'd still had value to Zelda and she'd been broken-hearted the morning she'd woken to find him gone. She knew she had to be thankful that he'd passed quietly in his sleep – and she was, because she'd have hated to see him suffer – but she did wish that it would hurry up and happen to her so she could join him.

Zelda reached for her tea and brought the mug to her mouth, but the handle slipped in her gloved hand, hot tea poured over her lap and the mug she'd had since 1953 – the last one of a set gifted to her by a family friend – fell to the tiles, where it smashed, pieces sliding off into dusty corners.

'That's it!' she muttered, pushing up to her feet as the skin of her thighs tingled from the tea and she threw the blanket from her shoulders. 'I have had enough.'

'There you go, my darling.' Mia Holmes placed a full cooked breakfast on the kitchen table in front of her youngest son, Joel.

'Thanks, Mum.' Joel smiled at her and her heart melted. He was such a handsome young man, and even though he had her brown hair and eyes, he reminded her a lot of his dad. 'I need this after that night shift.'

After finishing his shift late, something that often happened to Joel when he got stuck with a patient because he was too kind a soul to leave when his shift officially ended, he had come to Mia's for breakfast.

'Tough one, was it?'

While Joel ate and filled her in on the night's events, Mia made two mugs of tea and took them over to the table then sat opposite her son. She was so proud of him and his role as an NHS paramedic. He'd been a quiet and serious boy and she'd worried about him when he was in his teenaged years, fretted that he might not have the confidence to go to university or get a job. Then, at seventeen, he'd surprised her one day by telling her that he was going to join the local St John Ambulance division. It had brought him right out of his shell and helped him decide to become a paramedic. Now, at thirty-four, he was confident and assured, so different to the shy boy he'd once been. The only thing that worried Mia about Joel was that he hadn't found a partner yet. Not that he *had* to settle down, but she really wanted to see him happy and sometimes she worried about him being alone. She was aware that he'd never admit it, but thought he must get lonely sometimes. She certainly did.

'This is good,' he said, before taking a bite of buttered wholemeal toast.

Joel didn't live with Mia, hadn't done for some time, but he often popped in after a night shift for a cup of tea and Mia usually tried to feed him while he was there. One of her things as mum to three boys – or rather, men – was that she liked to cook for them and to listen to them talk about their jobs. It was only Joel she saw regularly, though, as Dane, four years older than Joel, lived in London with his wife, Debbie, and three sons, Bruce, Peter and Clark. An editorial director for a publishing house, Dane worked long hours. Her middle son, thirty-six-year-old accountant Stuart, had one daughter, Flo, and lived in Hereford with his horse-mad wife, Nikki. Stuart and Nikki owned a stables where Nikki worked, and Flo, who was in primary school, was also horse mad.

'Didn't you sleep well, Mum?' Joel asked as he put his fork down and reached for his tea.

'I had a few hours here and there.' Mia waved a hand as if it didn't matter. In all honesty, she'd been awake most of the night, kicking the duvet off when she got too hot then pulling it round her when she became cold. Rolling over and staring at Gideon's empty side of the bed always made her chest ache and she knew it would take time to adjust to her loss. It wasn't as if she didn't know what to expect because, after all, she'd been through it before.

'You look tired, Mum. Try to have a nap later on. You want me to check your BP while I'm here?'

Mia laughed but she reached up and touched the bags under her eyes, realising with horror that she'd have to pay extra for them if she was taking a flight. 'No, I do not. Just because you have the equipment and the know-how does not mean you have to check my vitals every time you come here.'

Joel nodded. 'I know, but I do worry about you. Are you eating properly? I don't see you having breakfast.'

Mia patted her stomach under her flannel pyjama bottoms. 'Believe me, Joel, I'm eating.' She sighed inwardly. Grief, like the menopause that had hung around for ten years, seemed to make her eat more not less. She knew some people lost weight on the so-called heartbreak diet, and looking back to when she'd lost the boys' dad, John Wiltshire, she had ended up like a twig, but then she'd had three young boys to run around after as well as her grief. With the school run for Dane and Stuart and entertaining two-year-old Joel through the days, she'd barely had a minute to think, let alone dwell. It was very different this time; she was alone and it gave her far too much time to grieve for what she'd lost and worry about the empty days, weeks, months and years that stretched ahead. She was only fifty-six, had become a mother at eighteen for the first time, and wondered how long she had left. If she was like her parents, not long, as they'd both died in their late fifties, but then, they'd been very heavy smokers and her dad had died of a heart attack, her mum of lung cancer. It was possible that she'd live to see her eighties or more if she stayed healthy – and the thought of that made her feel hollow inside.

'Are you getting out enough?' Joel tilted his head as he asked the question, his brown eyes filled with concern.

'Stop worrying about me, love. I'm fine.' Dismay filled her as the nature of his questions sank in. He was worried about her. She dropped her gaze to the red-and-white checked tablecloth then rubbed at a barely visible speck of food with a fingernail. 'I've plenty to keep me busy.'

And she did. For starters, she had Gideon's things to sort through. She'd been putting it off, knowing that packing up his clothes and belongings would make it all so final. It would be the end of an era she had loved. But it had to be done, so perhaps today would be the day she'd get round to it.

Or perhaps, after Joel went home to get some sleep before his next shift, well, then she might just cut herself a nice slice of the Victoria sponge she'd baked yesterday, make another mug of tea, and curl up in front of the TV and watch Netflix true crime all day . . .

'You want more tea?' She pushed her chair away from the table and stood up.

'That'd be great, Mum.' Joel handed her his mug, stifling a yawn with his hand. 'Then I'd best be heading to the flat to get some rest.'

'You better had, love. It's important to recharge your batteries.'

Mia filled the kettle and went about making tea, her mind already straying to Netflix and the true crime documentary she'd watched the previous day about the burglar who'd been stopped in his tracks by a ferocious black cat.

Mia didn't have a husband to keep her company. She didn't even have a cat. And although she'd never admit it to her beloved son, after losing two husbands, some days she simply felt that she'd had enough.

Chapter 2

'And here's your room.' Liz's sister, Nina Potts, opened the door to the spare room of her four-bed detached house and Liz followed her inside. 'What do you think?'

Liz looked around and swallowed hard. So this was what her life had come to – staying in her sister's spare room. It wasn't a bad room at all. In fact, it was light and airy and had a lovely view of Nina's back garden with its rectangle of grass, border of trees and small blue shed in the far-right corner. The bedroom had clean white walls and ceiling, a double bed with white sheets that Liz imagined would feel crisp and fresh against her skin, fitted wardrobes with mirrored sliding doors and an open door that led to a small en suite.

'You have your own shower, so you have some privacy and won't have to endure Kane's bathroom hogging in the mornings,' Nina laughed. 'And there are fresh towels in there on top of the washing basket.'

Liz opened and closed her mouth, trying to find the words to thank her sister. She should be grateful, of course she should, but something else was bubbling inside her as she looked around the flawless room. Nina had everything that Liz wanted, from the perfect husband who worked in finance in the City, to the perfect house in a beautiful village. And finally, the bit that made Liz's gut clench when she thought of their sweet faces in a professional photo Nina had sent her a few years ago, she had two perfect daughters.

Turning her gaze to Nina, she took in her sister's curvy figure in stretchy jeans and a navy-and-white striped Boden top; her freckly face was the same shape as Liz's, and her ginger hair the same colour. However, Nina's hair was cut and blow-dried into a neat bob, whereas Liz's was a wild mane unless she spent hours straightening it and taming it with serum and spray. Nina was a slightly older version of Liz, a slightly rounder version of Liz, and clearly a more contented version of Liz.

Liz felt so jealous she could have screamed.

Instead, she sucked in a deep breath and forced a smile to her lips. 'It's lovely. Thank you, Nina.'

'You can stay as long as you like.' Nina reached out and patted Liz's arm. 'We're very glad to have you here.' Then her face fell. 'Well, not *glad* exactly because, obviously, it's terrible that you felt you had to leave your home, but . . . you know . . . we're here for you.'

We . . .

Because Nina was part of a couple, married to a lovely man who would never dream of shagging the neighbour and ripping her life and her carefully planned future, to shreds.

'Great!' Liz realised she was still smiling manically as a ventriloquist's dummy, so she made an effort to relax her facial muscles and her grip on the handle of her suitcase. 'But, hopefully, I won't be here long. I'm sure he'll come to his senses and everything will be back on track soon.'

Nina's gaze slid away from Liz's face and she went to the window and straightened the blind. 'Is that what you want, Liz? I mean, I don't know the full story but it's obvious that he hurt you and, well . . . Do you definitely want to go back to him?' she asked without turning back.

Liz cleared her throat. Pushed a few strands of hair behind her ears. Licked her lips.

'Well, I-I mean, I . . . What else could possibly happen?'

When Nina turned to face her again, Liz saw that her sister's eyes were shining and that was more than she could bear. Pity was not what she wanted or needed right now. She was here to teach Rhodri a lesson, to give him time to think about what he'd done, to make him realise how much he missed her. In the meantime, she would be strong, enjoy a break from work and reset (the shame of having to ask the GP to sign her off for a few weeks because of what had happened in the head teacher's office and then in the reprographics room had made her cheeks burn and her armpits tingle), so that when Rhodri phoned and begged for her forgiveness, she'd be cool, calm and magnanimous. This was very important to her because she did not want to put on a repeat performance of what had happened that day in school. The deputy head, Doris Lynch, a quiet woman in her fifties – known for a passive-aggressive management style that made staff wonder if they were actually being reprimanded or instructed to do things – had found Liz in the reprographics room. After seeing the state of Liz and the room, Doris had gently led her to the staffroom, where she'd encouraged Liz to sit down then got her a glass of water. While Liz had stared at the pink lipstick mark on the rim of the glass that she suspected had been there for some time, Doris had suggested that it might be a good idea for Liz to go home and get some rest. Apparently, Mr Brownlow had expressed his concerns to Doris and asked her to find Liz and speak to her about her behaviour. Doris had lowered her voice when she'd said words like *Human Resources, Occupational Health and GP appointment*, and so Liz had silenced her with a retort about domestic difficulties made worse by high stress levels at work, then topped it off with a reference to her teaching union. The school was having difficulty retaining staff and had a high number of teachers and support staff on longterm sick leave, so Liz was well aware that the *S* word and the *U* word could strike fear into the hearts of senior management.

Soon after, Liz had stomped out of the school building, leaving the dirty glass on a table in the staffroom, the cloudy water untouched. She'd driven home, got into bed fully clothed and slept all afternoon. When Rhodri had returned just after five, she'd gone downstairs to see him and found him eating beans straight out of the can. Something about that had triggered her rage and she'd let rip, telling him how hurt she was and how much of an idiot he'd been, all the while staring at the bean juice staining the corners of his mouth. Rhodri had gawked at her as if she was mad, as if he had no idea why she was upset, then he'd made a hasty escape after telling her he hoped she'd be calmer when he returned.

But he hadn't come home for three days and when he had, Liz had become what she could only describe as a deranged harpy who'd thrown eggs at his head and emptied a bag of flour and a pint of milk over the keyboard of his laptop. When she'd finally run out of steam, she'd phoned Nina and sobbed incoherently to her about needing somewhere to go, then started packing her suitcase, grateful that her sister had insisted she come and stay. Early the next morning she put her suitcase in the car and drove to Nina's, singing along to Celine Dion's *Greatest Hits* all the way.

'I'll go and put the kettle on,' Nina said, blinking her big hazel eyes at Liz. 'Come down when you're ready.'

Liz gave a brief nod then closed the door and sank onto the bed. This had not been part of the plan at all.

Bloody Rhodri!

She covered her face with her hands and willed herself not to cry, because she knew that if she started, she might be unable to stop.

Goats and chickens fed, Zelda made her way back to the house. Her fingers ached from the cold and the chilly breeze pinched at her nose, making her eyes water. These early starts on winter mornings were not easy for a woman of her age but then, when she thought back, they'd never been easy. However, she'd always got up early and completed her chores before breakfast because she liked to get things done.

Her mother had been the same and Zelda believed it was a generational thing. These days, there was so much reliance upon virtual worlds that could be accessed from mobile phones and other screens, but in Zelda's day, the real world had always been right there, waiting for attention. There had been animals to feed, grass to mow, windows to clean and clothes to wash. It was so different now with electronic devices to do just about everything from washing to cooking to counting to teaching you foreign languages. Quite frankly, Zelda thought it was insane and it was one of the reasons why she kept to herself. She had no desire to become a part of a world where interaction was done via screens and where people sat on their backsides all day and ordered their food in. She knew about all this because she watched TV sometimes, saw such things on *EastEnders* and other soaps, listened to postman Marcellus moan when he delivered her post and, occasionally, when she wandered down to Little Bramble to the shops, she saw people walking along with their eyes glued to screens, white buds blocking their ears and faces pale from time indoors. They seemed to get sustenance from their devices in the way people used to from food and drink and it baffled her, made her feel like a relic of a past that was long gone.

That thought made her chuckle: Zelda the relic, an artefact that would one day be stared at in museums like the body in the marsh or some such item. Perhaps they'd reconstruct her kitchen as was sometimes done in museums, along with her comfy chair and weathered table, and they'd have her preserved in some way – or a waxwork of her made – and people would shake their heads as they mused about how people used to live.

When did she get so old? It felt like yesterday that she was just eighteen, filled with excitement about life and anticipating a future filled with love, laughter and adventures.

Zelda knew she was living in a world that had no place for her now, and the fact that the only person to ever come to her door these days was the postman was all the proof she needed of that.

Five black bags and three cardboard boxes now took up the floor space of Mia's bedroom. Each one contained some of Gideon's things. A life dismantled by the separating of clothes – smart, smart casual and scruffs, the latter the hardest to part with because they were the ones he'd worn most often and the ones that couldn't be saved – the sorting of things he'd collected over the years and the emptying of the drawers of his bedside cabinet. It was awful, agonising, and she found herself dissociating from her actions as if she was watching someone else do it all. That had helped, a bit, and she'd been fine until she'd found the shoebox of sentimental stuff when going through his shoes.

She'd slumped onto the bed and emptied the box onto the patchwork cover, stared at it for a moment wondering if she had the strength to go through it or if she needed to put it all back in the box and bury it at the back of the wardrobe. A bit like she'd done with her grief. Taking that and tucking it away had got her through the funeral and the burial, had kept her going through those first dreadful weeks where she felt as though her head was full of cotton wool. She'd only let it out when she was alone and able to howl into her pillow, to cry without worrying about having swollen eyes and a hoarse voice. And even then she let it build up for a few days first because letting go was so hard – and she sometimes worried that she wouldn't be able to drag herself back from the brink once she started down that route.

But she always came back, clawed her way back to sanity by blowing her nose and dabbing at her swollen eyes, by making a cup of tea and sitting at the kitchen table, pressing her palms to the wood and letting it ground her. Life went on, even when people died, and until it was her time, so would she, hard as it might be, painful as it might be. Mia had children and grandchildren, bills to pay and a home to run. She had to keep going, because if she gave up, what did that do to her loved ones? Her suffering was something she had to endure. There was also Gideon; she knew he'd have wanted her to keep going. He'd loved and adored her, had wanted the best for her, and if he'd thought for a moment that she wasn't getting on with things then she knew he'd have been devastated. His final comfort was knowing that Mia would still live, still be there for her family, remember him and the love they'd shared.

She touched a hand to her chest in the way Gideon used to do. He placed his hand there at the base of her throat to feel her breathing, said it comforted him and that he loved that part of her, how soft and warm the skin was, how he could feel the vibrations of her laughter there and see the flush of arousal after they'd made love. Mia knew her boys would be horrified at the thought that their mother had enjoyed a good love life with Gideon – because who wanted to think of their mum like that? – but she had. Gideon had been a friend first, lover later. They'd met through a mutual acquaintance and become friends, then, years later, suddenly looked at each other differently and realised they were in love.

When he became ill and knew he wouldn't get better, Gideon had told Mia to move on and find someone else when he was gone, that at fifty-six she was young and beautiful and entitled to fall in love again. Mia wasn't so sure. She'd loved two men in her lifetime and loved them deeply, then she'd lost them both. Wasn't that enough for any woman? Besides which, she wasn't sure she would ever be brave enough to face the prospect of another loss.

Losing two husbands was enough for one lifetime, surely?

Chapter 3

'Feel any better now?' Nina asked as she sat across the kitchen table from Liz.

Liz drained her mug then set it on the table. 'Much. A cup of tea solves all problems, right?'

Nina smiled. 'Perhaps not solves, rather . . . buys you some breathing space.'

Liz gave a brief nod. Perhaps her sister had a better understanding of what she was feeling than she'd given her credit for, even though she hadn't yet told her the details. Not that Nina had any *experience* of how it felt to find your fiancé in bed with his personal trainer, or how it felt to yearn to get things back to the way they were, but she might just have a tiny bit of empathy for Liz if she knew the full story. As it was, she was being very kind and Liz was grateful.

'What time do the girls get home?' Liz asked, looking at the kitchen clock. It was just gone eleven. She'd been up early to drive from Maidstone, had packed the night before and gone to bed hoping to lose herself in the oblivion of sleep, but found that she spent most of the night tossing and turning.

Breakfast had consisted of three strong coffees and a slice of toast that she'd picked at, her appetite not being back to normal since her horrid discovery.

'Demi won't be back until around five because she has revision after school, but I'll pick Cora up at three fifteen.'

'How are they both?' Liz realised she hadn't asked about her nieces since her arrival. She did stay in touch with Nina via text and a monthly phone call, as well as on Facebook – when she could be bothered to go on there, that was. Since pupils at school had pelted teachers with friend requests a few years back, she'd been reluctant to use the platform much and so only signed into her account now and then. Nina shared memes and competitions on there but not many photos of her family, once telling Liz that she didn't like to share too much because once something was on the internet, you couldn't get it back and she didn't like to do that to her daughters. It suddenly hit Liz like a bucket of cold water over her head that she didn't have a clear image what the girls looked like now. The version of them she had in her head was of a sweet eleven-year-old girl with her ginger hair in plaits, a spattering of freckles over her nose and a baby in a frilly dress and bootees. Had it really been that long since she'd seen them? She'd met up with Nina for lunch a few times but since she'd got together with Rhodri four years ago, that had lapsed into . . . once a year? A sinking feeling in her stomach made her feel queasy.

'They're good. Excited to see you.'

Liz doubted that. Why would they be excited about seeing an aunt they barely knew? Demi probably wouldn't remember Liz very well at all and Cora had been a babe in arms so would have no memory of her aunt. Had Liz been so busy trying to create her own perfect family that she'd neglected her sister and her nieces in the meantime? It certainly seemed that way. But then she had been trying to build her own life and so her behaviour was perfectly justified. *Right?*

Liz reached up and pulled at the neckline of her jumper. It suddenly felt restrictive and itchy.

'Why don't we go for a walk?' Nina took their mugs to the dishwasher then placed them inside. 'I can show you around the village and you can get your bearings.'

'A walk?'

'You haven't been to Little Bramble for a while and it's gorgeous here.'

For a while . . .

Liz hadn't ever had a grand tour of the village because in the past, when she had come here, she'd come for a spot of lunch and a brief visit then jetted off again. Nina and Kane used to live in a small cottage that they were renting, and Liz had tried to tell herself she was glad she wasn't stuck in a small Surrey village like they were, but the reality of it had been that she'd longed for that kind of cosy domesticity. That longing had driven her to stay away because she couldn't bear to see her sister living the life *she* wanted. Instead, she'd studied at university, gaining a first-class honours in History followed by a Masters in the Tudor period, and finally, a PGCE in secondary education. She had thought to inspire pupils with her knowledge of history and her love of all things Tudor, but it turned out that teenagers weren't always interested in what had happened in the past, preferring to focus on the latest celebrity drama, *Love Island* and TikTok craze. There were some pupils who enjoyed her subject, who paid attention, of course there were, but there were more who spent the lessons with their mobiles under the desks as they scrolled social media for the next big thing. Somewhat disheartened, Liz had decided to follow the pastoral route instead of applying to be a curriculum team leader, and had been a head of year for the past few years. She liked the role, liked how she could help pupils and get to know them better, but she'd still dreamt of getting married, having a family and leaving the world of work behind. At least, that was what she'd thought she wanted, although she did wonder sometimes if she'd be happy at home full-time when, eventually, the children she intended on having were at school. What did Nina do all day? She guessed she'd soon find out.

'Sure,' she said now, 'a walk would be good.'

Ten minutes later, wrapped up in coats, gloves and hats, they walked out onto the street outside Nina's home. The air was icy and their breath blew out like puffs of steam that drifted away on the breeze.

'I'll take you through the village this time, but another day I'll show you the woodland walk. We have the best of both worlds in Little Bramble, I think, with a gorgeous village, a rural feel with plenty of fields and trees nearby *and* we're not far from London.'

As they walked, Nina pointed out local landmarks like the park, playing fields and primary school where Cora went. It was a three-minute walk from their home, which Liz knew made Nina very lucky. She could roll out of bed in the mornings and get Cora to school on time with ease. Of course, she knew that Nina probably did no such thing and would be up at dawn making pancakes while birds sang at her window and mice in cute dresses and hats held up her petticoats like some kind of Disney fantasy.

'What's funny?' Nina asked, her eyebrows raised in question.

'Sorry?'

'You chuckled.'

'Did I?' Had she just laughed out loud? 'Just enjoying how lovely it is here.'

Nina smiled but she looked a bit confused, as if she was concerned about Liz's state of mind.

They passed a row of cottages to their right and a pub called The King's Arms to their left and then they were in the centre of the village with the green, a bistro, café and village hall up ahead.

The trees surrounding the green were bare, their branches stretching towards the grey sky like gnarled fingers, but at the centre was a large evergreen. It was still adorned with Christmas lights and more dangled from signs and lamp posts, remnants of the festive season. Liz wondered what it would be like to spend Christmas in Little Bramble, if it would be cosy and happy, a time of community joy as friends and family gathered together. Her Christmas with Rhodri had been strained, not their usual extravagant affair with delicious food from M&S and Waitrose, a Christmas Eve of sipping champagne in the bath, then a Christmas Day breakfast of caviar, smoked salmon and Buck's Fizz before hours of lazy lovemaking and a dinner they made together. The thought stopped her in her tracks and she feigned searching for a tissue in her bag so Nina wouldn't wonder what was wrong. Had they ever actually done that or had it been on an advert or romantic Christmas movie and she'd claimed the scene for herself? Sometimes she knew she was guilty of recreating her memories as a way of protecting herself. Instead of a happy holiday, Christmas had involved some rather disappointing gifts from Rhodri then him disappearing next door to get something. He'd been gone for over an hour and she'd tried to busy herself by sorting the wrapping paper into the recycling and finishing the champagne, by starting a new book she'd bought herself then running a bath, but she'd felt uneasy, as if something wasn't quite right. Now she thought about it, that had happened more than once over the course of the holidays, but she hadn't thought to question Rhodri about it because their neighbour was, after all, a mutual friend and a man. She'd put it down to Rhodri needing a male friend as their wedding got closer and to the fact that their neighbour, Pete, seemed a bit lonely, a touch needy, even. If only she'd known the truth!

Just past the village hall was another pub, The Red Squirrel, then a row of shops that curved around the green like a protective arm. There was a grocer, butcher, sweet shop, baker, charity shop and hair salon. It was like stepping back in time as all the shops seemed independently owned and not the chain stores that she was used to seeing.

'It *is* a lovely village,' Liz said, warming to it in spite of the fact that she didn't really want to. It wasn't that she didn't want Nina to be happy, because she did, but just sometimes she didn't want her to be *too* happy. It didn't seem fair that, out of the two of them, her older sister had landed on her feet and got the family Liz had always craved. And without even trying, Liz suspected, unless getting pregnant to get a man to marry you was trying. She was convinced that was what Nina had done, falling pregnant within weeks of meeting Kane and being able to quit her shop job to be a full-time wife and mum. Liz thought it wasn't very feminist to want to give up a career and independence to make a home, but Nina had done it and Liz knew why. It was the same reason she had wanted to do it; to create the childhood they'd lacked and both had wished for growing up. They'd spoken about it often enough as children, shared secret dreams of marrying a prince and creating a happy family life with him then living happily ever after. As Liz had got older, that dream had become a visceral need, driving her through a series of unsuccessful relationships with men chosen for their marital suitability rather than because of her love for them and theirs for her. The men she'd dated in her twenties and at the start of her thirties hadn't stuck around long and she suspected that her desperation to marry and procreate had oozed from every pore and made them run for the hills. But they didn't understand *why* she craved the stability of a family life and, even if she had explained it to them, she doubted they'd have got it. Instead, she'd played games to appear to be nonchalant about dating, had shrugged when they'd told her of planned weekends away with the boys and coffee with ex-girlfriends, had acted as if none of it mattered to her, had insisted she was *cool* with anything. Inside, though, she had secretly seethed as yet another relationship broke down and the prince in question transformed into yet another toad. For Liz, it seemed, there wasn't a knight in shining armour to rescue her damsel heart – again, not a feminist thought, because women were meant to be their own protectors these days, but even so she craved stability and romance, to have someone of her own to love. And so she'd kept on going, her career had been strong and she'd had money in her savings account. She was, despite her childhood – or because of it, she sometimes thought – strong and independent. And then, when she least expected it to happen, she'd met Rhodri.

'Shall we grab a coffee?' Nina gestured back the way they'd come. 'Or the café does takeout so we could take them on the woodland walk if you fancy doing it today.'

But Liz had frozen because there, in front of her, was the village church. A low stone wall surrounded the building and grounds with a Victorian lychgate at its centre. Gravestones dotted the churchyard for as far as she could see and, on the church roof, a shingle-clad spire pointed to the sky. For a history buff like Liz, it was like coming across a pot of ancient gold coins.

'That must date back to what . . . the twelfth century or thereabouts?'

Nina laughed. 'I have no idea but I'm sure we can find out.'

'Why is it surrounded by scaffolding?'

'It's going through some repairs. Last year there was some water damage following a few slipped roof tiles, so specialists have been called in to deal with it.'

'What a shame. I'd have loved a look inside.'

'It is a shame, but hopefully it'll be fixed soon. There is, however, an old yew tree in the far corner of the churchyard that some say is around 3000 years old. Legend even has it that the tree can cure fertility issues.'

Liz looked at her sister as if seeing her properly for the first time since she'd arrived. 'You knew I'd be fascinated by this, didn't you?'

'Liz, you're my baby sister. I grew up with you, listened to you talk about Henry VIII and Anne Boleyn as if you knew them personally, sat next to you while you read every book you could find about them in the library and traipsed around old churches and buildings on day trips. Of course I knew you'd like the old church!'

Something tingled in Liz's chest. It was vaguely familiar but she hadn't felt it in a long time. It made her think of sunny Sunday mornings with Nina in their small back garden in Tonbridge when they'd take their bowls of Rice Krispies and glasses of orange squash outside and sit on a tatty navy nylon sleeping bag with a broken zip laid out on the grass. They'd talk about their mum and how they missed her, about what they'd loved about her and how one day they'd tell their own children about her. Their dad, Jeff, would be sleeping off his hangover from the previous night or not home yet if he'd been playing at a gig too far to get a ride home. Now, the thought of leaving two such young children home alone would be scorned, but back then, no one had seemed to notice and the girls certainly hadn't drawn attention to the fact that they were often without adult supervision. Besides which, Nina had always been so mature and capable and Liz had learned from her. They'd used the money their dad left for them to buy groceries and Nina had organised their home, washing and ironing, baking and making their budget stretch while saving pennies for what she called 'a rainy day'. Their dad had been kind when around and sober, had brought them fish and chips, glass bottles of Cherryade and tubs of chocolate-chip ice cream, had sometimes taken them on trips to the cinema and the park, but more often than not, and certainly more often as they got older, he'd been absent from their days. Nina had told Liz that it wasn't his fault, that he'd been broken by losing their mum to ovarian cancer when Liz was just ten and Nina thirteen. Nina had said that playing in the band was his escape from his grief, that nights out with his friends helped him forget, but Liz had found it hard to accept how he'd all but abandoned her and Nina, had found Nina's apparent acceptance of it even harder to digest. Part of her had blamed Nina, only three years older than she was, for accepting it as she did. If Nina had made their dad realise that they needed him around more, then he might have been there for them, been the rock they needed in their lives. It had been easier to blame Nina back then because she was the only one there. Liz could see that now, but it was still hard to admit, even to herself. Nina had basically raised Liz and herself and she'd taken on the parental role along with the challenges it brought.

'Do you want to take a look around the grounds?' Nina pointed at the churchyard.

'OK.' Something made Liz reach for her sister and she slipped her arm through Nina's. Nina's eyes widened slightly but then she squeezed Liz's hand and Liz felt that strange tingling in her chest again. Nina was a warm, caring person and for far too long, Liz knew, she'd pushed her away for reasons that were almost too complicated to try to unravel.

But as they walked over to the lychgate and let themselves through, Liz had a sense that something was about to change. She just hoped it was for the better.

Zelda opened her front door and smiled at the postman, Marcellus David. He'd been delivering her post for years and she'd always found him very pleasant and amenable.

'Good morning there, Miss Grey. How're you today?' His Caribbean lilt was as strong as ever, despite him having been the village postman for around three decades.

'Not bad, thanks, Marcellus – the right side of the earth, as they say.'

'I agree, better this side than the other.' Marcellus chuckled at their exchange as he always did. 'Now, let's see what we have for you.'

While Marcellus pulled several envelopes from his trolley, that Zelda knew would be bank statements, pet insurance reminders, optician special offers and cremation plan quotes, she looked behind her at the clock in the hallway. It was gone eleven, but her house was on the outskirts of the village and by the time Marcellus had delivered the post to the rest of Little Bramble, then walked up to her home, it was usually past eleven; she didn't mind because it meant that she got a chance to speak to one of the very few people who ever knocked on her door. These days, even exchanging pleasantries with the postman was something to look forward to. It was as though Marcellus knew this, because he always knocked on her door even though he could simply have slipped her post through the letter box. Sometimes, she suspected that he even put some junk mail aside so he'd have an excuse to come to her home so he could check on her.

'Lookie here, we have a parcel for you too.' He waved a small box in the air and Zelda's heart gave a small flutter. *A parcel!* Whatever could it be? Then, as she accepted the box, something occurred to her . . . it was probably a repeat delivery of multivitamins.

'What's the date, then?' Marcellus frowned. 'It's not your repeat prescription, is it?'

'It's the ninth, so I don't think it's my prescription, more likely my vitamins,' she replied, wondering why that date rang a bell. 'Oh . . .'

'You all right there?'

'Yes. Fine. Just realised it's Mother's birthday.'

'And she'd be a grand old age then?'

'Yes, she'd be 103 today.' Zelda's hand went to her mouth as the enormity of that age hit her. 'Goodness, 103!'

'An age we'd all be lucky to see.' Marcellus gave a small nod. 'Likely you will see it too, Miss Zelda. You're as fit as a fiddle.'

'Ha! I wish.' She shook her head. 'Thanks, Marcellus. I'll see you tomorrow.'

'You will indeed.' He tapped the side of his cap at her, gave her a cheeky grin then turned and wheeled his trolley down the garden and out through the gate. Zelda watched him go, grateful for his kindness and consideration.

'Right then, Mother, I'd better get dressed and head into Little Bramble,' she said aloud. 'I can't believe I forgot it's your birthday, but don't worry, I'm on my way.'

She closed the door behind her then headed for the kitchen, glad to have a reason to break from her usual routine, even if it was to lay flowers at her mother's grave.

In the village shop, Mia dropped a bar of chocolate into her basket, then reached for another.

'Baking or spoiling those strapping sons of yours?'

She turned to find Kyle Greene standing behind her, laughter filling his emerald eyes, his dark brows raised.

'Oh, hello, Kyle.' Colour rushed into her cheeks as she realised her basket contained more chocolate than anything else. How many bars had she put in it, exactly? 'More comfort eating than anything else.' Self-conscious now, she started removing chocolate bars and returning them to the shelves.

'Don't put them back on my account,' he said. 'A little of what you fancy does you good. Anyway . . . How're you doing?' Kyle asked, his voice softer, and she felt tears pricking at her eyes.

'I'm . . . I'm OK.' She closed her eyes for a moment and breathed slowly, not wanting to have a meltdown in the village grocery shop.

'You know,' Kyle placed a hand on her arm and she opened her eyes to look up at him, 'chocolate is good for sure, but other things can help too. Why don't you think about coming to one of my tai chi classes? They're good fun, good for your mental health – and I'd love to see you there.'

Mia knew that Kyle had run classes at the village hall since not long after his arrival in the village the Christmas before last, but had never attended one. She'd always blamed being busy and having many other commitments, but what excuse did she have now? And he might be right, making a date to do some exercise might do her good. It certainly wouldn't do her any harm, anyway.

'I'll do that, Kyle, thank you. How're you doing, anyway?'

Kyle had been a whirlwind in the village since he'd followed his mum there. Clare Greene, now Wilson, had arrived in Little Bramble the winter before last and Kyle had come soon after. They'd both stayed with Clare's mother, Elaine Hughes, for a while but then Clare had fallen in love with village vet, Sam Wilson, and in December they'd got married in a beautiful ceremony at the green. Mia hadn't attended, despite being invited, as she'd been too immersed in her grief to move far from home, but she'd seen photos of the wedding on the village Facebook page and it had been lovely.

'All good, thanks. Just between us, I'm going to be investing as a partner in Country Charm Weddings with Hazel. Dad gave me some money for Christmas and I had so much fun at Mum and Sam's wedding that I think this could be the right direction for me.'

'That sounds very exciting.' Mia smiled at Kyle's obvious excitement. Hazel Campbell had come to Little Bramble last year and set up her wedding planning business, then arranged Clare and Sam's wedding. Mia knew that Kyle and Hazel had become good friends because she'd seen them around together, and with Kyle's effervescent personality she felt sure that he'd make a fantastic wedding planner. 'You'll be just perfect.'

'Hope so.' He gave a little clap of his hands and flashed her a dazzling smile. 'But as I said, come and join us in tai chi and, if you ever want a coffee and a chat, I'm around, as are Mum and Nanna and others. We have a great little community and we're all here for you, Mia. I can't begin to imagine how you're feeling but I'm a good listener and if there's anything I can do, don't hesitate to ask.'

'You're a remarkable young man, Kyle.' Mia squeezed his hand. 'Thank you so much.'

'Don't forget about tai chi!' He kissed her cheek then sashayed away along the aisle, leaving behind a waft of expensive aftershave and a rather emotional Mia.

Kyle was in his early twenties at most and yet he displayed an understanding and maturity beyond his years. Mia could definitely benefit from spending more time around him, so she'd make certain to attend one of his classes. Didn't they say that being active could help in many ways? Plus, making a date with a regular exercise class would get her out of the house and into a new routine.

She turned back to the shelf and resumed browsing, wondering if chocolate flapjacks would be a healthier option to snack on because they contained oats but would still provide the comforting chocolate hit she craved. She'd have preferred a hug from Gideon any day of the week but that couldn't be so she'd have to find something else to comfort her instead.

Chapter 4

Liz and Nina stood in front of the ancient yew tree and goosebumps rose on Liz's arms. 'Wow! Just . . . Wow!'

'Pretty cool, huh?' Nina grinned at Liz. 'I knew you'd think so.'

Liz peered up at the tree, taking in its size and shape. Its branches spread out like twisted arms to create a broad crown and the green needle-like leaves had a waxy appearance. The fluted trunk was covered with a reddish-brown bark that flaked away in places, exposing lighter patches.

'You could just crawl inside and live there.' Liz giggled at the thought of hiding inside the tree like some kind of wood nymph and never having to deal with reality again.

'And not have to pay Council Tax or extortionate energy bills.'

'Exactly!' Liz caught herself mid grin. Moaning about council tax and energy bills had been one of Rhodri's favourite pastimes. He'd follow her around the house turning off lights and plugs, turning the thermostat down and tutting when he saw how much water she'd run in the bath.

'What is it?' Nina stepped closer. 'You look so sad.'

'Oh, you know . . .'

'Rhodri the renegade?'

'Recreant, more like. And more . . . He really was ridiculous sometimes.'

'Oh, love.' Nina hugged Liz with one arm and Liz tried to relax into her sister's warmth. It didn't come easily after years of feeling that her sister had bested her in so many ways, but it was also, she was forced to admit, a little bit nice to be hugged and to have someone to care.

Knowing what she did about Rhodri and how deceitful he could be, she wondered if he'd tell the people they knew, like their mutual colleagues, some lies about her, make her look like the one in the wrong when he'd been the one who'd cheated. She hoped not, because it would make her return to their shared life even more awkward. Hopefully, he'd keep what had happened to himself. As for friends he might tell – well, not that there had been any really close ones, but those she did have she'd let slip from her life when she'd embroiled herself in her romance with Rhodri. She'd done the same with her friends as with Nina, their closeness fading with each disastrous relationship, letting each man become the centre of her world and look where that had got her. What an idiot she'd been!

'Ridiculous, ratty Rhodri!' Nina wrinkled her nose. 'Although . . .'

'What?'

'Well, I know he upset you and you seem very hurt but . . . I don't know why. You haven't really explained what went wrong.'

Liz felt the surge of sadness and shame rising and covered her eyes with her hands. At the moment, the only people who knew about what had happened were Liz, Rhodri and Pete – unless they'd told anyone about it, of course. If she told Nina, that would change. It might make it harder to go back to Rhodri; it might make it real. And yet the secret was churning around inside her, making her stomach clench and her heart race. She feared that if she didn't tell at least one person then it would continue to bubble like a gassy potion until she exploded. Or it would eat away at her like rust on iron and cause its own combustion reaction.

'It's . . . it's the shame of it all, Nina. It's so embarrassing. There I was, boasting about my wonderful wedding, my beautiful, expensive dress, trying to decide on w-which cake to get and there he was, sh-shagging his personal trainer!'

'Oh God!' Nina shook her head. 'I'm so sorry. What an arsehole! Was she . . . attractive?'

Liz lowered her hands and met Nina's eyes. 'Not *she* . . . His personal trainer is Pete Jenkins. Our neighbour.'

Saying it out loud made Liz feel wobbly. It was like betraying everything she'd had with Rhodri, like admitting that their relationship was some kind of sham. Now she'd told Nina, could she still go back to him? Could she still have the life she'd wanted?

Nina took one of Liz's hands but she didn't say anything. She just held on tight.

'And yes, in answer to your question, Pete is very attractive. He's hot, toned, confident, sexy and . . . and now he has my fiancé! Or at least, he did have him . . . *in my bed*! Oh Nina, I just want my life back! I don't want all this fear and uncertainty and pain and anguish. All I've ever wanted was to feel safe and secure.'

Liz staggered forwards and when Nina caught her in a hug, she sobbed into her sister's coat while holding on as if her life depended on it.

After she'd placed the bunch of flowers against the headstone, Zelda bowed her head. 'Dearest Mother, sorry I'm a bit late getting here. And hello, Father.'

A cold breeze ruffled the cellophane wrapped around the flowers and Zelda knew that she should probably remove them from the wrapping and put them into the pots of the headstone, but her fingers were so cold they ached and she suspected that the flowers would probably wilt quickly anyway, so instead she left them as they were.

'And . . . happy birthday.' Zelda pictured her mother's face, her expression seemingly one of perpetual disapproval that puckered her mouth and caused deep grooves in her forehead and it made her smile. For all her mother's grumpiness, inclination towards seeing the worst in every situation and pessimistic demeanour, Zelda had loved her. She had loved her very much despite everything that had happened and had often missed her over the past eighteen years. Not always, but sometimes, because it could be lonely living alone.

Zelda blew a kiss to the headstone then looked around. Winter still held Little Bramble in its firm grip even though spring was just around the corner. Trees were bare of leaves, planters appeared empty – although she knew that bulbs would be just beneath the surface – and the ground was hard with frost. The church itself was surrounded by scaffolding, as if it too needed help staying upright in what felt like a very long winter. Usually, Zelda would have gone inside the church and lit three candles, one for Father, one for Mother and one for . . . well, a third one for what might have been. But the church was currently closed, deemed unsafe until repairs had been made and so, for now, Zelda would have to content herself with leaving flowers and what often felt like a piece of her heart in the churchyard. But there was one grave she wouldn't visit today and that was because she feared breaking down if she ventured near it. In fact, she rarely visited it because the pain was still too great to bear.

She turned and made her way across the grass, feeling tired after her walk down to the village and craving a hot cup of tea. She could go to the café and get one, she supposed, but she'd just have a sit down on the bench at the side of the path first because her knees were throbbing and she felt a little breathless. A bit dizzy. Rather worn out.

Just a little rest . . .

Mia sat on the bench and placed the two takeaway cups of tea next to her. Goodness it was cold and she was in two minds about sitting down in case she froze but she wanted to take a moment to sit close to her husbands. Well, as close as she could get to them both and the bench was midway between their graves. John had passed away thirty-two years ago, so lay in an older section of the churchyard, while Gideon was laid to rest in a fresher plot, having only passed in November. She'd brought two teas out of habit; she always brought one for her husbands and after she'd drunk hers, she'd go and pour a bit over each grave. It was a thing she did; sharing a cuppa with her husbands as if they were still here. Though what John would have thought about it, she had no idea. He'd probably have reprimanded her for wasting good tea, then chased her around the house to tickle her until she promised she'd never do it again.

Oh John . . . How could it be over thirty years since she'd last seen him? He'd been her first love, the father of her three boys, just a young man of twenty-five when he'd died suddenly in his sleep. He hadn't been ill, had been seemingly fit and healthy, but one night they'd gone to bed and when Mia had woken in the morning, she'd been unable to wake him. Her world and her outlook on life had changed overnight. It was as if her innocence had been torn away from her with one traumatic event.

Looking up, she saw an elderly lady ambling towards her. Well, she thought it was an elderly lady because of the size and stance but the person was wrapped up in so many layers, it was difficult to tell. When she reached the bench, the woman looked up and met Mia's eyes.

'Oh . . . uh . . . Do you mind if I sit down?'

'Of course not.' Mia shuffled over, taking the two teas with her, and the woman slumped onto the bench. 'It's cold, mind.'

The woman chuckled. 'I have two pairs of thermal knickers on and a long vest underneath my outer layers so my bottom should be safe from frostbite.'

Mia smiled. Something about the woman was familiar and then she realised who it was. 'I'm sorry . . . are you . . .?'

'Zelda Grey.'

'Yes! I thought so. I haven't seen you around in . . . quite some time.' She swallowed the comment *ages*, not wanting to cause offence. But she hadn't seen Zelda in a *very* long time. Hadn't, she now realised, so much as thought about the elderly resident of Little Bramble in months. And here she was, quite frail-looking and in such chilly conditions too.

'I think the last time I saw you, Mia Holmes, was up at the allotment.' Zelda peered at Mia from behind silver-framed glasses, her bushy white eyebrows just visible underneath her woolly green bobble hat.

'I think you're right. How are you?' Mia asked, keen to move the subject on from the allotment in case Zelda asked about Gideon. The allotment had been his project and although Mia had accompanied him there from time to time, she hadn't spent as much time there as him – until last autumn, that was.

In fact, she hadn't thought about the allotment much since last year and now that she did, she wondered what would happen to it. Would she have to give it up because it had been in her husband's name?

'I'm rattling around, same as always.' Zelda cracked a grin, exposing tea-stained teeth. Suddenly she shuddered violently.

'Are you all right?' Mia turned to face her properly.

'It's just colder than I anticipated. Either that or I'm getting so old that the cold seeps through to my bones quicker. Still, it's chillier in that earth, right?'

Mia gasped then pressed her lips together.

'Oh, I'm so sorry, Mia. I wasn't thinking. My sense of humour takes some getting used to, I have to admit. You lost your husband, didn't you?'

'I did,' Mia sighed.

'That must be very difficult for you.'

'Yes.'

'I'm so sorry for your loss.' Zelda looked around. 'Isn't he back there in the older grav— I mean *section*, though?'

It dawned on Mia that Zelda didn't know about Gideon.

'Uh, Zelda . . . You're thinking of John. But I-I lost Gideon back in November.'

'Gideon?' Zelda visibly started. 'That big, strong chap of yours? But he was built like a bull. Strong as an ox.'

'That's him.' Mia took a sip of tea, swallowed it down with her pain.

'Dear heart, apologies for the animal comparisons. I was just so shocked. But I am terribly, terribly sorry. I had no idea. Being up there at my house, I don't always hear the local news and rely mostly on Marcellus for gossip. Perhaps he didn't tell me because he didn't want to upset me. He often does that, you know, tries to protect me from sad news and this is *incredibly* sad news. Gideon was awfully young, though?'

'Fifty-eight.'

'What . . . Do you mind me asking, what happened? Because I saw him a lot last year at the allotment.'

'He had pancreatic cancer. He wasn't well last autumn but kept going to the allotment as often as he could because it made him feel normal, even when he couldn't do much else. He didn't want the cancer to change him even though . . . obviously . . . physically it took its toll.'

'I'm devastated to hear this news.' Zelda hung her head. 'Absolutely devastated. It should be wrinklies like me going, not young 'uns like him. Oh Mia, my poor dear, what a shame indeed.'

Mia nodded, then concern filled her as she noticed that Zelda was trembling.

'Here.' She held the full takeaway cup. 'Drink this. It will warm you up.'

Zelda eyed the cup. 'What is it?'

'Just tea with a splash of milk.'

'Thank you very much.' Zelda accepted the cup and removed the lid. Steam rose into the air as she took a sip. 'This is terribly kind of you. But isn't it for someone else? You had two of them. Are you meeting someone? Oh dear, have I taken someone else's tea?'

Mia shook her head, not wanting to admit that she shared tea with her dead husbands. 'It was for someone I used to know, but it seems that he's not coming so you're very welcome to it.'

Mia sat back on the bench and drank her tea while Zelda did the same and they fell into an easy silence as they each thought about the people they loved who lay at rest in the graveyard, both secretly appreciating the company of the woman by her side.

Arms linked, Liz and Nina walked around the side of the church, passing graves that dated back hundreds of years. Liz was impressed by how well the graveyard was taken care of, even in the depths of winter.

When they reached the more recent plots, her heart sank at the ages on some of them. Losing a parent was hard enough but losing a child, however old they were, had to be the worst. She gave herself a little inward shake; whatever she had been through, at least it hadn't been that. She'd lost her fiancé, her plans, hopes and dreams but not suffered the devastation of losing a child.

'It makes you think, doesn't it?' she said to Nina.

Her sister stopped walking and turned to her.

'What does?'

'People lose loved ones every day but losing a child has to be the absolute worst thing a person can go through.'

Nina gave a brief nod. 'It must be horrendous. Being a mum, I can't bear to think about losing my two. However, all heartbreak is terrible, whatever form it comes in. Remember, just because someone else is unhappy, it doesn't diminish what you've been through. It's like saying that you can't be happy or enjoy something just because someone else has it better.'

Liz gazed into her sister's eyes, noticing the warm gold flecks in amongst the green-brown. They were such a lovely colour and seemed to change with the light.

'That makes perfect sense,' Liz said. 'Have you always been this wise?'

Nina laughed. 'I'm not sure, but getting older has certainly brought some clarity to some aspects of my life.'

Liz smiled but inside she felt uneasy. She'd been cold towards Nina in the past, had kicked out against her as if it was Nina's fault that their mum died and their dad wasn't around for them. Nina was only three years older than Liz but she'd been the maternal presence in Liz's childhood and then Liz had turned her back on her. And why? Because Nina had what Liz wanted? The security and family she craved. Was that fair of her when all Nina had done was fall in love with a good man?

'Hey, what is it?' Nina tilted her head and took Liz's gloved hands. 'You look really sad. Rhodri needs a good talking-to for hurting you. He should at least have been honest with you and not led you on like that.'

Liz shook her head then swallowed hard, considered shrugging her feelings away, but realised that she owed Nina better than that.

'I don't think I've been as nice to you as I should have been.'

'What?' Nina frowned. 'What are you talking about?'

'I've pushed you away for years. Ignored y-you, a-and . . .' Her throat constricted as if a snake had just wound itself around it. 'I-I . . .'

'It's OK, honey, just breathe. I'm here for you. I've *always* been here for you.'

'I'm just starting to realise that, Nina. I was so busy being jealous of what you had that I didn't appreciate what you've always done for me.' Admitting this was hard but after her confession about what Rhodri had done, she seemed to have opened the floodgates.

'I worried that you might feel a bit left out when I married Kane but I did try to include you in our lives.'

'I know . . .' Liz was trembling now and she didn't think it was from the cold. 'But I felt so resentful and I-I pulled away from you. I don't know why I'm only just realising it.'

'I think I do.' Nina sighed. 'It's because you're here following a painful life event. You've been betrayed by the man who should have had your back and come to the person you knew, deep down, would always be here for you.'

'Oh my God, Nina, you're right!' Liz flung her arms around her sister as gratitude flooded through her. In her darkest moment, she'd needed someone to run to and that someone had been Nina. The woman who'd always had her back. 'I love you so much, big sis.'

'I love you too, honey. Now come on, let's get back to the house and have a hot chocolate. I'm bloody freezing.'

Liz linked her arm through Nina's and they marched through the churchyard. As they let themselves out of the gate, Liz turned back and noticed two women sitting on a bench at the far side of the church. One was very small and wrapped up in lots of layers, the other appeared to be younger but from this distance, Liz couldn't tell by how much. Probably a mother and daughter come to lay flowers at a relative's grave, she thought, silently sending them her condolences. Family mattered, whatever form it came in, and she was incredibly grateful to have her sister at her side, right where she should have been all along.

Chapter 5

At the school gate, Liz stood next to Nina as they waited for the doors to open. She wasn't sure why, but her heart was thrumming like a trapped bird against her ribcage. Was she nervous about meeting her seven-year-old niece? Nervous about what other people waiting at the school were thinking about her – if they'd even noticed her, that was, because she very often felt invisible these days. She wasn't sure, but the feeling was unpleasant so she inhaled several times, exhaling slowly in an attempt to calm herself.

Part of her felt guilty for being absent from work, she was aware of that, because her classes would be with a supply teacher. The GP had signed her off with stress and anxiety, and she also knew that she was in no fit state to be at work right now. The pressure of planning and marking, of writing reports and meeting parents and of standing in front of her classes was hard enough when she felt well; right now, when she felt weak and vulnerable, she knew that her mask could slip, and losing it in front of the pupils was not something any teacher wanted to do. Plus, of course, there was Rhodri.

The fact that he worked at the same school made it a million times worse because she'd bump into him in the corridors, see him in the staffroom and hear the pupils talk about him. The whole school knew they were together – hell, she'd even made the mistake of telling them about her wedding plans – and the barrage of questions she'd face from staff and pupils about why she'd been off turned her cold. She didn't know if Rhodri would have said anything to anyone, doubted Mr Brownlow or his management team would have said anything – whatever faults they had, they were not in the habit of spreading gossip about staff – and so, on her return, she hoped to be able to find a way to explain that would sit well with her and with Rhodri. She didn't expect to be in Little Bramble for more than a few weeks, hoped it would be less than that, but until she heard from Rhodri, she wouldn't know.

'There she is!' Nina waved as a small girl burst from the school, ahead of her peers, and into the yard. 'Cora!'

Cora waved back as she ran towards them, her mass of ginger curls bouncing, her smile wide.

'Mummy!'

Cora reached them and Nina swept her into a hug and twirled her round. When she set Cora on her feet, they were both grinning, their delight at being reunited after a day of school clear for all to see. Liz's heart tugged with grief as she witnessed their bond, aware that with Rhodri's betrayal, her chance of motherhood was further away than ever.

'Did you have a good day?' Nina asked.

Cora bobbed her head and held up her navy canvas bag. 'I did you a drawing and wrote Daddy a story.'

'How wonderful.' Nina stroked Cora's curls then frowned. 'What happened to your bunches?'

Cora reached up to her head and wrinkled her nose. 'Oh . . . they fell out at break.'

'They *fell* out?' Nina's eyebrows rose.

'Mm-hmm.' Cora pressed her lips together and gazed up at her mother with her big green eyes.

Nina shook her head at her daughter. 'We'll have to comb your hair carefully tonight then.'

'Noooooo!' Cora rolled her eyes. 'But I don't have them lice things, Mummy.'

'You don't know that for sure, Cora, and if you have them then there's a good chance we'll all get them.' Nina turned to Liz. 'Now here is your Aunty Liz. She's come to stay for a while.'

Cora turned her attention to Liz, appraising her in a way that made Liz feel she should curtsy or perform a trick, anything to get her niece's approval.

'Hello, Cora,' she said, plastering on her brightest smile while giving her head a good scratch. Just the thought of headlice could do this to her and she knew she'd be itching all day now.

'Hello, Aunty Liz.'

They smiled shyly at each other.

'Mummy told me you were coming but I said I didn't remember you because I haven't seen you for a loooong time and you don't have any babies who would be cousins for me. She said you don't have babies because you are focused on your *cara* and that she didn't know if your boyfriend was good for you a—'

'That's enough, Cora!' Nina turned to Liz and mouthed *Sorry*, while her cheeks turned bright red. 'I was speaking to Kane at the time and didn't realise a certain someone was eavesdropping but when I did, I explained about you having a *career*. I didn't discuss Rhodri with my daughter, I can assure you of that. I just said that your *career* is important to you and as for Rhodri, well . . .'

'It's OK.' Liz shook her head. 'It's been a while since you saw me, Cora, and no, I don't have any children and I do work hard at my cara, also known as my career.'

Liz could see why Nina might have said that to Kane but she couldn't deny that it smarted. Nina was able to focus on her family and didn't have to worry about a job but until Rhodri had come along there had been times when Liz felt that her job was the only stable thing in her life. It had occupied her mind, stopped her dwelling on her loneliness, given her a reason to get up each day. She liked teaching, but there were other things she wanted to do and she had hoped that one day she would be able to sit down and research, then write, historical non-fiction books. When, exactly, she wasn't sure, but it had been in her future plans, simply not as paramount as getting married and having children.

'S'OK.' Cora shrugged. 'I have lots of friends anyway so don't worry about having babies to be cousins for me.'

'Uhhh . . . thanks. I think.' Liz shrugged too, making Nina laugh, if a bit nervously.

'Come on, let's get you home and you can read your story to Aunty Liz.'

'And to Daddy when he comes home. Can I have an ice cream?' Cora asked as they walked.

'It's a bit cold for ice cream, sweetie,' Nina replied.

'Can I have a hot chocolate then?'

'That I can do.'

Liz huddled down into her coat. It was definitely too cold for ice cream and the idea of hot chocolate appealed immensely.

By the time they arrived back at Nina's, Liz felt drained. Cora didn't come up for air; she talked constantly and a lot of it was about school, her friends and teachers, then the rest was about food and TV. She wondered how Nina stayed so patient and sounded so interested in everything Cora had to say, even asking about some of the people she named as well as answering all of Cora's questions. Liz's experience of working with children was mostly with teenagers and certainly no younger than eleven-year-olds, and while they did ask questions, it was nothing compared to the sheer number that Cora asked.

In the kitchen, Nina made hot chocolates for the three of them while Cora went to change and wash her hands.

'What do you think of your niece, then?' Nina asked as she set a plate of what appeared to be home-made chocolate chip cookies and three mugs of chocolate on the table.

'She's adorable. A bundle of energy, though.'

'That's not a bad thing.' Nina smiled.

'No, I didn't mean it as a bad thing, but I admire your patience in dealing with her.'

Nina chuckled. 'Yeah, being a parent does take a lot of patience. Especially with answering questions. There are *always* lots of questions. When Demi was younger, she was the same and I never got a moment's peace. And then they become teenagers and there are lots of huffs and grunts, as well as slamming of doors and muttering of swear words. The happy excitement about life fades away and they seem permanently disgruntled.'

'Is Demi like that?'

Nina nodded then pulled out a chair. 'There's such a contrast between a young child and a teenager. Demi used to be as sweet as Cora but now . . .?' She folded her hands around one of the mugs and sighed. 'Now she seems to hate me.'

'I'm sure she doesn't. Don't forget, I work with teenagers and they can be difficult with everyone.'

'Wait until you meet her. I love her deeply, I'm her mum after all, but right now, she's not the little girl I adored. She's . . . challenging. And sometimes she's not very nice at all.'

'I'm sure she'll grow out of it.' Liz sipped her hot chocolate, savouring the sweet cocoa comfort.

'Are you talking about Demi?' Cora pranced into the kitchen wearing what looked like a miniature wedding dress with a rhinestone tiara. She flicked a white wand with a star at the end in the air and Liz found herself ducking for fear of getting accidentally tapped.

'None of your business.' Nina frowned.

'Demi can be very mean to Mummy and sometimes to me.' Cora climbed onto the chair next to Liz and placed her wand on the table then reached for the remaining mug. 'She used to be the best sister in the world but now she's a grumpy guts. Daddy calls her *Demi Darkness* and it makes her soooo mad.' Cora giggled but Nina grimaced.

'You shouldn't talk about your sister like that, Cora. She's just got a lot on her plate right now.'

Cora nodded. 'Being a teenager is hard because of all the hormoze. My friend, Luna, she says her big brother is a big meanie to her and she wishes she could send him to Canada. His hormoze have made him have spots too and he spends ages looking at them in the mirror and trying to squeeze all the yucky yellow pus out of them.'

'Hormoze can be horrible. Spots too. Poor Luna's brother.' Liz winked at Nina. 'But why does she want to send him to Canada?' she asked, intrigued.

'It's where bears live and she said the bears are welcome to him.'

'Oh! I see.'

Liz met Nina's eyes over the table and they grinned at each other.

'Perhaps I could send Rhodri there,' she said quietly.

'Has he got hormoze too?' Cora asked, lowering her mug to reveal a chocolate moustache.

Liz stared into the steam rising from her mug. 'I guess so.'

'Right, Cora, why don't you read us your story,' Nina said, handing Cora her school bag, clearly trying to change the subject.

'Okey-dokey, but be prepared to grab a tissue and cry your bloody heart out because it's a sad one.'

'Don't say bloody.' Nina gave Cora a meaningful look that made the little girl grin.

As Cora pulled a book from her bag, Liz sat back in her chair and sipped her drink. The image of Rhodri being chased by a bear was quite comforting, although, try as she might, she couldn't picture the bear catching him. Why was that? Didn't he deserve to be hurt and scared, to be worried about what lay ahead of him in the same way she was? The man had taken her heart and ripped it apart, had ruined her life and her plans and for what? A shag with his hot personal trainer. Was it really worth losing their relationship over? Did she mean so little to him that he could cast her aside for someone else in the blink of an eye? Or was what he had with Pete Jenkins more than just a fling?

She shrugged the latter thought away. *Nope. No, no, no!* It would all work out in the end. Rhodri was going to be incredibly sorry when he came to his senses and Liz would need to be very understanding. She just hoped she had that in her.

'Are you ready, Aunty Liz?'

Cora's question dragged Liz back to the kitchen.

'Oh! Yes, of course. Can't wait.'

Liz leant forwards and placed her mug on the table then folded her arms in front of her. At least while she was here, dwelling on what might have been wouldn't be easy, especially with her niece insisting that she stay present in the moment.

Chapter 6

Mia paused outside the garden gate of the large old house. Was she doing the right thing coming here? Since she'd bumped into Zelda Grey at the churchyard, she hadn't stopped thinking about her. It was a welcome change because her thoughts had been absorbed by her own grief and sense of loss since Gideon had passed away, but it was also a bit strange, she thought. To have one's mind occupied by concerns about an elderly lady she hadn't seen in ages and hadn't thought about in just as long, was that normal? But then, after she'd sat with Zelda on that cold bench in the churchyard and they'd drunk their tea, she'd felt a certain connection to her. She knew that Zelda lived alone and had done since her mother had passed away a long time ago, and she knew from what Zelda had said that she only heard about village goings-on from Marcellus and the titbits she heard at the village shop, so she'd gathered that apart from the very occasional visit to the café, Zelda spent most of her time alone. That must be awful. Mia knew that some people liked their own company; she did to a certain extent, but she had her three sons, her daughters-in-law and grandchildren. She might not see them all regularly, but they were there if she needed them and she did see quite a bit of Joel, so she felt very lucky indeed. That was the thing with life; even when your own circumstances seemed dire, your own pain enormous, your own loneliness all-consuming, there was usually someone worse off than you. As far as she knew, Zelda didn't have any children or family – at least, not local anyway – and so she had no one to turn to.

The more Mia had thought about Zelda over recent days, the more she felt the need to go and visit her. She'd got out her bakeware the previous day then gone to the shop to get butter, eggs, caster sugar and a few other things, determined to make something she could take to Zelda. In the cupboard she still had some of the jams she'd made the previous year with the delicious fruit Gideon had grown on his allotment. How she would feel when it was all gone, she couldn't bear to consider, but for now there were plenty of jars of blackberry, strawberry and blackcurrant jam so she'd used some of it in a nice Victoria sponge that she now carried in a tin as a gift for Zelda.

She'd had to pass the allotments to get there and it was strange. Turning, she gazed at the plots just beyond Zelda's garden. Gideon had one of the plots closest to the fence and beyond that lay a stream. On a few occasions in the summer months, they'd brought a picnic with them to the allotment and sat on the bank next to the stream, listening to the birds singing in the trees and the gentle burbling of the water. Even though they were in their fifties, they'd lain on the blanket after they'd eaten and spoken about their hopes and dreams, held hands and kissed like young lovers. And why not? They'd still been passionate about each other, had shared a tactile relationship that had made Mia feel lucky and fulfilled.

The last time they'd taken the blanket to their favourite spot had been after his diagnosis and their picnic had lain neglected as they'd both tried to take in the enormity of what was happening to him. Having no appetite and feeling overwhelmed by it all, Gideon had lain down with his head in Mia's lap and cried. Her giant of a man with his broad shoulders and muscular arms, his thick beard and shiny bald head, had sobbed and Mia had cried too. But she'd cried quietly, wanting to be strong for her husband, to help him to deal with the battle ahead. Gideon had seemed too alive to be ill, too strong to be facing death. Later on, at home, when Gideon had fallen asleep, Mia had sobbed into a tea towel. She'd already lost one husband so how could she be facing the loss of another? It was simply too much to bear, a cruelty too far for one woman to deal with. But the cancer had won and Gideon had lost the fight. It was cruel and unfair and in the dead of night the frustration still filled her with anger that made her want to scream.

But she was still here. Still breathing. Still grieving. Utterly lost at times but holding on by her fingernails. Trying not to fall off the edge because if she did then she knew she might never come back.

She'd heard that people could die of a broken heart but losing two lovers had broken her heart with aplomb – and yet, she had not died. Her love for them still burned brightly so perhaps that was what was keeping her going, like a furnace that was stoked by the flames of love. And then there were her sons, of course, who gave her a reason to get up each day. Mia couldn't let her boys down and so she got up every morning and faced each day however tired she felt, however much she wanted to stay in bed and hide under the duvet.

What, then, kept Zelda going? Had she never fallen in love? Was that the secret to longevity? Well, Mia would rather love and lose than never love at all. Her love with John had given her three wonderful sons, her love with Gideon a cupboard full of jams. She snorted. Gideon had given her far more than that, but the jam thought was a funny one and it would have made him laugh.

She sighed long and low then opened the gate and headed up the path towards Zelda's house, hoping that the elderly lady didn't have any allergies. So many people these days didn't eat gluten or dairy and she'd had no way of checking if Zelda didn't eat any of those things. It she didn't, Mia suspected that the cake would likely go to her chickens instead.

Mia knocked on the door and waited. The front of the house looked tired, the frames of the sash windows needed a lick of paint, the door too, and weeds sprouted where the path was cracked. It reminded Mia of wrinkles and the hairs that sprouted as people aged. Mia had a few stubborn hairs that sprouted from her chin and she touched a hand to her face self-consciously. Gideon used to tease her about them, had given them names, and pretended to be sad when she plucked them. She'd been so comfortable with Gideon and she couldn't imagine ever having that with a man again. Couldn't imagine ever *wanting* that again.

The door swung inwards and Zelda stood there looking very . . . grey. She had on grey trousers, grey slippers, a grey cardigan and a grey scarf that was wrapped around her hair. Her blue eyes peered at Mia from behind her silver-framed glasses and her eyebrows rose in surprise.

'Hello?'

'Zelda . . . it's me. Mia.'

Recognition dawned on Zelda's face and she smiled but her eyes were wary. 'Mia. To what do I owe this pleasure?'

'I hope it's OK to call unannounced, but I brought you a cake. I hope you like cake. I know not everyone does and—'

'A cake?' Zelda reached for the tin and accepted it as reverently as if it contained the Crown Jewels. 'You brought me a cake?'

'Yes.' Mia smiled but Zelda's eyes were glued to the tin. Mia felt a bit awkward then because the tin was an old one that had once contained chocolates. She had far nicer tins with pretty floral patterns and could easily have put the cake into one of those instead, but she'd thought to leave the tin with Zelda. The elderly lady looked so delighted that Mia realised that using a better tin would have been a good plan, made the cake more special, perhaps. Why hadn't she used a better tin?

'Thank you. Thank you so much.' Zelda finally raised her eyes to meet Mia's gaze. 'But why did you bring me a cake?'

'Well, it was lovely seeing you earlier this week and I thought it would be nice to bring you something. I enjoy baking but don't have Gideon to bake for now and I thought you might appreciate a Victoria sandwich. If you don't like cake or if you have any allergies, it's no problem. I can always take it home and bake something else for you and—'

'A Victoria sandwich? Goodness me, how lovely!' Zelda's eyes were shining and Mia felt herself choking up. How could such a small gesture mean so much to someone?

'I thought it would go well with a cup of tea,' she ventured.

'Oh . . .' Zelda glanced behind her. 'Yes. With tea. I . . . I don't have many visitors and the house is a bit of a mess.' She chewed at her bottom lip. 'Quite a mess, actually. I would invite you in but—'

'Zelda, that really doesn't bother me. I raised three boys so I know what it is to have a messy house and anyway, I'm sure yours isn't messy at all.'

Zelda glanced behind her again then back at the tin and she seemed to make a decision. 'Would you like to come in for a cup of tea, Mia?'

'I would like that,' Mia replied. 'Very much.'

'Well, come on in, then.' Zelda stepped back and Mia followed her inside, closing the door behind her.

'It's just through here.' Zelda shuffled along, holding her breath as they squeezed past the books, storage boxes and black bags and through to the kitchen. Only in there did she release the breath, hoping that Mia was not already thinking of her as a mad old woman who needed to be moved to a care home. Zelda had no intention of leaving her house while there was breath in her body, but she also didn't want anyone, especially not someone as nice as Mia, thinking she was losing her marbles.

'Take a seat, dear, and I'll get the kettle on.' Zelda gestured at the table then she set the cake tin down carefully, resisting the urge to look inside until she'd made tea.

'Thank you.' Mia pulled out a chair and sat at the table.

Zelda made the tea, aware that Mia was looking around the kitchen and wondered what she thought about it. Old-fashioned? In need of a good blitz with a mop and some bleach? Too many knick-knacks?

'I love all of your plants,' Mia said, breaking into Zelda's thoughts and pulling her gaze to the windowsill, which was chock-a-block with plant pots, each one containing herbs or greenery of some form or another. There were more plants on other surfaces, including the worktops, and Zelda saw them properly for the first time in ages. She was so used to them being there that she didn't notice them anymore, they were just a part of her home. She fed and watered them, tended to them, but didn't *see* them. 'You have so many.'

'I have green fingers, I suppose. Or is it thumbs?' She laughed as she shook her head. 'I like growing things. Always have.'

'I have some plants but Gideon was the one with a gift for gardening.'

'He certainly had plenty growing at the allotment.'

'He did. The cake has jam in the middle made from straw-berries he grew.'

'How fabulous.' Zelda licked her lips, her mouth watering. 'I love strawberry jam. It tastes like . . . like summer.'

Mia shivered.

'Are you cold?' Zelda asked. 'The Aga provides the heat in here because I haven't got around to getting central heating installed through the whole house, but I can get you a blanket if you need it.'

'No, I'm fine, thank you.'

'Are you sure?' Zelda asked.

Mia nodded. 'It was because you said *summer*. It feels as though last summer was a lifetime ago. A time of innocence before we found out about . . . about Gideon. Before every-thing changed.' The last word emerged quietly and Zelda imagined it was the finality of it hitting Mia anew. Grief did that; she knew it all too well herself.

'I'm very sorry, my lovely. I wish I could say or do some-thing to help but I know there's nothing anyone can do to alleviate the pain of such a loss.'

'It's OK.' Mia's voice wobbled and she covered her eyes with a hand. 'I'll be OK in a minute. So sorry about this.'

Zelda carried two mugs of tea to the table and set one near Mia then got two small plates and forks. She opened the cake tin, glancing at Mia every so often, unsure whether the other woman would want to be left alone for a bit or if she should try to comfort her. That was the problem with not having much social interaction; you forgot how to behave when others were distressed. Thinking it was best just to carry on with things, she sat opposite Mia but something told her to at least try and offer some comfort, even if she wasn't very good at it. She reached out and patted Mia's free hand where it rested on the table.

'There, there, my dear.'

The aroma of freshly baked cake drifted from the tin along with the scent of ripe strawberries. It was as if the ghost of summer had risen between them in cake form.

Mia lowered her other hand from her eyes and sniffed. 'I'm so sorry. I don't know what came over me.'

'You're grieving, Mia. It's quite acceptable to cry.'

'But I came here to do something nice for you.'

'And you have!' Zelda pointed at the cake tin. 'You made me a cake. I can't remember the last time someone made me a cake. Actually, I can – it was my mother and that was almost two decades ago. So please don't apologise at all.'

'But I didn't mean to get upset. I've been doing quite well, really.'

'Quite well?' Zelda tilted her head.

'Yes. Not getting upset. Just . . . getting on with things.'

'Grief needs an out, Mia, and you shouldn't try to suppress it. It can eat you up and spit you out if you don't release it. So don't you apologise for crying here. There's no judgement in this house. Not since Mother passed away, anyway.' She met

Mia's eyes then laughed. 'My mother was terribly judgemental. I loved her but she knew how to make grown men quiver.'

Mia smiled sadly and they both dabbed at their eyes.

'Dear me.' Zelda pulled a tissue from her sleeve and blew her nose. 'There's you worrying that I'm judging you for crying while I'm here worrying that you'll think my house is a tip.'

Mia's brows met. 'What? But why?'

'Well – I have things everywhere. Didn't you notice that the hallway is rather crowded?'

'Oh . . . well, I suppose it is but I thought you were moving some things around. Perhaps decorating a room.' Mia gave a small shrug and Zelda heaved a sigh of relief.

'Yes, that's it. I'm decorating.' She snorted and Mia joined her and the kitchen filled with the sound of laughter. It was the laughter of relief, the laughter of embarrassment and the laughter of catharsis. It was a sound that made Zelda's heart swell with joy, because the last time she'd laughed with another human being in her home had been far too long ago to recall.

Perhaps there was something to be said for the company of others and she hoped that this wasn't a one-off, because she already liked Mia Holmes rather a lot.

'Now, let's have a slice of this rather delicious-looking cake, shall we?'

Chapter 7

'What did your GP say?' Nina placed a mug of tea on the side table next to the sofa.

'Thanks.' Liz picked up the tea. 'That she'll sign me off for another two weeks and then I should see how I go. She's a very understanding doctor and told me that she worries about the mental health of professionals like teachers.'

Nina sat at the other end of the sofa and tucked her legs underneath her while Liz sank back on the comfy cushions. She couldn't believe she'd already been in Little Bramble for two and a half weeks and in that time she hadn't heard from Rhodri once. Not a phone call. Not an email. And not even a text message. The forefinger of her right hand had itched to type a text to him, to try to prompt him to do what she was convinced he'd do sooner or later, but so far, nothing.

She sipped her tea, cradling the mug between both hands. Perhaps Rhodri was extremely embarrassed that he'd cheated. Perhaps he was overwhelmed with sadness and trying to figure out how he could win her back. Perhaps she'd even misunderstood what she'd seen and they had, in fact, been wrestling.

Although the latter was, she realised, a bit of a stretch. She'd indulged in more than one fantasy where he arrived unannounced on the doorstep and told her how much he loved her, how much he regretted his infidelity and how much he wanted to make it up to her. However, the strange thing was that when she had those daydreams, his face wasn't always that clear. Which was odd, really, as it hadn't even been three weeks since she'd seen him and she had hundreds of photos of him on her phone. But try as she might, whenever she imagined him coming to get her, his face blurred and changed and he wasn't the Rhodri she had known. As for her love for him, that was hard to summon up too. She knew she cared for him, but the thought of throwing herself into his embrace and feeling love and desire for him just didn't feel . . . right. She couldn't remember how it was to feel intense love and passion for him and when she woke in the early hours of the morning, heart pounding, perspiration on her brow, she had wondered if she'd ever felt that for Rhodri at all. It was like trying to get a TV signal on the old portable TV that they'd had when she was a child: some days it was simply impossible to get a clear picture of his face or of what she'd thought she felt for him.

Nina, Kane and Cora had been warm and welcoming. Admittedly, Liz found Cora quite tiring at times with her constant questions and boundless energy – the latter making Liz think about a springer spaniel she'd seen on a recent walk as it raced around the village green after a ball, seemingly never tiring – but she also enjoyed spending time with the little girl. It was impossible to be anything other than fully present when Cora was at your side. Demi, however, was an enigma, as Liz had found teenagers often were. Not that she hadn't been polite and civil, but she'd also been quite withdrawn and reluctant to spend much time around Liz. Nina had told Liz not to worry about it when Liz had expressed her concerns that perhaps Demi was spending a lot of time in her room because she was there, and had reassured Liz that Demi usually stayed in her room or went out with her friends. But with her experience of teaching teenagers, Liz had been worried that perhaps something else was wrong with her niece, and that if it wasn't her presence causing an issue, then it could be something she might be able to help with.

'So are you going to speak to the head teacher today too?' Nina asked.

'I'll ring him after I've had my tea. Although based on how he reacted the last time I spoke to him, he'll probably be glad I'm staying away. After my little . . . outburst in his office, I think he's a tiny bit afraid of me.' Liz grimaced, thinking about how upset she'd been that day and about the expression of sheer terror on Mr Brownlow's face. If only he hadn't chosen that moment to tell her that he was concerned about the interim results for one of her GCSE classes – she was currently juggling her own two and two others, due to staff absence within the department – and that he wanted an official meeting with her to review their progress. To be fair, he'd bypassed protocol as she should have had a meeting with her curriculum team leader first, but then her CTL was off with stress, as was the second in department, so Mr Brownlow had apparently decided to do what he could to help. Or rather, to do what he was known for, which was to exert more pressure on staff until they either brought a sleeping bag into school with the intention of living there or went off sick. The poor pupils deserved better, but while management were behaving as if they were part of a dictatorship where all the shit rolled downhill, nothing would be fixed in a way that benefited those who mattered most of all – the children. To have happy and successful pupils, a school needed happy and healthy staff, and right now Mr Brownlow didn't seem to understand that very straightforward equation.

'Who will teach the pupils with you and most of your department off?' Nina asked.

It was a simple question but one that made Liz's heart squeeze with guilt. A tear welled in her left eye and trickled down her cheek.

'Oh Liz, I'm sorry. I didn't mean to make it worse . . . I just wondered who will be covering all those classes.'

'He'll have supply teachers in, I suppose, although they're in short supply at the moment – pardon the pun – because no one wants that kind of pressure. It's all such a mess. Perhaps I should suck it up and go back in.'

'No! Absolutely not.'

Nina turned on the sofa to fully face Liz.

'I've seen how upset you've been over the past fortnight and you are in no fit state to be in work. You're barely eating or sleeping, you keep bursting into tears, you're not with it at all. No offence, Liz, but you can't stand in front of a class and deliver. I know your job is important. Being a mum means I know how hard it is when school staff are off, but I'm also your sister and I care about you and worry about you. You need rest and recuperation and to get your thoughts in order. Heading straight back into a high-pressured environment before you're ready will put you on your knees. I mean, while you look a tiny bit better than when you arrived, you're not fully recovered and you still need to sort some things out. Like . . . well, what you're doing about the wedding, the house, Rho— and all that other stuff.'

Liz sagged in her seat and wiped a hand absently over her cheek. 'I know you're right but there's so much guilt attached to my job. I want to be there for the pupils but I also know that I can't give them my best right now. Plus, it's worse, I think, because if I go in it won't exactly distract me from my worries because in school . . . I'll see Rhodri.'

'Do you know that he's going into work with no problem then?'

Liz sighed. 'When I checked my work emails, I saw the cover list. The school sends it out to all staff on a daily basis and Rhodri's name isn't on there, so he's clearly been going in as usual. It kind of makes me look worse, doesn't it?'

'Not really. He was the cheater who broke your heart. He's clearly tougher than you thought and – I hate to say it, in fact

I'm incredibly sorry to say it – he can't be nearly as upset as you are.'

Liz met Nina's eyes and saw only compassion there. 'I know you'd think so b-but I can't understand how he can't care at all.' She also wasn't sure that Rhodri *was* that tough, knowing what she did about his background, but feeling sorry for him right now only made her feel weaker.

'Has he phoned you?'

'No.'

'Messaged you?'

'No . . . but—'

'Are you still holding on to the hope that he will?'

Liz hung her head.

'You are, aren't you?' Nina shuffled across the sofa and took Liz's left hand between both of hers. 'Oh sweetheart, this isn't good for you. I think you need some closure.'

Liz stared hard at the log burner that glowed orange at the heart of the lounge, trying to summon some strength from inside as she thought about Nina's points. She'd had a glow inside her when her life seemed to be going the way she wanted it to; the way she had planned it. That glow had kept her going, got her up in the mornings and propelled her through her days, but now that her plans had been turned upside down, she felt cold, unlit, ashy.

Was she wrong to hope that Rhodri would come to his senses? She hadn't contacted him in the hope that absence would make his heart grow fonder, that he would realise how much he missed her and needed her in his life. He used to need her, didn't he? Liz had helped him to get his life back on track, had built his confidence, had done what she could to make him happy. She'd expected to hear from him every day since her arrival, keeping her phone turned on and fully charged at all times, sleeping with it under her pillow so she'd feel the vibration if he messaged during the night. It was why she hadn't even begun to start cancelling things like the ceremony and reception, the flowers or dress fittings. Why she hadn't contacted any of the guests to let them know what had happened. They hadn't officially announced that it was over between them, so surely that meant that there was still hope? Once Rhodri got this out of his system, he might still want to go through with it – but it would certainly take some time for Liz to adjust. The longer this separation went on, the clearer it was to her that she wouldn't be able to simply share their home and bed again as if nothing had happened, that they might need to attend counselling together and to rebuild their relationship slowly, but it was something she was prepared to do.

Wasn't she?

She'd been convinced it was at first but now . . .

With each passing day, she felt another piece of her heart crack, fragment and fall away, as if all the love and affection she had for Rhodri was crumbling to dust. It wasn't completely gone, but if he left it too long, she worried she'd have nothing left for him and that it would be too late. And as for love, when she thought about it now, she wondered if it really had been love at all or simply her desire to be married and be a mother; basically to have Nina's life. Nina's life was, after all, fantastic, but Nina was married to Kane and Kane was not Rhodri. Nina had lived a different life from Liz and Nina's husband had not had an affair. Nina had not had to consider whether she could forgive that level of betrayal but Liz did. Could she really share a bed with Rhodri again, trust him with her body, her heart and her mind as she once had? Intimacy was about connecting on so many levels and while she might be able to do so with her body – although right now she wasn't certain about even that, unless she pretended – she wasn't sure that her mind and her heart would be able to go along with a charade.

'Drink your tea.'

'Pardon?' Liz dragged her gaze away from the fireplace.

'Your tea's getting cold.'

'OK.' Liz sipped the warm beverage.

'And when you've finished it, go and get some warm clothes on.'

'Why?' Liz's eyes strayed to the window where outside the sky was gunmetal grey, a cold wind whipping the branches of the trees and scattering leaves around the ground. It did not look like a good day to be heading out.

'I think you need to clear your head before you do anything else and a walk is a good way to do that.'

'But it looks freezing.'

'All the better to blow the cobwebs away. After all, you haven't done much exercise since you got here.'

Liz bit her bottom lip. That was true. She'd gone running regularly in Maidstone but since she'd found Rhodri and Pete together, her energy levels had plummeted and going for a run had seemed like far too much effort.

Liz drained her tea then stood up. 'Where are we going?'

'To the allotment.'

'The allotment?'

'Yes.'

'You have an allotment?'

'We do.'

'You never said.'

'You never asked.' Nina winked at her.

'It's not something I would have thought to ask. You have a lovely garden so why do you need an allotment?'

'To grow things. The garden is great but it's also where Cora plays and where we sit and relax. The allotment is a space where we can grow fruit, herbs and veg and it's also a good walk from here so it gets me out when everyone else is at school and work. It's also a great place to socialise.'

'To socialise?'

'You meet all sorts of people there. It's nice.'

'But surely it's a fine-weather thing?' Liz eyed the window again, already feeling cold and she hadn't stepped outside yet.

'It's best in fine weather but it's also a year-round thing. There's always something to tidy up or prepare – and sometimes it's just nice to head up there and look around.'

'Really?'

'Yes, really. Come on, I'll show you where it is and then you can walk up there alone when you want some time to yourself.'

'Oh . . . OK.'

As Liz headed up to her room, the thought of going out into the frigid air of the late February day was not at all appealing, but the idea of having somewhere she could go when she needed to think was positive. She was enjoying spending time with Nina but knew that her sister needed some space too, and the last thing she wanted to do was to get under Nina's feet.

Especially not when they seemed to be getting closer by the day. Especially when it felt that while she might be about to lose her fiancé, she was in the process of rebuilding her relationship with her sister.

Chapter 8

Liz sucked in deep breaths as they walked, enjoying the sensation of the cold air filling her lungs, cleansing her from within. They left the main road and headed along the woodland path. To their right, behind trees and hedgerows, lay the village, while to the left fields and hills stretched out like a patchwork landscape. Liz glanced through the trees at the rural scene, currently sparse with winter, in a form of stasis before the spring arrived. Spring should be bringing her wedding and honeymoon closer, what she had thought of as the beginning of her life, but now she wasn't so sure.

Perhaps spring and summer would bring something else altogether . . .

Their feet pounded the mud path, scattering the wood chippings that had been laid to absorb the wintry showers. The air smelt of earth and woodsmoke that had drifted from the houses of the village and Liz's nose tingled from the cold. In the branches of a tree, a robin sang, a cheery repetitive whistle and Liz found herself swallowing hard. The robin didn't have a fancy wedding and expensive honeymoon to look forward to but it was simply content with sitting in a tree, enjoying the morning, singing its heart out. Why couldn't she find joy in such simple things?

After about ten minutes they came to a crossroads on the path and Nina gestured to the right. 'This way.'

'What's in the other direction?' Liz asked.

'If we kept going, we'd reach more trees and eventually train tracks but if we turned left, there are more fields, farms and Old Oak Stables. We're heading right, up towards The Lumber Shed and allotments.'

'The Lumber Shed?'

'Yes, it's a local business where they repair furniture or make new from reclaimed wood.'

Liz nodded her approval.

Soon they passed the entrance to the village train station to their left and more houses to their right. Liz realised that the village green now lay behind them and that they were heading in a north-easterly direction.

'It is quite a walk,' she said, breathing deeply.

'Good, right?' Nina grinned at her.

'Very.' Liz's heart was beating quickly from the exertion and not from stress, which she was glad about. She was warm now in her winter layers and she was enjoying the walk and the scenery. Being outdoors was definitely therapeutic and it made her realise how much she'd missed getting outside and raising her heart rate naturally through exercise. It provided a much-needed mood boost that in turn made her feel stronger than she had since her arrival.

After following a footpath that passed through a wooded area, they emerged into an opening where there was a small cottage surrounded by fields.

'That used to be rented out but I don't think anyone's lived there in quite some time.' Nina pointed at the rather neglected-looking cottage.

'What a shame,' Liz said. 'It looks lovely and it's in such a pretty spot.'

'It belongs to the owner of the big house.'

'What big house?' Liz frowned.

Nina stopped walking and pointed ahead. 'That one.'

'Wow! It's like an old manor house from a Regency drama.' Liz gazed through the trees at the house that stood behind high walls, its chimneys tall, its upper windows reflecting the wintry sky and racing clouds.

'And here we have the allotments.' Nina turned Liz around to show her a field of rectangular plots. Some had sheds, some had small greenhouses, and some had low fences separating them from the others.

'Which one is yours?'

'I'll show you.'

Nina slid her arm through Liz's and walked her around the outside of the plots towards one at the far end of the field. There was a small lockable shed and Nina pulled a key from her pocket and opened the door. The smell of wood and a musty enclosed space hit them both and Liz coughed. 'Been locked up for a while then?'

'I haven't been up here for about a month but we have a WhatsApp group where we share information about storm damage or escaped animals, as well as other things like spare vegetables and fruit available in the summer and autumn. It's a nice community thing, although not everyone gets involved. Not everyone has the time like me.'

Nina was a busy wife and mum but Liz knew she'd have more time than some to interact in a WhatsApp group. As a teacher, Liz barely had time to visit the toilet during the school day, let alone chat on phone apps, but it was different during school holidays when Rhodri was out, then she'd often lose hours browsing Facebook or Instagram, reading makeup and diet tips, admiring celebrity wedding and baby photos or watching TikTok videos. She doubted Nina wasted time, judging from what she'd seen of her over the past two weeks, but it was certainly easy to do and social media could be a rabbit hole.

Nina stepped inside the shed and picked up two foldable chairs that she handed to Liz, then she crouched down to reach something off a low shelf. 'Ooh! Looks like something has been living in here.'

'Careful!' Liz gripped the chairs tightly, imagining a giant spider or ferocious badger.

'Why?' Nina glanced behind her, eyebrows meeting quizzically.

'It might be dangerous.'

'Dangerous?' Nina giggled. 'Like a bear or a wolf? You do realise this is Surrey and not Canada, don't you?'

Liz laughed. 'No – I mean yes, but it could be a rat or a badger. They're vicious, aren't they?'

'I don't think it's either. Plus, as far as I know, badgers and rats only attack if scared and feeling threatened. I'm sure they'd be more likely to run away than attack.' Nina tilted her head and peered under the shelf. 'Looks like a hedgehog to me.'

'Is it alive?'

'I'm not sure.'

'Poke it.' Liz stepped closer to her sister.

'I'm not poking it!' Nina said. 'It might frighten the poor thing.'

'How did it get in there?'

'There's a small hole in the floorboard in the corner, so I'm assuming it climbed in through there.'

'What should we do?'

'Nothing for now. I'm thinking it's probably hibernating.'

'Oooh, it could be.' Goosebumps rose on Liz's arms. She'd seen stories like this on Instagram and instinctively reached for her phone, gasping as she realised it wasn't in her pocket. 'Shit!'

'What's wrong?' Nina rested on her haunches and looked up at Liz.

'I've left my phone in the house.'

'That's OK. Were you going to Google hedgehog rescue?'

'Uh ... yes.' Liz gave a curt nod. She wasn't. Her first thought had been to photograph the hedgehog for an Instagram post but on finding her phone missing, her heart had skipped a beat because if she didn't have her phone, what would happen if Rhodri tried to contact her?

'What's wrong, Liz? You've gone white as a sheet.' Nina stood up.

'My phone. I have to go back for it.'

'We can research what to do back at home. Looks like the little creature's been there for a while, judging by the nest he's built himself or herself, and he or she can get out if they need to, so I don't think it's an emergency. I'll find out what to do later.'

'It's not that.' Liz's heart was racing and she propped the chairs against the outside of the shed and placed a hand on her chest. It was so tight she was finding it hard to breathe.

'Liz?' Nina stepped in front of her and placed her hands on Liz's shoulders. 'Do you feel faint?'

Liz shook her head. Wheezed. 'I need . . . my phone.'

'It's OK. It'll be safe in the house.'

'It's not . . . that. I need it because . . .'

'What is it?'

'Rh . . . Rhodri might call and then—'

'Excuse me!'

They both turned to the voice that came from the path running between the allotments.

'Is everything all right?' The woman smiled tentatively at them, but her eyes revealed concern.

'Fine,' Liz said softly, still gripping her chest. 'I'm . . . fine.'

'You're clearly not.' Nina shook her head.

'You don't look fine. Would you like a cup of tea? That might help,' the woman said, holding up a flask.

'That would be brilliant, thank you.' Nina took charge and reached for one of the chairs. She opened it up and helped Liz sit down then pulled what looked like a sawn-off log from the shed and placed it next to the chair. The woman came through the small gate into the plot and placed a flask on the log then a tin cup. She opened the flask, poured steaming liquid into the cup and handed it to Liz.

'There you go, lovely. There's sugar in it.'

'I don't . . . take sugar,' Liz said.

'It'll do you good.' Nina gestured at the cup. 'Drink.'

Liz sipped the sweet tea and felt the heat spreading through her body, the sugar seeping into her bloodstream. It gave her something to focus on other than the tightness in her chest and her pounding heart. She wasn't sure exactly what had happened just then. She'd panicked about her phone and her heart had sped up and she'd felt overwhelmingly dizzy and not quite there, as if she was leaving her body and about to drift up into the sky.

Suddenly, she was aware of Nina and the woman talking and she tuned into their conversation.

'Anxiety, is it?' the woman asked.

'She's been through a difficult time.'

'Poor love,' the woman said, her eyes wandering to Liz's face. 'How're you feeling now?'

'Better. Thanks.' Liz rubbed at the back of her neck with her free hand. 'I don't know what happened.'

'Don't worry, lovely, we all go through difficult times.'

'Goodness!' Nina smacked her forehead. 'I've just realised! You're Mia Holmes, aren't you?'

'That's me.'

'Oh, I . . . I was so sorry to hear about Gideon.'

'Thank you.' Now Liz watched the colour draining from Mia's face.

'He was such a lovely man. I didn't know him very well but often saw him here working on his plot, that was . . . before he became *ill* . . .' Nina's face contorted as she whispered the last word as if it was offensive. 'I really am terribly sorry.'

'It's OK.' Mia blinked rapidly. 'I did join him here now and then, but more often after he . . . he wasn't able to do much other than sit and watch . . .'

'Yes, of course. I saw you here with him. I didn't like to intrude – and I'm embarrassed to admit it, but I didn't know what to say.'

'I understand. It's hard to know what to say to someone who doesn't have much time left. Gideon would have understood too.' Mia looked around them. 'He loved his plot. Last autumn, he couldn't go far but getting out seemed important, a break in the day, so I'd drive him as close as I could then push him the rest of the way in his wheelchair.'

Liz watched how her sister's eyes were glued to Mia's face, how they were filled with compassion. Nina was such a warm,

89

caring person. How had she ever doubted her sister? How had she ever been angry with her for having everything she did when she so clearly deserved to be happy?

'Would you like to sit down?' Nina asked. 'I have some mugs in the shed. I think that perhaps you could do with some tea too?'

'That would be very nice.' Mia gave a grateful smile as she sank into the other chair.

Liz emerged from the shed with two mugs. She poured tea from the flask into one and gave it to Mia.

'Help yourself.' Mia pointed at the flask. 'There's plenty there for us all. I don't know why I still use that giant flask when I have smaller ones in the house. Force of habit, I guess because Gideon used to moan if there wasn't enough tea. He could drink a gallon of the stuff in minutes.'

'Thank you.' Nina poured tea into the spare mug then leant her back against the shed.

'No, thank *you*.' Mia smiled. 'I came over to help and ended up getting upset myself. I guess I'm not coping quite as well as I think I am.'

'Give yourself time,' Nina said. 'It's very early days.'

'That's true.' Mia nodded. 'Same for you?' she directed the question at Liz. 'You've lost someone?'

Liz swallowed hard. 'Yes.' The word emerged as little more than a whisper.

'Oh my dear, I'm sorry.'

'Thanks.' Liz forced her lips into a brief smile.

'Well, here's to female support.' Nina held up her mug. 'And to sharing tea on a cold February day. Our circumstances might not have brought us together during the happiest of times, but right now I'm grateful to be here with you both at this lovely allotment.'

Liz stared across the allotment plots and up to the big house behind its boundary wall. Everything looked shut down and uninviting now but she could imagine how it might look in the summer months. The air was so fresh and clean, the plots surrounded by fields and trees, it was open and yet sheltered, the earth currently seeming to sleep but soon it would awaken and the allotment would offer an abundance of fruit, vegetables, flowers and more to those who worked the land. It made her think of relationships and how they could die if they weren't tended, watered and fertilised, or if the wrong soil was used. Her relationship with Rhodri had floundered for reasons she didn't fully understand yet but here she was, with two other women, possibly creating a new foundation for relationships that could grow and flourish if she tended them correctly. It felt surreal and yet it felt more real than a lot had in recent years now she thought about it.

'Cheers.' Mia tapped her mug against Nina's and then against the tin cup that Liz held.

'Cheers.' Liz smiled as she sat back in the canvas chair. It was true that the circumstances that had brought her to Little Bramble weren't ideal, but she liked to believe (sometimes) that everything happened for a reason. Right now, it seemed that the reason was for her to spend more time with Nina and, perhaps, to meet Mia, who seemed like another woman in need of some female friendship.

Loss came in many different guises, but thankfully, friendship did too.

Chapter 9

'Phwoar! Choc-chip banana muffins.' Joel reached out a hand and Mia tapped it playfully.

'No you don't!'

'What? But why? They smell incredible.'

'They should do. I've been baking for hours.'

'Feeling peckish?' Joel winked and reached for a muffin again but Mia got there first and grabbed one then handed it to him with a smile.

'Here you go. I made them to give to some friends.'

'Lucky friends.' He peeled the paper case aside and took a bite of the large muffin then closed his eyes as he chewed. 'That is incredible, Mum. It's a good job I moved out or I'd be twice the man I am.'

Mia laughed. 'Joel, you're so busy you couldn't get fat if you tried.'

Joel was tall and broad-shouldered with a muscular physique. Growing up, he'd been like a twig, but over the years he'd filled out as his body had changed from boy to man. He was her baby, her youngest, and her heart lurched at the glint of grey in his sideburns and stubble. At thirty-four, he was almost a decade older than his dad had been when he'd passed away, and Mia didn't think she'd ever stop worrying about her boys, ever take it for granted that they'd live into their eighties. Every single day of life was a gift. The thought that they might suffer their father's fate was too much for her to bear so she constantly pushed it from her mind.

'Sit down, Joel, and I'll put the kettle on.' Mia was used to trying to distract herself from the morbid thoughts that crept in if she let them. What was the point in constantly worrying when she couldn't control what might happen and could end up wasting her life fretting instead of living and enjoying time with her boys?

'Thanks, Mum.'

Today, Joel had come to visit after his day shift, the signs of a busy time evident in his messy hair (he had a habit of dragging his hands through it), stubble and the dark shadows under his warm brown eyes. It was a tough job, a challenging job, and although he insisted that he found it rewarding, Mia knew that it took its toll on him – especially when he arrived at a scene where it was too late to save someone.

While Joel sat down, Mia made two mugs of tea then sat opposite him. She bounced up immediately as if she'd sat on a pin and went to the oven then peered inside. The raspberry and lemon cookies she was baking looked fine; they were just beginning to brown.

'There are cookies too, so you can take some home when they're ready.'

'Bonus!' Joel swallowed the last bite of his muffin then picked up his mug. 'So which friends are getting these culinary delights?'

'Some ladies I met up at the allotment.' Mia smiled as she thought about earlier that day when she'd sat with Liz and Nina and drunk tea from Gideon's flask. They hadn't sat for long because it had been too cold, and although they'd had tea and seats, they hadn't had blankets or a fire, so when the flask was empty, they'd reluctantly tidied up and walked back into the village. Mia lived at the southern end of the village green so her walk home was not as far as Liz and Nina's but it was still good exercise for her. 'It's funny, actually. Earlier today I went up to the allotment for a walk and to check on Gideon's plot and I bumped into Nina Potts. She was there with her sister, Liz. I hadn't seen Nina for a while but I'd never met her sister before.'

'I know Nina . . .' Joel frowned. 'Tall, ginger hair, lots of freckles.'

'That's her.'

'I don't think I've met her sister, though.'

'You wouldn't have. She doesn't live locally but she's staying with Nina for a while.'

'That's nice.' Joel's eyes slid to the oven.

'They're not ready yet.' Mia laughed. 'Be patient, my boy. Anyway, we shared a flask of tea on Nina's plot and when

I got home I thought it would be nice if I took some cakes next time.'

'Tomorrow?'

'Yes.' Mia didn't know if Liz and Nina would even be at the allotment tomorrow but once she'd got the idea of seeing them again into her head, as well as taking Zelda more cakes, she couldn't get it out. She'd felt compelled to get baking.

'Glad to see you getting out, Mum.'

Mia met her son's eyes. 'Well, I doubt it will be a regular thing but I enjoyed today. We sat and had a chat. Liz, that's Nina's sister, seems to have been through a tough time and it just got me thinking.'

'Yes?'

'People all go through difficult times but the human spirit is incredibly resilient. I know I've not been myself lately, but I *am* trying. You know that, don't you?'

Joel reached his hand over the table and took hold of hers. 'Of course I do, Mum, and I appreciate how difficult a time you're having. No one, especially not me, expects you to *get over* losing your husband. Gideon was your world and while I know they say time can ease grief, it's only been a few months. You're entitled to be sad, low or furious at the universe. Don't beat yourself up for feeling these things. And, to be honest with you . . . I miss him too.' Joel's voice wobbled and he coughed then rubbed at his eyes. 'Sorry . . . didn't expect that to happen.'

'Gideon loved you.' She smiled sadly, aware that it wasn't only her who'd lost Gideon; her sons had too. And he'd been such a large presence in Joel's world because Joel lived locally and saw more of Gideon than his brothers did.

'Yeah, I loved him too, daft giant that he was. I see death and grief a lot at work, too often for my liking, but it's part of the job I signed up for, and I know it's part of life too. But when it happens within your own family sphere it's hard to accept. Gideon was too full of energy and zest for life to go, you know?'

'I do, love, I do. I still expect to hear his key in the lock, his footsteps in the hallway, his weight settling into bed next to me.'

Joel's eyes were glistening now. 'Oh Mum, I really wish I could make it better for you.'

'I'm OK! And I certainly don't expect you to do anything. You have your own life to live. Besides which, I'm a survivor if nothing else.' Mia shook herself and stood up; making her son sad was the last thing she wanted to do. She slid her hands into oven gloves then got the two trays of cookies out. 'These are done now.'

She placed the trays on the cooling rack, removed the oven gloves then went to Joel and stood behind him, placed her hands on his shoulders, her chin on the top of his head. 'I'm OK, Joel. I'm here for you whenever you need me.'

Joel placed his hands on top of hers and squeezed them. 'I know, Mum.'

She stayed there for a moment then pressed a kiss to Joel's messy hair. It smelt clean and citrussy, the scent of her son, and her heart gave a little flip because she loved him so much. Finally, she turned away and slid the cookies off the trays and directly onto the cooling rack. Once the baking trays were in hot, soapy water in the sink to soak, she placed two cookies on a plate then handed it to Joel.

'Are we comfort eating then?' he asked, his eyes clear but red-rimmed.

'We are. We deserve a treat.'

'I think I need the sugar to keep me going. Mind you, I did promise myself I'd go for a run later, so I guess it's OK to have these now.'

'A run?' Mia shook her head. 'I don't know how you do it.'

'If I don't do it, I feel worse.'

'I'm actually thinking about attending yoga and tai chi.'

'At the village hall?'

'Yes. I bumped into Kyle the other day and he said I should join the classes. It might do me good.'

'Go for it, Mum. I'm really pleased you've got some friends at the allotment and that you're thinking about joining some classes.'

'Well, whatever happens to us, life goes on, right?'

'Indeed it does.' Joel picked up a cookie and bit into it. 'Mmm-mmm. Delicious!'

Mia filled the kettle, planning on making more tea, a smile on her face. She had twice lost men she loved and she wasn't twenty-one any more, but perhaps there were still things in life she could enjoy, like making new friends, taking some classes and baking for her sons. She doubted the ache in her heart would ever go, but keeping busy might be some kind of soothing balm. Besides which, thinking about what she had instead of what she'd lost had to be a positive step to take.

Chapter 10

Liz marched along the woodland path, breathing deeply of the fresh morning air, making an effort to focus on the sights and sounds around her. She considered jogging but didn't feel quite ready to go for it yet, wondered if she'd ever be able to summon that level of energy again. The trees on either side dwarfed her, the path beneath the wood chippings was solid and dry and she could hear a robin in a nearby tree. She wondered if it was the same robin from the other day or if there were others in the vicinity. The scent of the richness of the earth rose to greet her and something else teased her as she neared the end of the path, a waft of frying bacon.

Her stomach grumbled, reminding her that she hadn't eaten much for breakfast after experiencing that tightening in her gut when she woke, when she remembered where she was and why. Anxiety was a horrid feeling and she wished it would go but until she had Rhodri back, their life together back and was back in their home, she knew it would drag in the pit of her stomach like a bag of rocks.

Distraction! It was key to passing her time here, to escaping the terrible pain in her chest and to being herself again. That was why she'd decided to get up, dress and leave the house after Nina had set off to walk Cora to school. Liz had accompanied them several times on the school walk, but she thought Nina might appreciate some time alone with her daughter this morning. As much as Liz was enjoying being around Nina and her family, she was conscious of not wanting to be a nuisance. She'd walk up to the allotment, have a look around up there, then stop in the village for some lunch.

After leaving Nina a note, she'd packed her small rucksack with a notepad and pen then she'd dressed warmly and set off. This time, though, she'd ensured that she had her mobile phone, not wanting to spend her time out worrying about missing a call from Rhodri. He hadn't tried to contact her yesterday: she'd checked as soon as she'd got home from the allotment, her heart sinking when she went through her messages, emails and WhatsApp. There had been nothing. With each day that passed, she felt her hope seeping away and wondered if this really was it, the end of Rhodri and Liz.

She stopped walking and leant over, gasping at the strength of the pain inside.

Not again, please!

Her eyes stung and her chest felt tight, she gasped as she tried to fill her lungs.

Oh God! Was this it? Was she having a heart attack?

Breathe, Liz! Breathe.

She focused on slowing her breaths, counted in for four, held it for seven then exhaled to the count of eight. She did this eight times, feeling her chest expanding, the knot in her shoulders loosening. She looked around her, focused on the sight of the sky through the branches of the trees, a heavy canopy in shades of brown and grey, no blue to be seen on this chilly day.

The sky was still above her; the air all around her; the earth beneath her feet. She was OK.

I am OK . . .

'I am OK,' she whispered to herself, the woods and the sky.

When she felt more together, she started to walk again, taking it slowly and doing her best to think about nothing other than her surroundings and where she was heading. *I am being mindful*, she thought, holding on to a flicker of pride in how she'd managed to calm herself.

Eventually, she reached the stone cottage that she thought looked sad and abandoned. The low wall surrounding it was green with moss, the front garden neglected, the windows dark and dirty, their net curtains shabby, a pile of decaying leaves blocking access to the front door. Liz could imagine what this cottage would be like if someone lived there and took care of it, gave it a good clean and a lick of paint. It was in such a lovely spot, surrounded by trees and fields, the allotments nearby and the village a short walk away. It was a perfect rural setting yet close enough to the village not to be isolated. Why didn't anyone live there? It seemed such a waste.

She made a mental note to find out more about the cottage; why, she wasn't sure, but something about it intrigued her. Perhaps it was the history buff inside her, keen to find out what secrets the cottage might hold.

When she reached the allotment, she made her way to Nina's plot. She'd grabbed the shed key that Nina kept hanging on a hook in the kitchen. When they'd got home yesterday, Nina had made a point of telling Liz that the key was there should she need it, as if she knew that Liz might want to head up to the allotment alone at some point. And she had.

Outside the shed, she paused. It seemed wrong to go inside without Nina, as if she was entering her sister's house when she wasn't there. But it was just a shed. If she went inside there would be nothing but chairs, gardening tools and . . . possibly a hedgehog. She shuddered. The thought of encountering the creature alone did not appeal to her so she tucked the key back in her pocket. Nina had said she would find out what to do about the hedgehog today, so it was probably best to leave it alone for now.

Looking around, she saw no one else. It was early and cold, so she shouldn't expect many people to be here at this time of the morning, but even so, she found herself hoping to see Mia again. It would be nice to chat to the kind older woman again and possibly share a cup of tea. Something in Mia's demeanour had reminded Liz of herself, as if they shared a sense of loss, even though Liz's partner was still alive and well.

She'd take a walk around the back of the allotments and see what lay in the other direction. That would occupy her for a while then she could head back down to the village and have some lunch.

Mia drove her car along the bumpy track then parked it just outside the gate to Zelda's home. She would have walked but didn't fancy carrying the tins of cakes and biscuits, so she'd decided to drive instead but she'd forgotten about the bumpy track. Gideon had made her laugh whenever she'd driven him along it, pretending that his teeth were chattering in his head and that his belly was sloshing around as if it was filled with jelly. Even when he'd been unwell, he'd made her smile. It was as if he could still be himself through using humour, still cling to the man he was and push the horrid disease that was destroying him aside. He'd been incredibly brave and strong, her beautiful husband.

'Bloody cancer!' she muttered, not for the first time, resisting the urge to pound her fists against the steering wheel because of the unfairness of it all.

She got out of the car, retrieved the tins from the boot then made her way to Zelda's door. Hands full, she couldn't knock so she gave it a tap with her foot and waited.

Nothing.

She tried again.

Perhaps the elderly woman couldn't hear her or perhaps she was out. Mia thought the latter more likely, and her heart sank. She'd been looking forward to seeing Zelda's face when she gave her the baked goods.

'Cooee!'

Mia turned around, frowning.

'Mia!'

Beyond the garden wall was what looked like a moving scarecrow, complete with wide-brimmed brown hat.

'Zelda?' She walked back to the gate, opened it with her foot then stepped out but it closed quickly behind her on its spring and gave her a swat on the bottom. She staggered forwards and almost dropped the tin of biscuits.

'Are you all right?' Zelda hurried towards her but Mia had regained her balance and she nodded.

'I'm fine, thanks. That gate closes so quickly, though.'

'I had to tighten the spring on it because the chickens kept escaping when I let them out of the coop.'

'Of course, you have chickens.' Mia glanced behind her.

'Yes, the coop is around the side of the house. They have an enclosed space to roam but sometimes I let them into the garden to have a scratch around. Cheeky little buggers have made their way down to the gate a few times, though, and if they can squeeze through, they will. More than once I've had to track them through the woods and get them home before dark or the foxes would have them.'

Mia nodded along, awe filling her. This tiny woman had been racing around the woods after chickens? Alone? That was resilience of spirit for sure.

'I have got some bruises on my old bottom, though, where the gate has closed quickly and caught me before I can get out of the way.' Zelda's lips turned upwards then her eyes alighted on the tins in Mia's arms.

'These are for you.' Mia held them out. 'Cakes and cookies.'

'Oooh!' Zelda grinned. 'Now you're spoiling me.'

Mia laughed. 'It's a pleasure to have someone to bake for other than my son. I just end up eating everything myself otherwise and . . . well . . .' She nodded her head at herself. 'I really don't need the calories.'

'Nonsense! You're a beautiful woman in her prime. You should be proud of your curves. It's all downhill when you reach my age. Between you and me, some of my curves actually touch my knees now.' Zelda chuckled and Mia joined in. 'Oh, I used to have a fabulous figure myself back in the day. Right Marilyn Monroe lookalike, I was.'

'Really?' Mia replied then her eyes widened. 'Goodness! I didn't mean that how it sounded. I'm not surprised that you looked like her, just—'

'Ha! Ha!' Zelda was waving a hand. 'It's fine. I know I don't look like her now, but in my youth I could have given her a run for her money. That was all a long time ago, though.' Zelda sighed. 'Anyway, shall I take those tins?'

'Wouldn't you like me to carry them up to the house for you?' Mia didn't want to offload the tins onto Zelda.

'Only as long as you let me put the kettle on.'

'You've got yourself a deal.'

Zelda opened the gate and they were about to enter the garden when movement over at the allotment caught her eye. 'I think that's Liz.'

'Who?'

'Liz . . . Gosh, I can't remember if she told me her surname but I met her up here yesterday. She's Nina Potts' sister. I was hoping to see her here today too.'

'Oh . . .' Zelda blinked. 'Don't let me stop you.'

'No, no, I wanted to see you but I also hoped I'd bump into Liz again. She's very nice.' Mia looked at Zelda then back at Liz.

'Well . . . if she's not busy, invite her in for tea too.' Zelda gave a nonchalant shrug.

'Are you sure?' Mia suppressed her smile. She'd had a feeling that Zelda might appreciate the company but she didn't want to suggest it herself. Also, something about Liz that she'd noted the previous day made her want to find out more. Liz had seemed so sad and anxious that Mia had recognised something of herself in the younger woman. Just as with Zelda. The three of them might be different ages but they were all going through their own difficulties. Gideon had always said that talking was good for people and that a problem shared was a problem halved. Mia wasn't 100 per cent certain about that, but surely the chance to enjoy some company, tea and cake was better than feeling alone? Liz might have Nina, but if she was anything like Mia then she wouldn't want to put on her family all the time, if at all.

Sometimes, the kindness of strangers could be a good thing – people you could talk to who wouldn't judge you but who would listen and even understand. Mia saw it often enough on the TV these days, about how being there for others was important, about how talking was good for mental health. Besides which, she had nothing better to do with her time and if she could help someone else simply by being there to listen, it would be a deed well done.

'Yes, why not?' Zelda said. 'Put the tins on the doorstep and go and get her. I'll put the kettle on and leave the door on the latch. Just come on in when you return.'

'Wonderful! Will do.' Mia trotted up the path and put the tins down then marched back out of the garden and to the far end of the allotment, only realising when she reached Liz how out of breath she was.

'Oh hello.' Liz smiled at the red-faced woman who'd just run towards her.

Mia nodded then pointed at her chest. 'Just . . . get breath . . . back.'

'Of course.'

Liz had walked around the outside of the allotments and down the banking that led to a stream. On the other side of the water were more trees and fields, giving the allotments the feeling of being completely rural. The more she saw of Little Bramble, the more she liked it, and the more she wondered how it would be to settle in a place like this.

'Sorry!' Mia smiled. 'I saw you and ran over here . . . but silly me, I forgot how unfit I am.'

'I don't know if I'd be able to run at the moment, either.'

'My youngest son, Joel, runs all the time. I don't know how he does it. He tells me he enjoys it, but personally, I can't understand the attraction. Having boobs doesn't help.' She patted her chest then laughed. 'Perhaps I just need a better bra. If I remembered to put one on this morning.' She frowned. 'Not sure I did. Uh . . . Anyway, I wondered if you have plans?'

'Right now?'

'Yes.'

Liz shook her head. 'I came up here for a walk in the hope it would clear my head a bit. I was considering opening up Nina's shed then I remembered the hedgehog and thought better of it.'

'A hedgehog won't hurt you.'

'Maybe not but I didn't want to disturb it in case it's hibernating. Nina said she'd contact someone about it today and find out what she should do. So I decided to go for a walk instead. It's so lovely here. I'm sure it's gorgeous in the summer.'

'It is.' Mia nodded. 'Absolutely beautiful. And in the autumn when the leaves on the trees change colour and . . . oh!' Her expression changed and her eyes clouded over. 'Sorry.'

'No, don't be sorry.' Liz watched Mia's face carefully. 'Are you all right?'

'I am . . . It's just that I've always loved the autumn and now . . . now it will be forever changed.'

'Is that when you lost your husband?'

'Back in November as autumn turned to winter. Quite symbolic, really.'

Liz tried swallow but her mouth had gone dry. She wasn't sure what to say in the face of such raw grief.

'Anyway . . .' Mia seemed to collect herself. 'I've been baking and I brought some cakes up for Zelda Grey.' She pointed behind her at the big house. 'The lady who owns that house. And she's invited us both for tea. If you'd like to join us.'

'For tea and cake?'

'Yes.'

Liz looked up at the large house. It was enormous. Did one woman really live there alone? It would certainly be a different way to spend the morning than she'd envisaged. She was here anyway so she'd just as soon make the effort to meet another villager, even though in her current mind frame she preferred the thought of hiding herself away under the duvet.

'I'd love to join you both.' She tried to inject some enthusiasm into her tone.

'Fabulous!' Liz clapped her hands. 'Come along, then.'

Liz let Mia take her hand and slide it through her arm, then they walked up to the house together. The more she thought about it, having tea and cake with two interesting women sounded a lot better than staring at her phone and waiting for Rhodri to come to his senses, plus it would be a good story to share with him when he did.

Zelda placed the teapot she reserved for when she had guests – which was never – on the kitchen table along with three mugs, a small jug of milk, the sugar bowl, a plate of cookies and one of muffins. She'd brought the tins in one by one, not wanting to leave them outside in case the chickens found them before Mia got back. Then she stared at the table. It didn't look right. It was old and worn and she had guests coming.

Guests!

Not just one but two if Mia's friend agreed to come.

'Do you hear that, Mother?' she said aloud. 'I have guests coming for tea and one of them even baked these for me.'

She could just imagine her mother's response: *Get a tablecloth out, Zelda.*

Of course! That was what she'd missed.

She opened one of the drawers and rooted through it then pulled out a white tablecloth. She shook it out and was hit by a wave of lavender from the small net bags her mother had always kept in the linen drawers. She cleared the table before laying the cloth over it then moved the tea things back. It looked so much better, covering the scratches on the table and the stain from where she'd knocked over a bottle of Christmas port, which had then seeped into the wood like blood and refused to come out despite many attempts at scrubbing it clean.

She touched a finger to the delicate embroidery around the edge of the tablecloth, small roses and lilies that her mother had once spent weeks on. Did people spend time doing things like embroidery anymore? It wasn't a form of instant gratification, so she doubted many would bother with it. She couldn't embroider now because of the arthritis that had formed bumps on her knuckles, making fine needlework difficult, but as a girl she'd had quite a talent for it. Her eyesight also wasn't good enough, despite her strong glasses.

'Helloooo!' She heard the voice from the hallway that she guessed was Mia's. 'It's only us.'

'Come on through!' she called back, a sudden bubbling in her stomach taking her by surprise. Was that excitement at the thought of having company for the second time within mere weeks? 'Just like buses,' she said, chuckling to herself. 'One day you can't get one and the next they all come at once.'

She straightened her jumper and went to stand at the end of the table, readying herself to welcome her guests into her home.

Chapter 11

Liz followed Mia through a long hallway. She tried not to stare at things but the house was like something out of a period drama, right down to the décor that seemed frozen in time. It smelt musty, as though the windows hadn't been opened in years. It wasn't an unpleasant smell but it wasn't one that Liz liked either. She knew that if she was there for any length of time she'd have to fight the urge to throw open as many windows as she could and to let the wind blow through the house and clear out the stale air. Growing up, Nina had been a big fan of opening windows, even in winter, and of drying washing on the line in the garden; she said it smelt better that way plus the ancient tumble drier ate the electricity from the token meter and having lighting was more important.

They made their way past closed doors, trying to avoid the piles of books, boxes and bags, and through a doorway on their right that led into a cosy kitchen. At the end of a long wooden table, an elderly lady stood with her hands, clad in grey fingerless gloves, clasped in front of her. She was small, with a shock of white hair that framed her head like a candyfloss wig, wearing silver-framed glasses, a long green jumper, what looked like stained riding jodhpurs and a pair of battered yellow wellington boots. Something about the vulnerability in the woman's eyes and stance made Liz's heart squeeze.

'Zelda, this is Liz. Liz, meet Zelda,' Mia said as they walked to the table.

'Hello,' Liz said, offering a polite smile.

'Hello, there.' The woman smiled back, raising one of her hands and gesturing at the chairs. 'Please sit down. I've made tea and we have delicious offerings from Mia to enjoy with it.'

Liz glanced at Mia, who gave a small nod as she pulled out a chair, so Liz sat down and pulled the chair closer to the table. Her eyes roamed the cakes and cookies before sliding across the kitchen to the Aga and surrounding mantel, to the stains on the wall above and to the cobwebs in the corners of the high ceiling. The window was in need of a clean and the curtains hung stiffly, as if they were ingrained with years of food and steam but there was greenery everywhere, with plants on every available surface. Liz had kept the house she shared with Rhodri spotless, in spite of having a full-time job, and had a window cleaner come in twice a month, more often if a storm made the glass dirty in the meantime. She bleached surfaces, sinks and toilets, stripped the bed weekly, washed curtains every few months and swept and vacuumed several times a week. Rhodri had often laughed at her, told her to leave the cleaning and come sit down and watch TV, but Liz couldn't rest if something needed tidying or cleaning. Where had that come from? She'd always kept herself busy, too busy to think, perhaps?

'Shall I pour?' Mia interrupted Liz's thoughts as she pointed at the teapot and Liz felt heat flood into her cheeks. Had Mia seen her looking around, perhaps known that Liz was judging the condition of the house?

'Please do,' Zelda said as she sat down. She looked even smaller on the chair, hunched over as if she might crumble in on herself at any moment. No wonder she wasn't cleaning from top to bottom, Liz thought; she was elderly and seemed quite fragile. 'Thank you so much for baking again, Mia.'

'It's a pleasure.' Mia handed Liz a mug of tea. 'I'm not sure if you want sugar or milk, dear, so help yourself. Zelda?'

'Just a splash of milk, thank you.' Zelda accepted a mug from Mia.

'I love baking but because it's only me now, I end up eating everything myself and it's not doing my waistline any favours. There is my son, Joel, but he works shifts and so although I can send some baked goods home with him, I tend to get through my fair share and then some.' She laughed but her hand slid down to her waist. 'Still, no one to look good for these days.'

'You look wonderful, Mia. You're a beautiful woman and I'll not hear differently.' Zelda winked at Mia and Liz was glad she'd responded first because Liz had been worried about how sad Mia looked when she said there was no one to look good for. Poor Mia was grieving deeply for her husband and Liz wished there was something she could say or do to help.

'You do look fabulous, Mia,' Liz added.

Mia laughed. 'Well, I'm hoping to do some work on the allotment this year to stay active and I'm walking plenty too. Also, I saw Kyle Greene the other day and he suggested going to the tai chi classes that he runs. I think I might go.'

'Tai chi?' Liz raised her eyebrows. 'I've never done that but I know it's meant to be very good for your circulation and your mental health.'

'Mental health?' Zelda huffed. 'Isn't there a . . . oh darn it . . . a thingamajig . . . a what do you call it . . .' She clicked her fingers. 'An app, that's it . . . for that, these days?'

'You can get apps for everything,' Liz replied. 'I have a mindfulness one on my phone and it's great.' She frowned as she thought about the app. When exactly had she used it last? She paid for it monthly, had used it when she'd first down-loaded it and found it good, but recently? She couldn't recall the last time she'd meditated.

'Well, I think I might go and try out tai chi. You two could come with me,' Mia said as she cupped her hands around her mug.

'I'll come!' Liz said quickly and nodded, thinking that it would be another way to keep her mind off Rhodri. 'While I'm here, I want to stay active.'

'Are you here for long?' Zelda asked.

'Not really. I'm staying with my sister for a few weeks but I'll probably head home around Easter. So in about four weeks. Although, I might go home before then . . .' *If Rhodri gets in touch,* she added silently.

'Where is home?' Zelda pushed her glasses back up her nose and Liz noticed that the wool of her glove was fraying around her thumb.

'I live in Maidstone.' Liz thought of the house she'd bought with Rhodri. 'I have a four-bedroom house built of red brick with a blue door, a garage and a driveway.' It sounded like a sales pitch.

She swallowed hard as the image of her house filled her mind. The first time she'd seen the house it had been a blueprint, a plot on a new estate ready to be filled. She'd been so excited at the thought of having a home of her own. Well, a home for her and Rhodri, a place where they could start a family and grow old together. The estate was lovely, filled with young families with shiny cars, neat lawns, clean windows, neighbourhood watch and personal trainers. Personal trainers who seduced your fiancé and ruined your perfect life . . .

'Here you are, lovely.' Zelda was holding out a tissue.

'Oh . . . thanks.' Liz accepted the tissue, suddenly aware that her cheeks were wet. 'S-sorry. I didn't realise I was crying.'

'That happens to me too.' Mia smiled kindly at her. 'It's so hard when your partner passes away.'

'Passes away?' Liz frowned. 'My Rhodri is still alive. I'm sorry, Mia, you must have misunderstood me. I was just thinking about our house and how much I loved it when we bought it. We paid a hefty deposit and had to wait for it to be built but it was so clean and new and fresh and totally ours.' She dabbed at her cheeks then blew her nose.

'Can I ask why you're sad then?' Zelda fixed her eyes on Liz. 'Because to me that all sounds rather grand.'

Liz sighed. 'Rhodri and I . . . we're having difficulties.'

'I'm sorry to hear that, my dear.' Zelda cleared her throat. 'But I do hope it's something you can work through.'

Liz tucked the tissue in her sleeve then picked up her tea. 'I'd like to think so too.'

'Life can be tough,' Zelda said, 'but I'm sure that if there's love there, you'll find a way to work it out.'

The three of them fell silent as they drank their tea and munched on cakes and cookies. When Mia broke the silence, Liz was surprised at how comfortable she'd felt just being in the company of the two women. Sometimes, simply sitting with others in quiet contemplation could be beneficial.

'So, ladies, are you both going to come and try tai chi?'

Liz nodded but Zelda's brows met above her glasses. 'I think I'm a bit old for all that.'

'Not at all.' Mia shook her head. 'It's low-impact and suitable for anyone. I googled it.'

'Uhhh . . .' Zelda picked at a loose thread on her glove. 'Weeell, in that case I think I could give it a go.'

'That's settled, then.' Mia grinned. 'There's a class early on Saturday morning. I'll come and pick you up, Zelda, shall I?'

Zelda looked at Mia then at Liz. 'I can make my own way down to the village.'

'I know that, but at least if I come and pick you up, I can make sure you find your way there.'

Zelda chuckled. 'Are you suggesting that I might not come?'

'Not at all.' Mia waggled her eyebrows. 'I just want to ensure that you get there safely.'

'I'm going to have another muffin, then, because it seems I'm going to need all the energy I can get.' Zelda reached for the plate and Liz was happy to see some colour in the elderly woman's cheeks now. It must be hard living alone in a house this big and Liz could imagine that some company and delightful baking would make Zelda feel a bit better, especially when it was from Mia, who Liz was liking more by the minute. Despite recently suffering such a devastating loss, Mia really seemed to have a heart of gold and plenty of kindness to share around.

Later that day Liz was massaging moisturiser into her face following a shower when she heard a loud bang. She froze, wondering what had made the noise. As far as she'd been aware, she was in the house alone. Nina had told her she was taking Cora shopping for new school shoes after she'd collected her from school, Kane would still be at work and Demi didn't usually get home until later on.

For a few moments there was silence then the sound of someone climbing the stairs and heading into the family bathroom. There was nothing unusual about that, but the bang had been, so she wiped her hands on a towel in the ensuite then went to the bedroom door and opened it.

The door to the family bathroom was closed and she could hear laughing. Or was that crying?

She crept across the landing and stood in front of the door, straining to hear.

There was definitely someone crying in there but whoever it was, they were trying to do it quietly. It sounded female so wasn't Kane and if Nina had come back she'd have Cora with her. So it must be Demi.

Suddenly, the toilet flushed, so Liz darted back to her room and pushed the door behind her, leaving it open a fraction so she could peer through the crack.

The bathroom door swung open and there she was: Liz's sixteen-year-old niece. Since arriving in Little Bramble, Liz hadn't seen much of Demi, and what she had seen hadn't been that pleasant – Demi had been quite cold, but then Liz had noticed that Demi seemed to treat her parents that way too. Demi seemed very angry and Liz had decided not to take it personally, knowing how teenagers could be.

Demi paused on the landing and Liz sank back into the shadows behind the door, wary of being spotted, but Demi pulled her smartphone from her pocket and held it up. She swiped the screen, her eyes flickered across it as if she was reading something, then she growled. It was an animal noise, filled with anguish and fury, and when she lowered her phone,

Liz saw the tears trickle down Demi's cheeks. She couldn't rush to Demi and hug her because then Demi would know that she'd been spying on her and she didn't think Demi would react well to that or to a hug from the aunt she barely knew, but Liz's heart squeezed. Whatever Demi had read or seen on her phone had made her sad and Liz wished she could do something to help.

Suddenly, Demi wiped the back of her hand across her eyes, sniffed hard, tucked her phone back in her pocket then stomped down the stairs and straight out the front door, slamming it behind her.

Liz emerged from her room and peered down the stairs, wishing she had a closer relationship with her older niece so she could ask her what was wrong.

Chapter 12

As Liz walked to the allotment later that week, it was still cold but not as icy as it had been when she'd arrived in the village. Something about the promise of spring in the air reflected in her step. At the sides of the path, she noticed snowdrops that had opened their delicate bell-shaped flowers to make the most of the slightly milder conditions. Further along were primroses, seeming to have appeared within just days, their pale-yellow blooms and fresh green leaves a sight that lifted her heart. She caught herself, surprised at how she could feel this way when everything in her life had seemed so gloomy recently, when she still hadn't heard from Rhodri. Not so much as a whisper.

What had changed since her arrival in Little Bramble to give her this sliver of hope, even when her heart was still so heavy?

She'd been able to spend time with Nina and her family. That had been pleasant and made her start to question her behaviour towards her sister. There had also been time with Mia and Zelda. They were two women of different ages, different generations to her and yet . . . there was something about them that made Liz feel that they could understand her, offer her advice and envelop her in a friendship born of compassion and empathy. Age was irrelevant, it seemed, when making new friends as an adult, and while she didn't know them very well, she suspected that she soon would. She found them intriguing and wanted to know more about them, to learn about their lives and how they'd dealt with the challenges they'd faced over the years. Not having had a mother or maternal figure in her life, apart from Nina who was just a few years her senior, it was nice to spend time with older women, women who'd been through tough times and yet were still standing. They were resilient in ways that Liz wanted to be and she suspected they had a wealth of experience to share, plenty of wisdom to impart. Just like the snowdrops that returned every year, storing up their strength in their bulbs and emerging from the ground to face the sun again, Mia and Zelda kept going, kept smiling, kept on facing each day.

Liz reached the allotment slightly out of breath after her brisk walk but she also felt invigorated and knew that she would soon be ready to run again. She was gathering strength, rebuilding herself slowly and while she didn't yet know what her future would look like, the longer she spent in Little Bramble, the more she was able to believe that she'd be OK. She still thought that she wanted to go home to Rhodri, to know that he'd try to make things up to her, but she was coping well, she thought, and would survive whatever the outcome.

Hopefully!

'Zelda!' she called, spotting the elderly woman at the edge of the allotments. 'Everything all right?'

Zelda raised a hand in greeting. 'Lost some bloody chickens, haven't I?'

'Hold on.' Liz jogged around the outskirts of the plots and towards her friend. 'What happened?'

Zelda was dressed in jeans, wellies and a baggy brown jumper. She had a grey hat on her head and her familiar fingerless gloves. Even she had apparently cast off her coat with the advent of spring.

'I let them out of the pen this morning and they had a good roam of the garden but then I had a delivery of chicken feed and while the driver had the gate propped open with a box, the birds got out. I managed to get them all back except for Henrietta, Mother Clucker and Dr Pecker.'

Liz nearly snorted but caught herself in time and asked, 'M-Mother Clucker?'

Zelda raised her eyebrows. 'They all have names.'

'They're great names.' Liz smiled. 'Want some help catching them?'

'If you don't mind, dear. But be careful with the cockerel, Dr Pecker.'

'Why?'

'Why'd you think?'

Liz frowned. 'Because he pecks?'

'He can do if you catch him on a bad day.'

'Chickens have bad days?' Now she really had to hold back giggles.

'You'd be surprised, dear.' Zelda gave a solemn nod.

They walked past the allotments and towards the stream. On the other side of the banking, Liz saw a flash of white. 'There!' She pointed.

'Where?' Zelda leant forwards and peered into the undergrowth.

'I saw one dash behind that tree. How did they get across?' she asked, looking around. The stream was about two feet across and looked about a foot deep. 'Can chickens swim?'

Zelda nodded. 'But I doubt they'd want to right now with the water still being so cold. They've probably used the stepping stones further along.'

Liz blinked. Chickens could have bad days, swim and use stepping stones? How had she never known about this? Mirth bubbled inside her and she had to grit her teeth to stop herself from laughing out loud.

'Go on, then,' Zelda said, gesturing at the water.

'I'm sorry?'

'Jump in.'

'Pardon?' Liz scanned Zelda's face. Was she really suggesting that Liz should jump into the stream?

'Well, the chickens won't come back without some encouragement.'

'I know but . . .' Liz looked down at her trainers. If she went through the water she'd get wet and cold.

'I thought you wanted to help.' Zelda's blue eyes twinkled behind her glasses.

'Are you serious?' Liz asked.

'Of course I'm not serious!' Zelda grinned. 'I was teasing you.'

Relief coursed through Liz. 'I thought you were. I just . . . I think my sense of humour took a setback when my fiancé . . . well . . . when things went umm . . .'

'There he is!'

'Rhodri?' Liz gasped.

Zelda scowled at her. 'Rhodri?'

'Yes. No. Uhhh—'

'I meant Dr Pecker.' Zelda pointed across the stream at a large cockerel. It was strutting along with two chickens in tow. 'Look at him, leading his ladies astray. He's a mischievous bloody cockerel.'

'He's gorgeous,' Liz said, admiring the cockerel with his dark-grey speckled feathers, red fleshy coxcomb and matching red wattle. Realising that she knew the strange names, she smiled inwardly. Reading comprehension activities for pupils often used factual texts and clearly she'd absorbed those details without being aware of it.

'He's a Maran. They all are, in fact. Beautiful birds that lay lovely dark-brown eggs and plenty of them.'

'Are they tame?' Liz asked, wondering why the birds would run away if they were.

'Very, but they still like a good old roam. Problem is, they don't realise how much danger there is out there. They're so greedy they head out looking for food but could easily be snatched by a fox or bird of prey.' Zelda placed a hand to her chest. 'I would hate for that fate to await them.'

'Well, let's get them safely home then.' Liz pushed her shoulders back. 'Where are the stepping stones?'

'Follow me.'

Zelda led the way and they passed her house with its protective wall and emerged in a clearing. Off to the right, a series of large flat stones led across the stream.

'Right, I'll go over and try to shoo them back this way.'

'Are you sure?' Zelda asked. 'I can do it if you wait here to lead them home.'

'No, no, it's fine.' Liz smiled at Zelda. The idea of leaving the octogenarian to race around the woods after her chickens seemed awful, so Liz was happy to help. She pushed up the sleeves of her fleece. 'Right, here I go.'

Zelda watched as Liz gingerly crossed the stones and reached the bank opposite. Snowdrops spread out around the trees for as far as she could see like an inviting soft, white blanket. She could understand why her chickens would want to roam over there but also feared for their safety. If they stayed out there too long, she might struggle to get them back and if darkness fell then goodness knows what fate might befall them. She had to get them home even if it took the rest of the day.

Liz weaved between the trees until she was on the far side of the birds then she started to usher them along. Henrietta squawked a few times and Dr Pecker flapped his wings, but they headed towards the stones.

'Go on, Dr Pecker! Hurry up, Henrietta!' Liz clapped her hands and the birds hurried along, clearly not impressed at having their morning adventure disturbed. 'Get a move on, Mother Clucker!' Liz met Zelda's eyes across the stream and they both giggled. 'I'm sorry!' Liz grinned. 'It's such a fab name.'

Zelda bobbed her head. She'd given thought to naming her chickens and had chosen each name to ensure it was different. Mother Clucker was a particularly mischievous hen and often quite vocal so it had seemed perfect for her. Plus, though Zelda wouldn't admit it out loud, she liked seeing the surprise on people's faces when she called the name.

When they reached the stones, the birds tried to turn around but Liz was there, arms spread wide, legs too, and she hopped from foot to foot to encourage them to cross. Seeing no other way, the birds crossed the stones and headed towards Zelda, the human they knew and trusted.

'Stay behind them and I'll lead them home,' Zelda said.

'No problem.'

And like a strange kind of Pied Piper, Zelda headed for her garden gate then held it open while her birds trotted through. She shut the gate quickly and leant against it.

'Thank you so much, Liz. It would have been much harder if I'd had to do it alone.'

'You're very welcome.' Liz's cheeks were rosy and her eyes shone. 'I quite enjoyed myself.'

Zelda looked at Liz's pretty face. She looked a bit better today but she knew that the younger woman was keeping something back, that she had a secret pain inside. Always one to stay active, Zelda knew the benefits of manual labour, of working the land, which was one of the reasons why she'd held on to the allotment for so long.

'Do you have any plans this morning?' Zelda asked.

'No, why?'

'Well, if you fancy some more exercise, I have some work that needs doing on the allotment.'

'Ooh! I'd love to help.'

'Wonderful. Let me just get the chickens secured then we can go to my plot and I'll show you what needs doing.'

'OK.'

'Come and see the chicken coop if you like.'

'Thanks.' Liz came into the garden and carefully closed the spring gate behind her then they walked around the side of the house.

After Zelda had shown Liz where she kept the chickens and settled the runaways with some food, she pulled a set of keys from her pocket.

'I keep my tools in the shed in the corner of the garden. Here's the key. Go and grab a spade and a trowel then I'll show you what needs doing.'

Liz nodded, then went to the shed.

Zelda had recognised something in Liz's eyes that she'd seen in hers in the mirror. It had faded somewhat now with the passage of time but she still knew what it was. Liz was heartbroken about something or someone, and while Zelda would never pry or push for Liz to tell her, she would do what she could to show quiet support and, hopefully, Liz would be able to start to rebuild her strength. Zelda didn't have any answers to how to heal a broken heart but she did know how to live with heartbreak, how to keep going even when she hadn't felt like getting out of bed in the mornings. She'd hate to think of Liz living like that, though, and so she'd do what she could to help her see that whatever had happened to her, there was always hope that things would work out in the end. Whatever form that end took.

'Put these on.' Zelda handed Liz a pair of gardening gloves when they reached her allotment plot. 'They're an old pair but they're sturdy.'

'Thanks.'

The gloves were made of a thick material and felt quite heavy in Liz's hands. She rested the spade and trowel against the low fence then slid her hands into the gloves. They were a bit big but better than risking blisters or splinters.

'What do you want me to do?' Liz asked as she looked around Zelda's plot. It was separated into different sections with small wooden dividers and there were four raised beds on one section.

'Weeding.'

'Weeding?'

Zelda gave a brief nod. 'Damned weeds get into the soil and they're a nuisance to get out. It's hard for me to get down and dig them out now, what with my ageing bones and bumpy fingers, but you're young and supple so it'll be easier for you.'

'Right, OK. No problem. What are you going to plant this year?' Liz grabbed the trowel and knelt in front of the larger section of earth, trying not to sigh at the sight of the weeds that were already raising their heads above the rich brown soil.

'This year I was thinking I'd grow potatoes, peppers, chard, herbs, rhubarb and more.'

'Wow! That's quite a selection.'

'It's surprising what you can grow. But it's no good planting out until the earth is weed-free and it's also better to warm the plot first.'

'How'd you do that?'

'With cloches or clear plastic sheeting.'

'That doesn't sound very environmentally friendly.' Liz wrinkled her nose.

'Using plastic?' Zelda asked.

'Well, yes.'

'Darling,' Zelda placed her hands on her hips, 'I've been using the same length of plastic for years. I don't use it then throw it away. I recycle it annually. I was a war baby and we didn't throw anything away. Your generation's not the first to reuse things.'

'Oh.' Liz's cheeks grew warm. 'I'm sorry. My mistake. And I'm also sorry for sounding judgemental.'

'Not at all, Liz. Honestly, it takes a lot to offend me. I understand where you're coming from and I'm sure that there are other products on the market that are better for the environment but I'm pretty old school in that I rarely throw anything away. Reduce, reuse and recycle, as the advert used to say!' Zelda chuckled and Liz couldn't help smiling.

'That's an excellent philosophy.'

'I think so.'

'Right, I'm going to get to work.'

'Thank you, dear. I'll just pop back to the house and see if I can find my kneeling pad. I thought I'd left it in the shed but I might well have taken it inside by mistake. My memory isn't what it used to be. Won't be long.'

Liz looked at the plot in front of her. She could see what appeared to be some well-established weeds, though she didn't have a clue what they were called, so she'd start with those then work through the rest.

As she worked, she grew warm. Weeding was not for the faint-hearted. It took physical perseverance, manual dexterity and soon she felt the need to remove her fleece. She stood up and pulled it over her head then knelt back down and resumed her efforts to extricate a particularly stubborn root from the ground. She wondered how Zelda usually managed, because while the elderly lady was no shrinking violet, she would find it hard to spend any significant amount of time on her knees in this position.

When she finally dug the root free, she dropped it at her side and sat back on her haunches. The sun had made an appearance in the blue sky and she felt perspiration at her hairline but realised she didn't mind. She wiped her arm over her brow to stop the sweat from running into her eyes. She'd been working for about forty-five minutes and in that time, she hadn't thought about Rhodri at all. She groaned inwardly as it dawned on her that she'd just thought about him, but even so, being here in the great outdoors with mud on her jeans, the gloves and even up her arms, she felt good. She was doing something worthwhile, something with an end result, and she found herself wanting to see what Zelda would plant and thinking how fascinating it would be to watch things grow. It must be so satisfying to eat produce you'd grown from seed and it was something she'd never done. Well, except for cress when she was at primary school and each pupil had grown some on a piece of kitchen roll then they'd eaten it in egg mayo sandwiches. Liz had spent her life purchasing fruit, veg and herbs from supermarkets, sometimes farmers' markets, but if she had a plot of land like this she'd be able to grow her own. It would be a different type of lifestyle altogether and she felt sure that she would waste far less if she knew how much effort had gone into growing it.

'Ha ha! Look at you, dear, you have mud everywhere.'

Zelda had appeared at Liz's side without her noticing so she pushed up to her feet and stretched out her back. 'Do I?'

'All across your forehead and in your hair.'

Liz grinned. 'It's OK. I've quite enjoyed myself although I think a soak in the bath later will be good.'

'You certainly deserve it. You've done a wonderful job.' Zelda appraised the plot. 'I brought the kneeler, found it under the sink of all places so I think I must have stuffed it under there when I was fixing a leaky pipe.'

'You fix pipes?'

'You'd be surprised, Liz. I learnt to do a fair bit over the years. Mother was a terrible snob but she was also incredibly tight with money so she learnt how to do all sorts of jobs herself and, in turn, taught me. She wouldn't allow me to call someone in if she could take care of a job herself. Although she did draw the line at gardening.' Zelda's gaze slid away and she seemed to go somewhere else for a moment.

'That's amazing. I wish I had more practical skills.'

'I'm sure you have plenty, Liz, but I'm always happy to share my knowledge with you.'

'Thank you.' Liz gazed at the tiny little lady at her side and wondered why Zelda didn't seem to have any family around her. Had she suffered the loss of a partner like Liz had or a different kind of loss? Or, had she never fallen in love? Zelda had grown up in a different time, of course, and from what she'd said about her mother, it seemed that the woman had been strict and domineering, so perhaps she'd stopped Zelda from having a significant relationship. It seemed such a shame because Zelda had so much wisdom to impart; she was just like the grandmother Liz had always imagined having.

'I almost forgot.' Zelda tapped her forehead as if in exasperation. 'I've made us some lunch.'

'Lunch?'

'Yes. Nothing fancy but I had a tin of red salmon at the back of the pantry – I promise it's not from the 1940s! – and some nice brown bread, so I made some sandwiches and cheese and crackers.'

Liz's stomach growled. 'Sounds amazing.'

'Simple food but tasty, right?'

'Definitely.'

'Well, dust yourself off and let's go and eat.'

'I haven't quite finished, though.' Liz pointed at a patch of weeds in the far corner.

'That's all right, they'll keep. To be honest . . .' Zelda pursed her lips. 'I was wondering if you might fancy helping me a bit with the allotment this year. While you're around, that is. I have plenty of seeds and some seedlings growing in my small greenhouse and it would be lovely to have some help.'

A warmth spread through Liz's chest and through her limbs. 'You'd really like my help?'

'I don't want to put on you, Liz, but if you have time, I'd be very grateful.'

'I'd be delighted to help.'

'You'll get your share of the crops, of course.'

'That's very kind, although I doubt I'll still be here then.'

'Well, if you are, you'll be welcome to them. And on that note, I have a basket of eggs at the house for you to take home.'

'Fresh eggs?'

'Free-range, too.'

'Fantastic.'

'Come on then, Liz, let's go and eat lunch and wash it down with a nice mug of tea.'

Liz picked up the spade and trowel, along with the kneeling pad that she'd managed without, and they made their way up to the house. Liz felt lighter than she had done in days at the thought of having a project for the next few weeks and at the thought that she could be seen as useful and helpful. So often with Rhodri she'd felt as if she was expecting too much of him, that wanting a hug or a chat at the end of a long day was putting pressure on him. He'd even asked her not to speak to him in the mornings until he'd read the news on his iPad because he'd said Liz was far too chatty first thing. That had stung but she'd swallowed down her hurt and made every effort not to be irritating, not to be loud and had found herself tiptoeing around the house before work. Being away from Rhodri, Liz could see exactly how much she'd changed herself to fit what Rhodri wanted. And even after all that, he'd still gone and had an affair. So what, really, was the point in trying to be what she wasn't?

But letting go of one way of living was hard and she wasn't sure that a life without Rhodri was what she wanted. She needed to take things day by day and to see how she felt when Rhodri did call her. Which he would do. Soon. She was almost certain of it.

Chapter 13

'I was thinking that we could have some breakfast after the session,' Mia said as she reached into the back of the car for her bag. 'What do you think?'

Zelda nodded. 'That would be lovely. I haven't had breakfast out in years.'

'Really?' Mia said, then instantly regretted it. Perhaps Zelda hadn't had breakfast out because she'd have had to do so alone. Not that there was anything wrong with treating yourself, of course, but Mia liked to have company when she ate out and could understand that Zelda might do too. 'Perhaps Liz will join us.'

'I hope so. I got to spend some time with her yesterday when she helped me to get the chickens back into the garden and then she did some weeding at my plot. She's a lovely girl and a great beauty too.'

'She *is* lovely and yes, a beautiful young woman,' Mia agreed. 'That's nice that she helped you.'

Zelda nodded. 'She came to the allotments for a walk. I'd lost three of my bloody chickens because the buggers had run off into the woods so she helped me get them back. I blame Dr Pecker. He's such a show-off and was leading the girls astray. Probably planned to find them some food then enjoy an alfresco threesome.'

Mia snorted. Zelda said some funny things.

'Thanks again for the fresh eggs.' Mia thought of the large box of dark brown eggs Zelda had given her when she'd picked her up.

'You're very welcome. They lay so many that I can't possibly eat them all. Marcellus gets his fair share but I was thinking that they might come in handy with all that lovely baking you do.'

Mia smiled. 'Aha! You had an ulterior motive.' She winked to show she was teasing.

'You saw right through that one.'

'I'll certainly make some cakes with them.'

Zelda patted her hair. 'Do I . . . do I look OK?'

'You look lovely. Very smart.'

'Thank you. It's just . . . I know you probably think it doesn't matter what I look like with me being a wrinkly and all that but—'

'Of course it matters. I think you're wonderful and I hope I look half as good as you when I – *if* I reach your age. You're very cool, Zelda.'

'Cool? I'll take that, thank you.'

Zelda had clearly made an effort that morning. The past few times Mia had seen her, Zelda had been dressed in faded, threadbare or stained clothing that she clearly wore to feed and clean out the goats and chickens or to work in the garden or at the allotment. Today, though, she was wearing a pair of black leggings with thick socks that came up to her shins, white plimsolls and a baggy black top with long sleeves. She had brought a red wool coat with her but it lay folded over her arm. She also had a black scarf tied around her head with tiny silver half-moons on it that shone in the morning light. She did look cool.

'I do like your trousers,' Zelda said and Mia looked down at herself. The zebra stripe yoga pants had been a recent purchase, along with the black yoga top with a knot at the front that sat over her belly. She'd put on a long black vest top underneath it and had thought she looked ready to exercise when she'd checked out the overall effect in her bedroom mirror. Gideon had loved her in yoga pants, telling her that they hugged her curves in all the right places. He'd have liked these ones, she thought sadly, wishing he was here to accompany them to tai chi. Not that he'd have been keen to have a go, believing in exercising in the fresh air with long walks and gardening, but he might have come along had Mia tried to persuade him. Her heart wrenched; this wasn't easy at all.

'Ooh, look, there's lovely Liz.' Zelda pointed at the village hall, where Liz stood chewing at a fingernail. 'Isn't she tall? I hadn't realised how tall she is. Kind of like a model. I always wanted to be tall but I didn't grow much in my teens. However, I did have something of Marilyn Monroe about me. I had plenty of admirers in my day, not that Mother would have let me date any of them, though—' Zelda bit her bottom lip and Mia frowned. Why had she stopped talking?

'You looked like Marilyn Monroe, did you?' she asked, wanting to encourage Zelda along this positive train of thought. Zelda had told her before that she'd looked like Marilyn Monroe in her youth, so it was clearly a source of pride for her.

Zelda sighed. 'I did. I had the slim waist, the hourglass curves, the blonde hair and long dark eyelashes to die for.' She raised a hand and touched it to her face as if she was remembering. 'If only we treasured youth when we had it, realised it's fleeting. Inside, I don't feel any different – but how the outside of me has changed!'

'Did your mother fight the boys off with a broom, then?' Mia gave a laugh to show she was joking but Zelda didn't smile. Instead, she looked devastated.

'Mother was very . . . strict. Not at all keen for me to fall in love or get married and—Well, it doesn't matter now.'

Mia shook her head. 'I'm sorry.'

'Don't be. It was a long time ago and what doesn't kill us makes us stronger, right?'

'I guess so.' Mia hooked her bag over her arm then locked the car. She wondered what else Zelda had been going to say about her mother. Whatever it was, she had a feeling it wasn't a pleasant memory. 'Do you have any photos of you in your Marilyn Monroe heyday?' She hoped the question would return the pleasant memories for Zelda.

'I do have a few photos, somewhere in that big old house. Goodness knows where, though. Perhaps you can help me look for them sometime?'

'Absolutely. Just let me know when you'd like to do that.'

They crossed the road and approached the hall. Liz spotted them and waved, a smile lighting up her pretty face.

'Hello! I'm so glad you're here. I arrived stupidly early and felt like a right idiot standing here on my own.'

'You could have gone inside,' Mia said.

'But I don't know anyone and I'd be far too self-conscious.'

'Kyle's a lovely person and he'd have put you at ease, I'm sure.' Mia knew that Kyle, with his warmth and amiable smile, could relax most people. 'Although he can be a bit of a tease too.'

'Well, you're here now so we can all go in together,' Liz said, looking relieved. 'Like the three musketeers.'

'I used to love the film they made of that in the 1970s with Michael York and Oliver Reed. Michael York was such a dish when he was younger,' Zelda said. 'I had a huge crush on him back in the day.'

'A dish?' Liz asked.

'Yes, you know – tasty.' Zelda tapped at her teeth. 'What is it you say these days? Oh I know . . . hot!'

'I see.' Liz laughed. 'Michael York was hot?'

'Indeed he was.' Zelda chuckled. 'I'd wouldn't have kicked him out of bed.'

Mia hooted with laughter as they climbed the steps into the village hall. Hearing an eighty-two-year-old woman call someone hot was a new one for her. 'I liked him in *Romeo and Juliet.*'

'With Leonardo DiCaprio?' Liz asked.

'No, that was a far more recent version.' Mia shook her head. 'The other version was made in the late 1960s and he played Tybalt.'

'Well, you learn something new every day,' Liz replied.

'Indeed you do.' Zelda pushed the door open and stepped inside. 'Even at my age.'

Inside, the hallway was warm, a pleasant contrast to the cool air outside. It smelt as Mia remembered, like a school – of paint, chips and people. The noticeboard in the entrance advertised classes including yoga, tai chi, baby band, Zumba and crochet.

'Wow! That's a lot of classes available,' Liz said. 'You'd never be bored living here.'

Mia and Zelda exchanged a smile. They'd both lived in the village for years and Mia had never taken a class there, had rarely gone there, even when it had been the old hall, the one that burnt down. But then she'd been a busy mum, had a job and a house, and after a while she'd had a second husband too. Time had been precious and the years had flown. Yes, she'd taken the boys to the village hall when they were little, had gone there for shows and events, but she hadn't used it as often as many other villagers had. Now, widowed and with her children gone, perhaps it was time to embrace the hall and all that it offered.

'I haven't actually been here in ages,' Zelda said. 'I used to attend the Christmas shows in the old hall but I've been to this one less than a handful of times. I just haven't had a reason to come here, I suppose.'

'But today we do – and let's hope it's the start of something regular.' Mia meant what she said.

'That would be something to look forward to every week.' Zelda tilted her head and beamed at Mia. 'Shall we go in and see what tai chi is like, then?'

'After you.' Mia held out her hand for Zelda and Liz to go in front of her then she took a deep breath. It would be good to create a new routine for herself so she had things on the weekly calendar. Some structure to her days would be a positive step forward. Even if it was a step in a direction that led her away from her life with Gideon. But Gideon was gone and, as much as Mia might wish it was different, he was never coming back.

The hall was bright and airy as they walked towards the stage. Zelda's stomach fluttered and she held her coat against her, squeezing it tight as if it could ward off harm. She didn't think she'd be facing harm, of course, but being surrounded by people after so long was daunting. She wasn't accustomed to being with others like this, but a glance at her companions told her that neither of them felt particularly comfortable right now either. Mia was smiling but her face was pale and Zelda knew it would be difficult for her, this moving on with life after losing the man she loved. It was still so soon after Gideon's death and Zelda was filled with admiration for Mia's bravery and resilience. As for Liz, the younger woman was looking around her uncertainly, as if she was wondering if someone would tell her she didn't belong there and send her packing.

'Well, hello there!' The voice stopped the three women in their tracks and they looked up at the stage, where a figure stood gazing down at them.

'That's Kyle Greene,' Mia whispered. 'Hello, Kyle,' she said louder.

'So you decided to give tai chi a go, did you?' He stepped forwards and Zelda admired his outfit, a red fitted T-shirt with baggy black trousers that ballooned around his legs then ended in elasticated cuffs around his ankles. He had dark brown hair that looked as if he'd just run his hands through it then swept it in different directions and thick dark brows. She couldn't tell what colour his eyes were from this distance but they were lighter than his hair so she guessed they were green or blue. 'I'm so happy you're here.'

'This is Zelda and Liz,' Mia said. 'My friends.'

Zelda felt her throat constrict at Mia's use of the word *friends*. Mia saw her as a friend and that filled her heart with joy.

'Hey, Zelda. I'm delighted you could make it at last.'

'Hello, Kyle.' Zelda gave a small wave, wondering how Kyle knew who she was, but then, most people in the village knew of other villagers even if they didn't know them personally. She suspected she was probably talked about as 'the weird old woman in the big house near the allotments'.

'Hi,' Liz said quietly, seeming to try to hide behind her long ginger hair.

'I don't think we've met, have we?' Kyle said and Liz's cheeks flushed.

'No. I'm staying here with my sister, Nina Potts.'

'I know Nina.' Kyle nodded. 'Good to meet you, Liz, and you are very welcome to join us whenever you like. Right, you lot, turn off the volume on your phones, find a space and get ready for a gentle warm-up.'

Zelda watched as Mia pulled her phone from her bag, muted it, then carried her bag to the side of the hall and set it down with her coat, while Liz did the same.

My friends, she thought, with pride.

Liz stood on the spot and took some slow deep breaths as Kyle had instructed. She found her eyes wandering around, observing others initially, admiring their workout gear, wondering who they were and how often they attended classes. Considering that it was early on a Saturday morning, there were quite a few people there, varying from late teens to early twenties and up to eighty-something, judging from Zelda and an elderly-looking man who was there with a younger woman with a short brown pixie cut. From time to time, the woman glanced sideways at the man as if checking on him and Liz wondered if she was his daughter. It would be nice to attend something like this with a parent, she thought, although the idea of doing so with her own father was as likely as catching a lift home on a unicorn.

Liz was standing between Zelda and Mia and she felt grateful for their presence, knowing that she'd have found it much harder coming here alone. What had happened to her? She'd always thought of herself as a confident and independent woman, as someone who could go anywhere alone and not feel self-conscious, but recently, that seemed to have changed. Was it the effect of Rhodri's betrayal or did it go further back than that? Had she been pretending to be confident and self-assured all along when really she was still an insecure little girl inside?

'OK then, class, you should be feeling nice and warmed-up now,' Kyle said from the front, dragging Liz from her thoughts. 'Try to follow what I do. Don't worry if you can't keep up at first and don't do anything that feels like it's straining, especially our new members, but do keep breathing nice and deeply. This is meant to be fun, energising and relaxing.'

Liz made an effort to focus on Kyle and to push her musings away. What was the point in being here if she wasn't going to immerse herself in the experience?

Kyle bent his legs slightly then began sweeping his arms in wide arcs. His movements were calm and controlled, his shoulders low, his face a picture of concentration. He was elegant and graceful and his movements reminded her of water flowing. As Liz concentrated on copying him, the room around her slipped away, the people in front and behind her disappeared, and it was simply Liz looking up at Kyle on the stage in front of her, as if he was pinpointed by the glow of a spotlight.

A warm energy flowed through her limbs, connecting her body and breath, and her mind cleared of everything other than the beautiful force that glowed golden inside. It was the happiest she'd felt in ages and she basked in the joy of her body and breath, in being here in this village where she had been welcomed with warmth and acceptance.

When Kyle finally stopped moving and stood still, palms together, feet together, facing out from the stage, Liz imitated his stance. The energy she'd experienced sat gently in her belly and she wanted to keep it there, treasure it, tend it like a project filled with potential. Her lungs felt cleansed, her limbs light, her head clearer than it had been for some time. It seemed that this ancient practice really worked.

Curiosity made her slide her gaze to her left. Zelda stood there, eyes closed, palms touching; a statue of tranquillity. To her right, Mia was smiling, eyes fixed on Kyle, chin raised as her chest rose and fell slowly. Liz cared about these two women already and was gladdened by their relaxed states, happy to see that they had enjoyed the session too.

'Well done, everyone,' Kyle said, his face serene. 'I hope you enjoyed that. You all did so well. Hazel and Jack, you've both come along brilliantly and should be proud of yourselves.'

Liz peered at the couple near the front, who seemed to have eyes only for each other. When the man, Jack, reached out and tucked a strand of blonde hair behind the woman, Hazel's ear, Liz's throat tightened. That was the action of man deeply in love. As if oblivious to the presence of everyone else, Hazel went up on her toes and pressed a kiss to Jack's cheek and he bent his dark head and kissed her swiftly on the mouth.

Liz lowered her gaze to the floor, not wanting to torture herself by witnessing true love when her own heart was broken. But despite the pain inside, seeing such tenderness also gave her hope. People did fall in love and they did treat the ones they loved with respect. She had just been very unlucky with Rhodri. She had, she was starting to accept, put her energy into caring for a man who simply did not feel the same way.

'All right, darlings, don't forget I'm running a Sunday-morning yoga class too and there's also another tai chi on Wednesday evenings.'

Kyle blew kisses at them all then picked up his water bottle from the stage and jogged to the steps that led down to the floor.

'How did you find that?' Mia asked.

'Good.' Liz bobbed her head. 'I enjoyed it.'

'Me too,' Zelda said. She looked so tiny in her workout clothes, with her white hair sticking out from underneath a black silk scarf, that Liz was hit by the urge to hug her. She resisted, of course, not sure how Zelda would take to a hug from a woman who was still practically a stranger, but

Liz knew that part of it came from her own compassion for others. It was one of the things that had led her into teaching. One of the things that had led her to fall in love with Rhodri. His past had not been easy and she'd glimpsed something of herself in him and wanted to take his pain away by looking after him. That had been part of her problem, she suspected: the need to try to fix others at the risk of losing herself and putting her own needs aside. 'Is it time for breakfast now? I'm ravenous.' Zelda rubbed her tummy.

'Definitely. Let's head to the café for coffee and bacon sarnies,' Mia said. 'I'm peckish too.'

They grabbed their things and Liz pulled her phone from her bag to check it, on the off-chance that she might have a message, and almost fell over when she saw that she did.

And it was from Rhodri!

Chapter 14

Mia held the door to the hallway open for Zelda then turned back to Liz, but she was standing in the main hall holding her phone in a trembling hand.

'Liz?' Mia called but Liz's eyes were glued to her phone. 'Liz, are you all right?'

Liz glanced at Mia then back at her phone. 'I-I'll catch up with you.'

Mia looked around for Zelda. The elderly lady was talking to Marcellus David near the front door to the hall, so she returned to Liz.

'Don't you want to come for breakfast?' she asked.

Liz raised her eyes from her phone and concern filled Mia at Liz's expression.

'Have you had bad news?' she asked. 'Can I do anything to help?'

Liz opened her mouth, closed it, opened it again. 'I . . . I've had a message from Rhodri.'

'Your partner?' Unease churned in Mia's gut.

'Yes. H-he said he wants to speak to me. And . . . see . . . that's all I've wanted to read for weeks. I've been longing to hear from him. But now . . . now that he's messaged me . . . I'm scared.'

'Does the message say anything else?' Mia looked from Liz's face to the phone she was gripping so tightly her knuckles had turned white.

Liz held the phone out and Mia read the message.

Hi Liz,

Need to talk. Let me know when you're free.

R x

'OK . . .' Mia shifted her bag on her shoulder. 'Well, that could be good, right?'

She wasn't sure why Liz hadn't heard from her partner for weeks but doubted it was a good sign.

'I don't know. I mean, perhaps he's come to his senses and he wants to apologise and make up, but what if . . . what if he doesn't and he wants to cancel the wedding plans?'

'Wedding plans?' Mia winced at the surprise in her tone. She hadn't realised that Liz was meant to be getting married, had only known that Liz had seemed sad about something and that it involved a man. 'When are you meant to be getting married?'

'July.'

Liz looked so bewildered that Mia wrapped an arm around her shoulders. Liz was about the same age as Joel; could easily have been Mia's daughter. Around them some people were still chatting before heading home, Kyle was performing a rather noisy impression of someone for his mum, Clare, and her husband, Sam, and the caretaker had appeared to check windows were closed and that the hall was left clean and tidy. Mia was aware that this was not the best place for them to talk. They needed privacy for a conversation like this.

'Right, sweetheart, let's head to the café and get a warm drink and some sugar into you, then we can talk.'

'What am I going to say to him?' Liz asked. 'If I tell him I can speak to him today then he might give me bad news and I don't know if I can cope with hearing it.'

'You'd be surprised what you can cope with and with how strong you are. However, I think we need to be sitting down somewhere a bit warmer and more private before we discuss this any further.'

Liz pressed her phone to her chest. 'Yes. You're right. Never act in haste. Take the time to think things through. Nina would say the same.'

'I'm sure she would.'

Mia led Liz towards the doorway and thanked a woman who held it open for them. Zelda was saying goodbye to Marcellus, so Mia gestured at the front door of the village hall and Zelda nodded her understanding.

Mia wasn't sure what was going on with Liz but she had a better idea now that it was related to her fiancé and that something distressing had happened. She'd do what she could to help Liz deal with the situation. Her losses had been of a different kind, but they'd still been losses and grief was grief, whatever had caused it and whatever form it took.

Zelda followed Mia and Liz into the café. It was warm and cosy inside, the early morning sunshine finding its way through the windows and draping itself lazily across the café floor. A few tables were taken by individuals reading newspapers or books, couples, and families, but there were several still free.

Mia led the way to a window table, pulled out a chair and nodded at Liz. 'Here, sit down.'

Liz did as she was instructed but Zelda stayed standing, happy to head to the counter.

'Take a seat, Zelda, and I'll go and order.'

'I can do it,' Zelda said, keen to avoid being seen as helpless or a nuisance.

'It's fine, I'll go.' Mia smiled confidently so Zelda decided to concede this time but to cover the bill when it came.

Zelda pulled out a chair opposite Liz, hung her coat over the back then sat down.

'I'm going to order some drinks, so you can both warm up a bit, and when I come back we can have a look through the menu and decide what we want to eat.' Mia met Zelda's gaze but then her eyes strayed to Liz and Zelda saw the concern there. What had happened between them feeling relaxed and contented after tai chi and leaving the village hall? Now she took a good look at Liz, she could see that the young woman had gone very pale and that she looked troubled.

'Good plan,' Zelda said when Liz didn't reply.

After Mia had left them, Zelda rested her elbows on the table and looked at Liz.

'You doing OK, lovely?'

'I . . . not really.' Liz seemed to realise where she was. She removed her coat then hung it on the chair behind her.

'Want to talk about it?' Zelda sat back a bit and gazed out of the window so Liz wouldn't feel under pressure. 'You don't have to, obviously, but if it would help to talk, I'm a good listener.' She returned her gaze to Liz, trying to infuse it with compassion.

Liz gave a small smile. 'Thanks.'

'I take it that it's complicated? As most things are.' Zelda worried that she'd been too pushy and offered Liz a way out in case she was feeling awkward.

Liz pulled her phone from her pocket and Zelda suppressed a sigh. Was she going to be blanked now while Liz got lost in her virtual world?

Bloody technology.

But Liz swiped her finger across the screen then set the phone on the table in front of Zelda.

'Look at that,' Liz said.

Zelda peered at the screen. 'What is it?'

'A message from my fiancé.'

'You're engaged? How lovely!' Zelda grinned but Liz shook her head and tapped the phone screen, so Zelda read it again, wondering what she was missing. 'He says he wants to talk to you.'

'Yes. Exactly.'

'Uhhh . . . I'm sorry, dear, but I don't understand.'

Liz pressed the top of the phone and the screen went blank then she sighed. 'See, we're having problems. Things aren't good, so if he wants to talk to me, I'm worried about what he's going to say.'

'I see.' Zelda steepled her fingers and rested her chin on them. 'I am very sorry to hear that.'

Liz glanced up as Mia joined them. 'I forgot to ask what you both wanted so I ordered three pots of tea but if you'd prefer coffee or something else I can go back and change the order.'

'That's fine by me,' Zelda said.

'Tea is great, thanks.' Liz pushed her long hair back from her face and scooped it over her shoulder. She had such lovely hair, Zelda thought, like a bright copper waterfall. 'I was just telling Zelda about the text message.'

'Right.' Mia knitted her brows.

'Yes, I was explaining that Rhodri and I are having some trouble.' Liz leant back and ground her knuckles into her eyes. 'Who am I kidding? I have a terrible feeling that we're over.'

When she lowered her hands, her eyes were red, the skin around them white from the pressure she'd exerted.

'Is there anything we can do to help?' Zelda asked, feeling somewhat out of her depth. She'd had her own heartbreak, of course, but that had been a long time ago and she wasn't even sure she could articulate what she had been through back then. Some days it was as raw as the day it happened but others she felt detached from it, as if it had happened to someone else.

'I don't think so.' Liz's eyes filled with tears that sat on her pale eyelashes like translucent beads.

A waitress appeared with a tray holding three small teapots and three mugs, so they waited while she set them down along with a jug of milk and a bowl of sugar cubes.

Mia lifted the lid off one of the teapots and gave the contents a stir.

'It's all such a mess, you see,' Liz said, her voice thick with emotion, when the waitress had gone.

'I'm taking it that he hurt you?' Zelda asked.

'He did. Very badly.' Liz pulled a napkin from the dispenser on the table and dabbed at her eyes. 'We were meant to be getting married but . . . I came home early from a run after I'd got a cramp a-and I found him in bed with our neighbour.'

'Goodness!' Zelda placed a hand on her chest. 'That must have been awful.'

'It was.' Liz looked crestfallen.

'Was she a friend too?' Zelda said.

'It was a he and he was Rhodri's personal trainer.'

'I'm sorry, darling.' Mia reached out and squeezed Liz's hand.

'Me too. How dreadful for you.' Zelda shook her head. 'Being cheated on by the person you thought you were going to spend your life with would be truly awful.'

'I came here to stay with Nina for a while so I could think. Rhodri and I work at the same school and I couldn't face going in every day and seeing him there, so I've taken some sick leave. I hate doing that but I just can't bear to be so close to him every day and . . . and things not be the way they were between us. We have a lovely, lovely home but I couldn't stand being there either and there's no way I could sleep in our bed after knowing they'd been in there together and . . . Oh!' Her eyes widened. 'I just realised that even though I loved that house, I can't live there again. Not without Rhodri and not with him, either, because I'd see them together every time I stepped into our bedroom and looked at our bed and . . .' Her bottom lip wobbled. 'Oh God!'

Liz started trembling violently and Zelda worried that she would faint or vomit.

'Take a deep breath, Liz, and have some tea.' Mia poured tea into the three mugs then added milk. She picked up one of the mugs and placed it in Liz's hands.

Obediently, Liz raised it to her lips and drank. Slowly, some colour returned to her cheeks and Zelda was flooded with relief. She'd been growing more and more concerned as Liz had told her story because she'd looked worse with every word.

'Would you like me to phone your sister?' Mia asked. 'I can let her know you're not feeling well.'

'No!' Liz turned her gaze to Mia. 'Please don't. I don't want to worry her. Nina's being so wonderful and the last thing I want is to be a nuisance. She has enough to deal with as it is.' Liz frowned, then added, 'With two children, I mean. She's a busy mum.'

'Of course,' Mia replied. 'Just wanted to check. In that case, let's see if Zelda and I can help. We've notched up a few years between us and plenty of life experience, so we might be able to offer some advice.'

Liz nodded. 'I know I need to reply to his message, but I don't know what to say or how to say it. I've been longing for him to contact me, desperate to hear from him in case he wants to try to find a way through this. We used to be friends and then we fell in love . . . or I thought we did . . . and I was keen to marry and I thought he was too. But as the wedding got closer, he seemed to become distant. I assumed it was nerves or something else because he didn't have the easiest of childhoods. And then . . . then I found him with Pete.' She raised her mug and took a gulp. 'I wish this was vodka.' She laughed wildly and Zelda and Mia smiled sadly.

'I can pop to the shop if you'd like,' Zelda said. 'Although I'm not keen on vodka. I'm more partial to a drop of sloe gin myself.'

'No, it's fine. If I start drinking now I might not stop and then I'll feel worse tomorrow. I like a gin and tonic but in the right circumstances and I don't think this is a good time.'

'Very wise.' Zelda raised her own mug. 'Tea it is then.'

Liz sucked in a shaky breath. 'The message he sent. It's vague, which means I don't know how he's feeling.'

'Is that the first time you've heard from him since you came to Little Bramble?' Mia asked.

'Yes,' Liz said. 'Since I left our home and came here. I had a bit of a . . . a breakdown at work and so I knew that I had to get away. It was all too claustrophobic, living and working in the same place and having his lover living next door.'

'I imagine it was like a pressure cooker,' Zelda said. 'About to explode at any moment.'

'I did!' Liz giggled, surprising herself. 'I shouted at the head teacher when he said something completely unlinked to my domestic situation then I stormed into the reprographics room, threw some paper around and kicked the broken tray off one of the machines.' She covered her mouth with a hand as if the memory was too shocking to think about.

'Oh dear!' Zelda chuckled.

'We've all been there.' Mia winked. 'Sometimes a good explosion is just what you need. But it's good that you came here to your sister. Good that she's here for you.'

Liz's smile dropped. 'She's always been good to me, but at times I haven't been as . . . kind to her as I could be.'

'It sounds to me like you give yourself a very hard time, Liz,' Zelda said. 'Time, now, perhaps, to give yourself a break.'

Liz looked up and met Zelda's gaze. 'Do you think so?'

'I do. We're often our own harshest critics.' Zelda put her mug down. 'I'm guilty of it and I suspect Mia probably is too.

We think we can fix the world and everyone in it and when we can't . . . we beat ourselves up. I spent a long time trying to make my mother happy.'

'Did you succeed?' Liz asked, eyes wide.

'That's a story for another time.' Zelda picked up a menu. 'But the moral of it is: whatever you do, you can't help others until you've put the oxygen mask on yourself. If you can't breathe properly, how can you help everyone else?'

'You're very wise, Zelda.' Liz was looking at the older woman with an awe that made her feel guilty. She could say the words, yes, but she wasn't always good at putting them into practice.

Around them the sounds of a regular Saturday morning at the café filled the air: cutlery clinking, the murmur of multiple conversations, the coffee machine frothing, the constant hum of the large fridges. Aromas of toast, cakes and bacon floated around them, and steam rose into the air from the mugs of tea. Everything appeared to be normal, or as normal as things could be, and yet . . . something was shifting.

Zelda could feel it deep inside.

Liz had shared her heartache, what was probably one of the saddest moments of her life, with Mia and Zelda. The last time someone had shared something so personal with Zelda had been a very long time ago, way before mobile phones were glued to people's hands and before Liz and Mia were born. Back then the world had been very different and yet people were not really that different at all, it seemed. They fell in love, they cheated, they were cheated upon, they disapproved of their children's choices. But they kept on going, fell in love and trusted others. It was part of being human.

'So . . . What should I do?' Liz asked, looking at her phone again.

'If you don't hear what he has to say, you'll never know what to do.' Mia shrugged. 'I suppose that, as hard as this is, you have to start somewhere.'

'It's true,' Zelda agreed.

'Right, then.' Liz nodded sagely. 'I'll have something to eat then I'll phone him and find out.'

'And we'll be right here with you.' Mia took Liz's hand and Zelda took the other, linking the three of them in a multi-generational chain.

'Thank you,' Liz said. 'Even though we haven't been friends for long, I feel stronger knowing that you've got my back.'

Zelda blinked hard, wondering how on earth she'd managed to get something in her eye. At least, that was what she was telling herself, but she suspected that the way her vision blurred at Liz's words hinted at another reason entirely.

Chapter 15

Fortified with plenty of tea and a heavily buttered teacake, Liz stepped out of the café and into the Little Bramble morning. Mia was paying the bill (she'd insisted) and Zelda had popped to the loo, so Liz had excused herself so she could step outside and get some air.

She looked around, getting her bearings. To her left was the village hall and to her right the vet surgery and a bistro. She was aware that the woodland path ran behind the café, obscured from view by trees and bushes. Again, she marvelled at the way the village blended so easily into such a rural area. Nina had chosen a lovely location to live and to raise her family.

After checking both ways, she crossed the road and came to a stop on the grass of the village green. A squirrel raced past, a blur of grey, and bolted up a nearby tree. It happened so quickly that Liz wondered if she'd actually seen it all, but then she spotted it scampering across a branch. It must be wonderful to be so light and agile, to move so quickly from one place to another, to be free of emotion and the baggage human beings often carried around with them.

A heaviness settled over her as she remembered what she had to do next. Phoning Rhodri would not be easy but she knew she had to do it and find out what he had to say. Not speaking to him or seeing him had allowed her to exist in a kind of limbo, one where uncertainty ruled and where she didn't have to make any tough decisions. If she spoke to Rhodri and he asked her to forgive him, then she'd have to decide if she had it in her to do that; something she wasn't certain about at all, now that it could happen. However, if he told her that he wanted out of their relationship, that it was over between them, what would she do then? The ache in her chest that had dulled to a throb during breakfast now intensified to a sharp pain and she hugged her hands to her chest. So much pain. So much sadness. In losing Rhodri, she would lose not just her fiancé but her friend, the person she had envisioned spending her life with, her hopes and dreams. Letting go of that sense of security would be tough and she would have to decide what to do next, decide where to live, where to work – she didn't think working at the same school as him would be an option. Liz would have to decide who she wanted to be from this point on.

Be yourself, Liz. Be true to yourself . . . Be you. Take a chance on you.

She turned around looking for the source of the voice but there was no one nearby. Had that been her mind playing tricks on her? Was it her mum, sending her a message from beyond the grave? Was she going mad?

It was time to do this. Before she lost her courage completely. Delaying any longer would simply make it harder; not knowing wasn't an option long-term.

She glanced behind her and spotted Mia and Zelda coming out of the café. She held up her phone and motioned at a bench on the green and they nodded. They would give her space to make the call then be there afterwards. *Thank goodness!*

Once she was sitting down, Liz swiped the screen of her phone then went to favourites.

There it was.

Rhodri Langley <3

His image displayed in a tiny circle to the left of his name. It was a photograph she'd taken of him on the night when they'd decided to get married. They'd gone out for a meal to celebrate their one-year anniversary and somehow, over dinner, they'd got engaged. Well, it hadn't been that random. A colleague of theirs at work had been showing off her ring following a whirl-wind wedding over the summer holidays to a woman she'd only been with for six months. It had made Liz question what she and Rhodri were waiting for. They were happy, they got on, they had a house together. If someone could get married as quickly as their colleague and be that happy then perhaps they could do it and find some happiness of their own. Although, after that evening they'd been engaged for two years before they'd started to make wedding plans. Neither of them had pushed for it and they'd sometimes joked that they were happy just being engaged. Had they both known, deep down, that something wasn't right? It had been a random comment from a friend that had led them to start planning the wedding and, even then, Rhodri hadn't seemed into it all. Liz had let herself get caught up in the glamour and the fairy tale, but this was real life and no fairy tales were make believe.

Now, Liz's hand shot to her mouth. Had it been that . . . unromantic? Had she been that desperate to be married that she'd do it regardless of whether she was or wasn't madly in love with her fiancé? Just because it seemed like the right thing to do?

'Oh, Rhodri, what have we done?' she whispered, stroking a finger over his image. 'We were fools to think that was the right reason to get engaged and married.'

Being away from him, away from their life, Liz had found the time and space to think clearly for the first time in a long time, and the clarity was incredible.

She touched a finger to his number and his image filled her screen.

Mia watched as Liz sat on a bench staring at her phone. A small grey squirrel scampered down a tree trunk and scurried across the grass of the green to the next tree then disappeared up the trunk.

'My cat Flint loved chasing squirrels.' Zelda chuckled. 'He'd have been up that tree and along the branch after it.'

'I can't imagine how a cat and squirrel fight would look,' Mia said, frowning. 'Probably be pretty awful.'

'The squirrels always got away.' Zelda nodded. 'But that bloody cat still enjoyed the chase.'

'Flint isn't around anymore?' Mia asked, trying to work out if she'd seen a cat at Zelda's.

'Passed away just before Christmas. Peacefully, in his sleep.' She sighed. 'I miss him though.'

'I'm sure you do.'

'Not that it's anything like what you've been through.' Zelda's eyes widened. 'Just that, well . . .'

'Grief is grief, Zelda,' Mia said, her eyes returning to Liz to check that she was all right. 'It doesn't matter who or what you're grieving for. It's the same emotion.'

'Yes, but a cat and a husband?'

Mia laid a hand on Zelda's arm. 'Was Flint your constant companion?'

'For seventeen years.'

'That's a long time.'

'I know.'

'I'm sorry for your loss.'

'And I'm sorry for yours.'

Mia took Zelda's hand and slid it through her arm. 'Shall we wander for a bit while Liz is on the phone, then we can make our way back to her when she's finished? I feel that if we stand here staring at her it will put her under pressure.'

'That's a very good point.'

They strolled along the pavement, passing the village hall then The Red Squirrel pub. It wasn't open this early on

Saturday morning but even so, the aromas of beer and chips emanated from the place.

'Gideon enjoyed many a pint in The Red,' Mia said.

'Did he?' Zelda asked.

'Sometimes, when he'd popped to get something from the shop, I'd receive a text to say he'd bumped into a friend and they were going to have a quick pint.' Mia rolled her eyes. 'He never stayed for more than one, unless it was pre-arranged, but I knew that if I sent him to pick something up to go with dinner, I'd have to turn the oven down.'

Zelda chuckled. 'Sounds like he was bit of a rascal.'

Gideon's smiling face filled Mia's mind, his salt-and-pepper beard, laughing hazel eyes, balding head that he often joked about polishing. His big strong arms that he'd wrap around Mia, making her feel safe, making her feel like she'd come home. How she missed those arms, that smile, his uplifting scent, waking up to find him in bed next to her, his big, solid frame a comfort through good times and bad.

As they approached the row of shops, Zelda slowed down. 'While I'm here, I'd like to pick up some sweets. That OK with you?'

'Of course.' Mia turned and looked across the green. Liz was still on the bench, phone to her ear, and every so often, she nodded. 'Looks like Liz is OK for now so we should have time.'

Inside, the shop reminded Mia of those from when she was a child. It was decorated to resemble an old-fashioned sweet shop and had mini jars of sweets on a central island in the middle of the shop then shelves on every wall holding bags and boxes of sweets. Behind the counter there were large jars of sweets including cola cubes, cherry lips, rhubarb and custard, lemon sherbets and more.

'My mouth is watering just looking at them all,' Zelda said. 'I think I'll get a basket.'

Mia's eyes fell on a jar of butterscotch sweets wrapped in gold foil. For a moment, she thought, *I'll buy some for Gideon.* 'They're his favourites,' she said, then she started.

'Pardon?' Zelda's eyebrows rose above her glasses.

'Oh – nothing. Just thinking that Joel would probably like some . . . chocolate eclairs. I'll get them for him.'

They walked around the shop together and Mia enjoyed the scents that permeated the air, from zingy citrus to berries to peppermint as well as the paper of the bags for self-service. Zelda picked up a few bags that she placed in her basket then she paused in front of a display of Belgian truffles packed in square black boxes with a red ribbon around them. She placed two boxes in her basket then moved on. Mia selected two bags of chocolate eclairs for Joel, glad that she had someone to buy for other than herself. Not being able to get anything for Gideon was hard but at least she could get something for her son.

'Takes you back in time, doesn't it?' Zelda popped a bag of mint imperials in her basket.

'It really does,' Mia agreed. 'Everything in here is geared towards making you spend money, from the colours to the smells to the memories.'

'It's a lovely little business. What a good idea someone had creating a shop like this but I guess there's always money in food and nostalgia. Right, I think I'd better stop there or I'll have no teeth left in my head by the time the month is out.'

'You've filled your basket.' Mia laughed.

'Indeed I have!'

They paid at the counter then left the shop with their purchases in recycled brown paper bags with paper handles.

'I hope these handles are reinforced because I don't fancy chasing my sweets around the green.' Zelda held up the two bags she was carrying.

'Would you like me to carry them for you?' Mia was concerned about Zelda carrying too much but the older woman shook her head.

'I'm fine, thank you, dear. A bit of weight-bearing does me good. I was a bit suspicious of that HRT stuff when I was going through the change and so I've always done my best to stay fit and healthy. Being active is one way I do that. Not that I didn't suffer some nasty effects of that damned menopause and I'm so glad the research proved me wrong and there are more options for women these days.'

'I'd have been lost without HRT.' Mia nodded, thinking about the difference it had made to her quality of life when she'd started taking it. 'When the hot flushes kicked in, I knew I couldn't live with them indefinitely but HRT put a stop to them.'

'Ooh, don't remind me!' Zelda shuddered. 'Those years were no fun at all.'

'Looks like Liz is off the phone.' Mia pointed across the grass at where Liz was sitting on the bench. She had her elbows on her knees and her phone in her hands. She was gazing at it as if it had all the answers to her questions.

'Let's get back to her, poor girl.'

Mia took Zelda's arm; it seemed like the natural thing to do. She just wasn't sure whether it was for Zelda's benefit or her own.

Chapter 16

Liz looked up as Mia and Zelda approached her warily, as if worried she would bolt if they startled her.

'All right if we sit down?' Mia said.

'Of course.' Liz sat back and stretched out her long legs in front of her.

Mia turned on the bench to look at Liz. 'No pressure, Liz, but if you'd like to talk about how it went, we're here to listen.'

'Thank you.' Liz sighed. 'We talked and it was all very civil. Rhodri said that while I've been away he's had some time to think and he's decided that it's for the best if we split up.'

She bit down hard on her bottom lip as emotion welled inside her.

'I'm sorry, sweetheart.' Zelda patted Liz's arm.

'Me too,' Mia said softly. 'I know that this is going to be a difficult time for you, but if there's anything I can do to help . . . anything at all, then please just let me know.'

'Same here,' Zelda added.

'Thank you. You're both very kind.' Liz cleared her throat. 'I'm not sure what I feel right now. I knew it would be one thing or the other . . . you know . . . split up or try again but hearing him say the words hit me like a sledgehammer. I thought I'd prepared myself but I hadn't . . . and even though, deep down, I know this is probably the best decision for us both, it still hurts.'

She crumpled over and hugged herself, letting the tears fall as she played Rhodri's words through her mind.

It's over, Liz.

We both need to admit it.

You weren't really happy.

I haven't been happy for ages but I wasn't sure what was wrong.

We can still be friends . . . in time . . . I'll always care about you and love you. Just not in a romantic way.

While Liz cried, Mia held her one hand and Zelda gently rubbed her back. It made Liz feel that she could let go, that she could pour out her feelings on a bench on the village green and not be embarrassed. She'd been holding everything in for such a long time and now it was as though something had been uncorked and it was going to come out, no matter what.

'W-what's wrong with me?' she said eventually as she sat up, aware that she had tears and snot running down over her mouth.

'Darling girl, nothing's wrong with you.' Mia placed a tissue in her hand. 'You're a beautiful young woman with your whole life ahead of you.'

Liz shook her head then started to howl again.

'There's something . . . very wrong . . . with me . . .' She choked the words out through her tears. 'It hurts so much!'

'What hurts?'

Liz froze. The question hadn't come from Mia or Zelda but from a male voice.

She looked up, surreptitiously wiping at her face with the tissue but feeling as if she was spreading the snot up her cheek.

A man with kind brown eyes, thick chestnut hair and a shadow of dark stubble across his jaw was crouched down in front of the bench.

'Oh! I . . .' Liz blinked hard. She wasn't about to pour out her woes to this stranger.

'She's not in physical pain, Joel. Well, not of the kind we need you for,' Mia said. 'This is my son, Joel. And Joel, this is Liz. You know Zelda, I think.'

'Hello.' He gave a small wave and a smile that exposed straight white teeth.

'This is your son?' Liz asked.

'Yes. Joel is the youngest of my three boys.'

'I haven't seen you in a while, Joel,' Zelda said. 'You've grown up into a fine-looking man.'

Joel laughed and a faint blush appeared in his cheeks. 'I guess I have. Well, I mean uh . . . I've grown up but I don't know about the fine bit.' His blush deepened. Then his expression changed. 'So you don't need medical assistance?'

'I'm fine,' Liz said. 'Just suffering from a broken heart.'

'I'm sorry to hear that,' Joel said. 'Whoever broke your heart is a fool.'

He stood up and Liz's eyes travelled with him, taking in how tall he was, how broad-shouldered, how strong he looked in his long-sleeved black top and jogging bottoms. Even though tears were still drying on her cheeks, she found herself intrigued that this man was Mia's baby, and she couldn't help comparing him with Rhodri. They were complete opposites. Rhodri was five foot nine, the same height as her, and she never wore heels because she dwarfed him when she did – which he didn't like. Rhodri was slim with narrow shoulders, pale blue eyes with fair lashes and thin sandy hair. But how Rhodri looked hadn't mattered to Liz; she'd cared about him and who he was. Who she *thought* he was. This man was handsome enough to be a Hollywood actor, reminded her a bit of a young Robert Downey Junior, and she felt sure that he must be married or at least in a serious relationship. But what struck her most about him was his beautiful brown eyes and the kindness and compassion she saw in them.

'You OK, Mum?' Joel asked.

'I'm fine, love. What time are you working?'

'I've got the night shift. A colleague wanted to swap as he's got some family party so I offered to take it for him.'

'You're too kind for your own good, Joel,' Mia said.

Joel shrugged with a smile. 'I didn't have anything planned so it's no bother.'

'You coming round for dinner tomorrow?'

174

'Try and stop me.' He leant over and gave Mia a hug. 'Well . . .' His eyes flickered to Liz again then back to his mother. 'If I'm not needed, I'll carry on with my run. See you tomorrow.'

'Bye, love,' Mia said.

He jogged off and the three women watched him go.

'Joel's a paramedic,' Mia said. 'That's why he was worried when he thought you were hurt. He's always the same with people. His training kicks in as soon as he thinks someone needs help.'

'He's a lovely lad,' Zelda said. 'And so handsome, don't you think, Liz?'

Liz swallowed then dabbed at her face with the damp tissue. 'Uhhh . . . yes. He seems nice.'

She glanced at Zelda and was sure she caught sight of a mischievous glint in Zelda's eyes, but it could have been the light reflecting on her glasses.

'Liz!' Nina was heading towards them with Cora in tow. 'Is everything all right?' she asked when she reached them, her eyes scanning Mia and Zelda.

'I'm fine,' Liz said. 'I just spoke to Rhodri and got a bit upset.'

'Awww, Liz.' Nina leant forwards and tried to hug her but there wasn't much space and her bag slid off her shoulder and hit Zelda in the face.

'Ouch!' Zelda leant sideways.

'Oh my goodness, I'm so sorry.' Nina tugged her bag back onto her shoulder and stepped back.

'I'm OK.' Zelda rubbed her nose. 'I've had worse.'

'Are you sure?' Nina's face was filled with concern.

'Absolutely. I'm just worried about this lovely girl.' Zelda turned to Liz.

'I think we all are,' Nina said. 'Cora and I are on the way home if you want to join us. We got her the pencils she wanted and then picked up some things for lunch at the shop.'

Liz nodded. 'I will do, thanks.' She yawned. 'I'm quite tired now. Tai chi was good, though.'

'Yes? I'm glad you enjoyed it.'

Nina looked a bit harried, as if she wanted to speak to Liz but didn't want to say too much in front of Mia and Zelda.

'I'll tell you all about it at home,' Liz said to Nina and her sister nodded. Then, turning and hugging Mia and then Zelda, she said, 'Thank you so much for being with me through that. I'm so grateful.'

'Any time.' Mia smiled.

'Stay strong,' Zelda said then she shook her head. 'I shouldn't say that. You *are* strong but you need to deal with this in your own way and to let it all out when it feels overwhelming. I'm here whenever you want to chat.'

'Thank you.' Liz stood up and tucked her phone in her pocket. 'See you soon?' she asked hopefully.

'I'll be at the allotment on Monday morning,' Mia said.

'OK, I'll see you there.' Liz smiled. 'You too, Zelda?'

'Well, of course.' Zelda winked. 'See you there.'

Liz walked away with Nina, feeling exhausted after the emotion of the morning.

'Are you OK, Aunty Liz?' Cora asked, sliding her small hand into Liz's.

'I am, thank you,' Liz said.

'Why were you crying?'

'I spoke to my . . . fiancé and he made me a bit sad.'

'Why?' Cora peered up at her. 'If you want, I could give him a piece of my mind like Mummy does when she's cross at Daddy.'

Liz looked at Nina, who rolled her eyes and mouthed *Only when he deserves it.*

'No, thank you, Cora. That's a very kind offer but I'm all right. It's just that it seems we're not getting married now and it made me a bit sad.'

'I'm sad for you. Did you have a beautiful dress to wear?'

The question made Liz gasp because the answer was *Yes!* She had bought the most beautiful wedding dress, veil and tiara. She'd felt like a princess when she'd tried them on and now she'd never get to wear them.

'I did.' She swallowed back her tears. 'But it doesn't matter. I can see if the shop will take it back or I could sell it to someone who *is* getting married.'

'You could put it on eBay,' Cora said then she frowned. 'But what if it doesn't fit them because you're big and tall and lots of people are short and—'

'Cora! That's enough questions for now. Let Aunty Liz catch her breath. When we get home you can help me make some cheese toasties because I think that's exactly what Aunty Liz needs right now.'

'Cheese toasties?' Liz smiled. 'That sounds perfect.'

'Cheese toasties and hot chocolates and Disney on Netflix will make you feel better, Aunty Liz. It always makes me feel better when I'm sad or when I have a cold and feel poorly,' Cora said.

'I'm sure it will,' Liz replied, not sure it would but trying to engage with Cora's innocent positivity.

They walked the rest of the way in silence with Cora between them, hopping and skipping and occasionally looking at Liz and smiling. As sad as Liz felt, it was hard not to feel some hope in Cora's unworldly take on things. Yes, Liz's life would be different to how she'd imagined it but that wasn't the end of the world. There was still so much beauty to be found. Still much to enjoy if she was prepared to open herself up to the possibilities.

Chapter 17

Zelda let herself into the field and closed the gate behind her. She double-checked it, knowing that her three goats were quite capable of letting themselves out of the field if the bolt wasn't slid fully across.

'Bloody goats,' she muttered as she tramped across the grass.

'Maaaaaa!' Snowball had spotted her and trotted happily towards her.

'Maaaaaa! Maaaaaa!' Midnight and Cocoa came too.

Snowball reached Zelda first and started nudging her side, clearly sniffing out the apple in her coat pocket.

'Hey! Hey! Slow down, eager beaver.' Zelda chuckled as she reached into her pocket and pulled out the apple slices wrapped in kitchen roll. She gave each goat several pieces then trudged over to their shelter.

Zelda had commissioned the shelter the previous summer from Connor Jones, the owner of The Lumber Shed. He'd made the large shelter from reclaimed wooden pallets and put in three and a half walls, leaving room for the goats to come and go as they pleased, along with some shelves for them to climb on. It was an impressive shelter and Zelda had been delighted with Connor's work.

She went about her morning chores, humming Frank Sinatra songs, mucking out the shelter, replacing the bedding and then filling the hay racks and replacing their water. Snowball followed her as she worked, occasionally nudging her for a scratch and once, when Zelda dropped the rake and bent over to pick it up, Snowball nudged her bottom and pushed Zelda over. Luckily, she landed in a pile of fresh hay, but even so, it took her a while to stop laughing enough to stand up again.

'Bloody hell, Snowball! Be careful, girl.' She rubbed the goat's chin, making eye contact with her. 'I know you like attention but one day you're going to push me over and I won't be able to get back up again.'

'Maaaa!' Snowball responded.

'I know, girl, I know. Right, that's all clean in there, you can have your breakfast and I need to go and have mine.'

She gave Snowball one last scratch, waved at Midnight and Cocoa, who were already tucking into their breakfast, then made her way back across the field and up to the house.

Keeping goats was hard work but eight years ago, when a local widowed farmer had fallen ill and had to be taken into a nursing home, she'd heard about the animals of his that needed rehoming. He'd reared the three female goats on his farm and treated them like family members. Zelda had land free and couldn't bear to think of the goats being separated or culled, so she'd adopted them. It had been a steep learning curve, and she'd known there would be work involved in caring for the goats, but what else did she have to do with her time? More recently, though, her worries about what would happen to the goats if – or when – something happened to her had crossed her mind. She'd spoken to the manager of a recently established rescue centre and the woman had agreed to take the goats and chickens in, should Zelda fall ill or pass away. Zelda had, of course, made a substantial donation to the rescue centre and included an even larger donation in her will, so that had given her some peace of mind.

At the gate, she let herself out then slid the bolt across. Snowball was still watching her from across the field so Zelda waved then smiled and the goat turned and joined her sisters for breakfast. Snowball had grown very attached to Zelda, a bit like a cat or dog would, and Zelda found the bond heart-warming.

Back at the house, she found Marcellus waiting on her doorstep.

'Good morning, young man,' she said. 'You're early today.'

'Ahhhh . . . good morning, Zelda. And what a fine one it is too. I came up this way first for a change.' He grinned at her. 'You been for a run, have you?' He winked.

'In my wellies and warm coat?' She laughed. 'And with my creaky knees?'

'Ha! Ha! I know that feeling well. To feed the girls, then?'

'Yes indeed and they're all well this morning.'

'Here's your post.' He held out a brown envelope and a seed catalogue.

'Looks like a bill or invoice for something,' she said. 'So nothing exciting. Thank you, kindly, though.'

He doffed his cap. 'As always, you're very welcome. I shall see you in the morning.'

'You will.' *Hopefully,* she added silently, never one to take life for granted.

Zelda headed inside and removed her woolly hat and coat but kept her fingerless gloves on. Her hands were chilled this morning. She needed to water the plants and to get the kettle on.

In the kitchen, she filled the kettle and set it on the hot plate then she picked up the envelope. She opened it and pulled the letter out.

Her eyes travelled over the back ink and her jaw dropped.

'What on earth?'

On her walk to the allotment, Mia thought about the previous day. Joel had come for Sunday dinner, helped her to peel vegetables then whipped the cream to go with the apple tart she'd made. Joel had opened a bottle of sauvignon blanc and they'd sat at the table while dinner cooked. She loved those times with him when they sat and chatted and he entertained her with stories from his job; some of them making her laugh and some bringing tears to her eyes. He certainly worked hard for his money and she was in awe of his emotional resilience because the things he saw on a daily basis and the situations he went into would break a lot of people. And yet, he remained fresh and enthusiastic and hadn't become jaded the way that some might. Her one remaining wish for him was to see him find a partner and fall in love.

He'd had relationships, one in particular had seemed like it might last, but then the woman had ended it after telling Joel that his work hours didn't offer the lifestyle she wanted. Mia could understand how it would be difficult being with a paramedic who worked long shifts and often didn't get home on time because they couldn't walk away from a job just because their shift had ended. Joel was devoted to his job, there was no denying that, and she could see how it would be a problem for some people, but Mia couldn't help thinking that it would be nice for him to have someone to go home to. What had made her a bit uneasy, though, had been how Joel had asked a few questions about Liz; to the untrained ear they would have seemed innocent enough but to a mother they hinted at more than just a passing concern for the pretty young woman. Liz was fresh out of a relationship, was heartbroken, and while Mia liked her very much, the last thing she wanted was to see her son get involved with her new friend and get hurt.

She reached the footpath at the north of the village that led to the allotments and paused for a moment to gaze around her. The sky was clear today, a bright blue, and the wind was cold but fresh. A perfect day for being outdoors, as long as you were wrapped up warm, of course.

She walked on, enjoying the feeling of strength in her legs and the strong beat of her heart. The walk to the allotments was a good one and she enjoyed doing it, aimed to do it more often. Although bearing in mind the letter she'd received that morning from the chairman of the allotment association, things could be about to change. Was Leopold Biggins really as powerful as he'd implied in his letter?

Spotting Liz and Zelda standing at the edge of the allotments, she raised her hand and waved then held up the cool bag she'd brought, which held portions of apple tart and a pot of cream. When she'd made the apple tart, it had been mainly for Joel, but she'd also thought of her two friends and how they'd enjoy some of it too.

With her free hand she patted the pocket holding the letter about Gideon's allotment. She'd brought it with her because she hoped Zelda would be able to advise her about what she could do.

'Hi, Mia.' Liz smiled at her friend. 'How're you today?'

'I'm good, thank you. What a lovely morning it is.'

'Indeed it is,' Zelda said. 'And what do you have there?' She gestured at the cool bag.

'I made apple tart yesterday and thought you might like some.'

'Gosh, I am enjoying your baking, Mia.' Zelda licked her lips. 'I've never eaten so well.'

The elderly woman seemed to have a bit more colour in her cheeks this morning and they appeared slightly fuller, as if she'd gained a little weight, which was good because when Liz had first met her she'd thought Zelda very frail-looking. Almost gaunt.

'Shall we sit down and have this with a cuppa?' Mia asked, keen to look after her friends. 'I've got the flask and bowls in my rucksack.'

'Brilliant.' Liz nodded. 'I'll get the chairs from the shed.'

As she reached for the chairs, she smiled when her gaze fell on the empty spot the hedgehog had occupied. Nina had spoken to a local hedgehog rescue charity, and they'd advised her to leave the hedgehog alone so it could wake from hibernation when it was ready. And that was how it had happened; one day the hedgehog was there and the next it was gone.

Once she'd unlocked Nina's shed and got the chairs out, along with the sawn-off log table, they sat down and Mia poured them all tea then handed them recyclable bamboo bowls containing apple tart.

'I have cream in here too.' Mia held up a small carton and offered it round.

They chatted about the weekend and the weather while they ate. Liz thought it was the best apple tart she'd ever tasted, the tang of the apple married beautifully with the hint of cinnamon and the richness of the thick cream. Washed down with tea, it was one of the most delicious Monday morning snacks she'd ever had.

'Thank you so much,' she said after she'd dabbed at her mouth with a paper napkin. 'That was amazing.'

'I'm glad you enjoyed it.' Mia smiled. 'It's so nice to bake and know that other people will enjoy it. Joel had his fair share yesterday, mind you, but I told him to leave some for us.'

Joel . . . The handsome paramedic who'd shown such concern for Liz on Saturday at the village green. She could still picture the kindness in his lovely brown eyes and the way he'd looked at her. Not that there would have been anything in the way he'd looked at her, she admonished herself, because he was simply showing concern but even so . . . the fact was that he had made eye contact with her and that was far more than Rhodri had done in a long, long time. The more she'd thought about it, Rhodri had avoided eye contact for as long as she could remember, had not complimented her on anything in just as long and so to have a man actually look into her eyes – even if it was out of concern for her health – had struck a chord with her.

Liz gazed out across the plots, noticing that there were a few other people there today, digging, weeding, planting seeds. Some plots already had patches of greenery where bulbs had poked their shoots above the soil and others had early tulips and daffodils brightening the area with their gorgeous array of colours. Spring seemed to have arrived suddenly, as if one night it had gone to bed and decided that the next morning it was going to take winter's place. She watched as a man stretched out a length of clear plastic over part of his plot then pinned it down at the corners, wondering what he was growing underneath it. Nina had told her that she'd bring Cora up soon to begin planting seeds as they hoped to grow some berries there this year as well as salad and potatoes.

'What are your plans for the rest of the day?' Zelda asked before licking her spoon and setting it in the empty bowl.

'I'm going to start contacting everyone I need to regarding cancelling the wedding.' Liz's stomach lurched at the thought.

'That's a bit grim,' Mia said.

'Yeah, but it has to be done.'

'Didn't your ex offer to do any of it?' Zelda said.

Liz shook her head. 'I did all the planning anyway and I don't think he'd know where to start. It's easier if I take charge because otherwise we could end up doubling up and it'll just get messy.'

'That's sensible.' Zelda bobbed her head. 'But not very pleasant for you.'

'I'll let him cancel the morning suits, though. That's his responsibility. Oh . . . and he's going to phone some estate agents to get our house valued.'

That was the worst one for Liz and she was glad Rhodri had texted last night and offered to do it. She would try to take the valuation and sale of the house one step at a time. Before it could happen, she'd need to decide what to do with her belongings and her share of the furniture. Not that she felt that she wanted any of it because she knew looking at it would make her think of Rhodri and now she knew for certain that it was over, all she wanted was to lick her wounds and make a fresh start.

'You poor thing,' Zelda said. 'I haven't even been able to bring myself to sell the cottage.'

'What cottage?' Liz asked.

'The one you'll have passed on your way in. I used to rent it out but I haven't had the energy or inclination to do that in years.'

Liz sat forwards. 'You have a rental cottage?'

'Yes.'

Liz's brain kicked into gear. If their house sold quickly and she quit her job – something that had occurred to her more than once – then there was nothing to keep her in Maidstone. Why would she want to stay there and be reminded of Rhodri every day? To drive past the estate they'd lived on? To risk bumping into Rhodri and Pete when she went into town? Here, in Little Bramble, she had Nina and her family. She had two wonderful new friends. She already loved the village and its location and if she had somewhere to live then everything would be a lot easier.

But that depended on a lot of factors and Zelda had said she couldn't be bothered to rent the cottage. But then she hadn't had a tenant ready to move in, had she?

'Zelda . . . Would I be able to take a look at the cottage? I mean – oh, that sounds terribly forward, but if you were to consider renting it out again to someone, then I might be looking for somewhere to live. Even if it was just a short-term rental . . .' She bit the inside of her cheek, wondering if she'd overstepped the mark of this new friendship.

The elderly lady frowned. 'You'd like to see my rental cottage? As a potential home for you?'

'Well . . . I'm going to need to find somewhere to live and while I don't know if moving to Little Bramble is a long-term solution, I do know that I can't stay with Nina indefinitely. She's very kind and has said I can stay as long as I like, but sooner or later I'm going to need my own space and she'll need her home back.'

Zelda nodded as she listened and Liz dug her fingernails into her palms, hoping she hadn't offended her. Liz glanced at Mia and was heartened to see that Mia was smiling.

'I don't see why not. In fact, that's quite a lovely idea! Oh, but I have to warn you – the cottage is in quite a state. It needs some tidying up.'

'That doesn't scare me,' Liz replied. 'I don't have much to do right now – other than cancelling plans – so I'd be happy to roll up my sleeves and get stuck in.'

'Then I'll go up to the house and get the keys. No time like the present and all that.' Zelda stood up. 'Ah . . . I nearly forgot.' She removed an envelope from her pocket. 'I received a rather snarky letter this morning from the chairman of the allotment association.'

Mia jumped up. 'I did too.' She pulled a letter from her pocket. 'What did yours say?'

'Something that I am not very happy about at all. Walk up to the house with me and I'll tell you all about it.'

'I'll tell you about mine too.'

While Liz put the chairs back in the shed, Zelda and Mia walked up to the house. Liz was now desperate to know what was in the letters too, but she'd hopefully find out when her friends came back. And, if she could, she'd try to help them decide what to do about whatever it was that had bothered them both so greatly.

Chapter 18

'Right, are you ready to take a look at the cottage?' Zelda asked Liz. She plastered on a smile but her stomach was churning with trepidation because she had no idea what it would be like inside. It had been a while since she'd stepped over the threshold and she wasn't looking forward to seeing it. However, Liz needed somewhere to live and the idea of renting the cottage to her was very appealing. Of course, it might need too much work done and it might not be a viable option as somewhere for Liz to live, but until they took a look, Zelda wouldn't know.

'I'm looking forward to seeing it.' Liz smiled.

'Me too. I haven't ever seen inside the place,' Mia said, 'although I've walked past it on hundreds of occasions.'

'It's a lovely cottage . . .' Zelda worried her bottom lip. Well, it *had* been a lovely cottage and when she was younger she'd spent some significant times there. Then tragedy had struck and she'd never been able to see it in the same way. 'It was a successful rental place over the years. After Mother passed away, I still rented it out for a time but keeping it running, along with the house and the allotment and everything else, just took too much energy so I closed it up – although I must admit that it's a terrible waste to have it sitting there empty.'

They walked down to the cottage and Zelda wrapped her hand around the keys inside her coat pocket. The letter she'd received that morning was still in there too. She'd spoken to Mia about it but wondered what Liz would think about it as an outsider to the village.

'Liz, we haven't told you what was in the letters we received from the allotment association and I'd like your opinion and I'm sure Mia would too.'

'Absolutely. It's outrageous!' Mia tutted.

'Apparently, Leopold Biggins, the chairman of the allotment association, who is probably all of twelve years old,' Zelda sniffed, 'thinks that Mia and I should relinquish our plots.'

'Relinquish your plots?' Liz asked, knitting her brows.

'Yes. He said that as I'm . . . ahem . . . advanced in years, it might be sensible for me to consider handing the plot over to someone else now. There are no vacant plots, you see, and there's a waiting list. I suspect, though, that he has the plots earmarked for one of his cronies.'

'Ugh! Cronyism. Nepotism.' Liz shuddered. 'Both are rife in education too.'

'I find it shocking, but I've been around a long time and so I know how the world works.' Zelda sighed. 'It's sad, but people are who people are.'

'The letter he sent *me* said that seeing as how Gideon has passed away, they would like the plot back. My name wasn't on it and so I have no right to it.'

'What? But that's appalling. Shouldn't he ask if you'd like to keep the plot?' Liz asked.

'It would have been the considerate thing to do.'

'I don't know this Leopold very well,' Zelda said, 'In fact, I've not set eyes on him since he took over as chairman because he certainly hasn't spent any time at the allotments himself, but there's something about his tone in this letter that sets my teeth on edge. It's . . .'

'Smarmy?' Liz asked.

'Exactly that and then some.'

'And then some?' Liz raised her eyebrows.

'Self-serving, I think. I suspect that the allotment association is a stepping stone for him. Marcellus told me that he was an office clerk, working for the parish council, and he jumped on the chairman position when his uncle retired. It's not a lot of power but it's something. He's likely the type to climb the rungs of the career ladder by greasing some palms.'

Liz giggled then slapped a hand over her mouth. 'Oh, I'm so sorry. I know it's not funny, but it's like being involved in an East End gangster novel.'

Zelda snorted. 'I guess it is. Bloody annoying man! How dare he assume that he can come along and upset the apple cart?'

'Too right!' Mia said. 'I want to keep Gideon's plot. At least for a year or so, anyway. Surrendering it right now would be like giving up a part of him and I already feel I've lost enough.'

'And my father donated the land for the allotments!' Zelda exclaimed. 'It used to belong to our estate. I doubt Leopold would know that as he's only been here for five minutes.'

'Sounds as though he's going to have a fight on his hands.' Liz chuckled. 'Poor man.'

'Poor man nothing! He'd better look out, that's all I can say.' Zelda pulled the keys from her pocket when they reached the cottage. 'OK, then, let's head inside.'

Liz's eyes roamed over the low stone wall that surrounded the cottage like two protective arms separated by a small wooden gate. Moss appeared to be thriving on the wall, a spongy, grey-green beard. The cottage looked neglected, uncared for, and her heart sank. Perhaps this was a silly idea. Perhaps she should forget about renting in the village. Or ask around and see if anyone had a newer place available to rent. And yet . . . the cottage was in such a lovely spot and something about it called out to her. She could imagine standing on this doorstep and listening to early morning birdsong, inhaling the heady scent of roses that could be trained to climb around the front door and placing pretty tubs of flowers in the front garden once she'd cleared away the winter debris. The shabby curtains could be replaced with new ones or with clean and trendy blinds, the windows replaced or repaired and cleaned, the doorstep swept and the door given a fresh lick of paint. This could be a perfect little home if it was given some attention. She sighed inwardly; she was getting ahead of herself – she didn't even know if Zelda would agree to her living there anyway.

Zelda pushed the key into the lock of the front door and tried to turn it. Nothing happened. She pulled it out, inspected it then tried again.

'It doesn't seem to want to turn,' Zelda said.

'Might need some WD40,' Mia said. 'Do you have any, Zelda?'

Zelda laughed. 'Probably, but it'll be up at the house.'

'Shall I try?' Liz asked.

'Be my guest.' Zelda placed the bunch of keys into Liz's hand. 'It's the silver key.'

'Thanks.' Liz stepped forwards and put the key in the lock. She tried to turn it but nothing happened, so she pulled it out, breathed on it then stuck it back in. She wriggled it from side to side then pushed it hard as she turned it and, finally, the lock gave and the door opened.

'Well done, Liz!' Zelda patted her back. 'You must have magical powers.'

'Just used to dealing with a sticky lock.' Liz grimaced. 'As a child, we often had problems with our front door and had to go through a similar rigmarole every time we came home.' The lock of the house they'd rented had been a nightmare on both cold and hot days, so Nina had developed a range of techniques for trying to open the door. Liz had learnt from the best.

Liz turned around to move out of the way for Zelda but the older woman shook her head. 'It's fine, dear, you go on in first.'

'Are you sure?' Liz said.

'Absolutely.' Zelda inclined her head.

Liz pushed the door wide and it creaked loudly, making the three of them giggle nervously. 'There won't be anyone in here, will there?' Liz asked, thinking not just of human beings but of giant rats and bats, as well as other creatures that could have made the cottage their home.

'Of course not!' Zelda squeezed her shoulder. 'If we couldn't get the door open with a key then no one else would be able to do it without one.'

The hallway was dark and smelt damp and musty, as if the air in the house hadn't been disturbed in years, which Liz suspected was true. A thick layer of grey dust lay on the floorboards of the hallway, adding to the air of abandonment. Liz wondered if she was making a big mistake even expressing interest in the place. It was such a far cry from her lovely new-build home in Maidstone.

There was a door to her right so she took hold of the handle and turned it and the door swung inwards, allowing light to pour out into the hallway. The room was dual aspect, with a window at the front and one at the back. There were two sofas covered with dust sheets and a small coffee table in the centre of the floor. The open fireplace still had logs in it and there was a rag rug laid in front of the hearth. On the internal wall behind the door was a bookshelf but it was empty, so presumably there hadn't been books on it when Zelda rented it out or if there had then she'd removed them. At least, that was what Liz hoped because she'd hate to think that there had never been books on it or that the books had turned mouldy with damp and decay and been thrown out. However, in spite of the smell that had greeted them in the hallway, the lounge seemed to be quite dry, the thick stone walls keeping the worst of the weather out.

'It needs a good dusting in here too,' Zelda said. 'And probably a lick of paint. What colour would you paint it, Liz? I'm asking because you're young and with it and would know what's fashionable these days.'

Liz turned around, gazing at the whitewashed walls. 'I'm not sure. You could stick with white or go with something darker, like blue or green, but then, because it's quite a small room, a lighter shade would probably be better.'

Zelda nodded her approval and something inside Liz lifted a little.

'I'd stick with a neutral shade then add colour with your furnishings.' Mia went to one of the sofas and lifted the dust sheet carefully, exposing a brown leather sofa. 'Sofa looks fine. The good thing about leather is that it's durable. The cushions will probably need a good airing and you could always get a few throws to spruce the sofas up. You can get some lovely soft ones these days that will come in handy in the colder months too.'

'It looks fine, doesn't it?' Liz ran a hand over the arm of the other sofa which she'd uncovered and was surprised to find that the leather felt smooth and warm to the touch.

'I invested in good-quality sofas years ago when I was still renting the cottage out and although they got a bit battered-looking, I always thought that they looked better for it.'

'I like the lived-in look,' Mia agreed.

Liz realised that she did too. The furniture she'd bought with Rhodri had all been new and immaculate, symbolic of their fresh start together, but it had meant that they'd both been terrified of spilling anything onto the cream cushions or marking the oak coffee or side tables with a mug or glass. They'd also been anxious about getting anything on the carpets or kitchen worktops and so they had, it dawned on her now, lived their lives as if on eggshells, forever afraid of shattering the perfectly erected façade. What an awful way to live that had been, she now realised. The tension would have been constant, even if they hadn't been consciously aware of it.

'At least you won't have to worry about spilling anything or dropping a few biscuit crumbs if you do take the cottage,' Zelda said as if reading her thoughts. 'These sofas have stories to tell and you'll just be adding to them.'

Liz smiled as she scanned the room again. She could imagine it on a cold winter's evening with the fire lit and the golden glow of lamps warming the corners. She could curl up on one of the sofas and enjoy a glass of good red wine while she read a book. It would be a very cosy place to live.

They went back out into the hallway where there was another door to the left of the staircase and a short corridor that led to what Liz guessed would be the kitchen.

'That's the dining room in there.' Zelda pointed at the door. 'It's empty apart from a table and chairs, and it could be used as a dining room or as a study.' She smiled at Liz. 'Whatever the tenant fancied.'

Mia had already gone ahead to the kitchen and pushed the door open. Liz followed, her heart fluttering as she admired the solid oak cabinets, the granite work surfaces and the apron- fronted sink in front of a window that overlooked the back garden.

'It's perfect!' she said as she went to the window and looked out at a small cottage garden. It was overgrown with brambles and a rickety swing stood in the one corner, its chains dark with rust, but there was also a shed and some well-established trees. The back door led straight out to the garden and she could imagine how nice it would be in the warmer weather to open the door and take her morning mug of tea outside or her mid-morning coffee. The house she'd shared with Rhodri had a large rectangular back garden, but as it was overlooked by the houses behind and on either side, it wasn't very private. It had been one of the things that she'd felt was a shame about the lovely house, but it had seemed a small price to pay to have a lovely new home on a good estate, a home that the agent showing them around said would certainly increase in value within a short space of time. *A home that would have been the perfect place to start a family . . .*

Liz shook the thought away, vowing to be positive going forwards. She had a strong feeling that she could be happy in this little cottage if she was able to rent it. She could start over, begin a new life close to her sister, brother-in-law and nieces and enjoy being in the countryside surrounded by trees and wildlife and not far from her two new friends. She could find a new teaching job or even try something new – could take some time out to think about what she wanted and do supply teaching in the meantime to pay the bills. She could go to classes like tai chi and for meals in the village pubs and not have to worry about spending all weekend cleaning, scrubbing away at the house as if she could scrub away her doubts and fears. She'd no longer have to fret about how she was going to pay for the canapés and champagne that they would serve at the fancy hotel when the wedding guests arrived, or about how she would post perfect photos of her Instagram-perfect life to her account to show her colleagues how perfectly happy she was.

As if she had something to prove . . .

Because looking at it from her new perspective, she had.

She'd been trying to prove it to other people but all the time the main issue with it had been that she was trying to prove it to herself.

Since her arrival in the village, she hadn't even opened her Instagram app and hadn't wanted to. Living with Rhodri, she'd spent hours taking photos with filters, trying to get them just right so she could post them along with the most popular hashtags.

It seemed exhausting now to even think of living like that.

No wonder she'd been feeling a bit burnt out.

No wonder Rhodri had distanced himself from her and their life together. He must have been tired of trying to pretend too. At least now they could both be true to themselves and live as they were comfortable living – and if that meant not being afraid of spilling a drink or a few crumbs, being able to sit in the garden in her pyjamas with bed hair and deleting her Instagram account, then so be it!

She realised that Mia and Zelda had left the kitchen so she went out to the hallway, noting the footprints in the dust, and followed them up the stairs. There was a small window on the landing, two doors to the left and one to the right.

'Main bedroom there,' Zelda said, pointing to the room above the lounge, 'and second bedroom there next to the bathroom.'

One bathroom? Liz realised that was very different from her new-build home that had a downstairs toilet, a family bathroom upstairs, two en suites in the master bedroom and another of the double rooms. There had only been two of them so what on earth had they needed all those toilets for? The children they had discussed having and never would now? Come to think of it, Rhodri had never expressed a strong desire to be a father; it had been Liz who'd pictured them having two or three children to fill their house with love and laughter. What would have happened to the carpets and perfect sofas had that been the case she had no idea but suspected she'd have been frazzled trying to keep everything clean and tidy. It was hard enough keeping house with just two adult people living in it, alongside a full-time job, let alone with a brood of little ones running around with sticky fingers and muddy feet.

As they went from room to room, Liz admired the small bedroom with a window that had a view of the fields and trees out front then the small but perfect bathroom complete with claw-foot tub. Across the landing, they entered the main bedroom that was dual aspect like the lounge directly below. There was built-in storage under the eaves and a double-bed frame in the centre of the room.

'We'll have to get a new mattress as the last one was thrown out, but the frame is pretty sturdy.' Zelda patted the head-board. 'Again, it needs a lick of paint but that's easy enough to sort out.'

'I'm sure one of Joel's friends is a decorator,' Mia said, frowning. 'Let me message him and check.' She pulled out her phone and, while she typed, Liz went to the window that had the same view as the kitchen one, only better, because she could see beyond the back wall and the trees and across to the allotments.

'This is such a lovely spot, Zelda,' Liz said. 'I'm sure you could sell the cottage for a fortune if you chose to do so.' Her heart lurched at the thought because then she would need to find an alternative property and now that she'd seen the cottage, she couldn't imagine wanting to rent anywhere else.

'I could have sold it years ago, but I wanted to hang on to it.' Zelda sighed as she shuffled to the door. 'I . . .' She placed a hand to her mouth and her eyes misted over as if she'd drifted to another time and place.

Liz watched her, wondering what she was thinking, aware that Zelda seemed to be wrestling with emotion.

'I couldn't bear to part with it, to be honest,' Zelda went on. 'There's so much . . . history within these walls.' She sighed again then turned and left the bedroom.

'He's replied already,' Mia said, interrupting Liz's musings about what Zelda was talking about.

'Who has?' Liz asked, confused.

'Joel. He said he'll message his friend and check if she can fit you in.'

'That's wonderful, but Zelda hasn't even confirmed that I can rent the cottage yet.'

'You can!' Zelda called from the landing. 'If you want it, it's yours. I'd be so happy to have a dear friend living here, especially one who has quite clearly fallen in love with the cottage and will care for it, even breathe new life into it.'

Liz placed a hand to her chest as the enormity of what could happen welled inside her. If she wanted to, she could live here. This could be her home. Not Rhodri's, not a different man's, not anyone's but hers. Well, it would belong to Zelda, but Liz could live here and be her own person, find out who she really was away from the relationship she'd thought she wanted and the life that had never really been hers to have.

'You'll be happy here.' Mia squeezed her hand. 'The village has a way of getting under your skin and into your heart and you may well find that once you move here, you'll never want to live anywhere else.'

'I can imagine.' Liz smiled as she looked around. 'I've got to be honest, though, I don't know if I need help painting. I could probably do it myself. After all, I have the time.'

'Well, wait and see what Joel's friend says and you could always have her paint one or two rooms while you do the rest. Mind you, Joel loves painting too, so I have a feeling he'll offer to help. If you'd be happy for him to give you a hand, that is. He wouldn't expect payment, of course. Well . . . except for some home-baked cakes, probably. He has such a sweet tooth. Oh dear, I hope I'm not rambling. It's boring when people go on about their children, isn't it?'

'Not at all.' Liz shook her head. 'It's wonderful to see how much you love him. He's very lucky to have a mum like you.'

The pride in Mia's eyes as she spoke about her son warmed Liz right through. Mia clearly loved Joel very much. He did seem like a nice man – and although the thought of accepting help from anyone was something that she found difficult, she also suspected that it was a part of village life. People knew their neighbours here and had close friends nearby. So did Liz now, in her sister but also in Mia and Zelda. Turning away offers of help would be churlish and could cause offence and she would hate to upset anyone because of her reservations. She had erected walls around herself a long time ago, built strong defences around her heart – defences that had probably kept Rhodri out without her realising it – but if she was going to stay in Little Bramble then she'd clearly have to learn to lower them and to let people in. It wasn't easy but she'd already made a start with Mia and Zelda, had accepted them for who they were as they had done with her, so perhaps she could do the same with Joel and others.

Panic at the thought of trying to change who she'd become instantly filled her. Could she really change? Could she adapt and become the person she'd like to be?

One step at a time, she said inwardly. *One step at a time and everything will be just fine.*

'I don't know about you two but I fancy a cup of tea now,' Zelda said when they were all downstairs again. 'There are no teabags or milk here so do you fancy coming up to the house?'

'Try and stop me!' Mia said. 'I always fancy a cup of tea.'

'Yes, please.' Liz took Zelda's hand in both of hers. 'And thank you.'

'Whatever for, dear?' Zelda fixed her blue eyes on Liz.

'For considering renting the cottage to me. For . . .' Liz's throat tightened. 'For giving me a chance to leave my past behind.'

'Goodness me, Liz, it's only a cottage. I'm not wiping your mind clean, like in some kind of sci-fi movie.'

'No, I meant that—'

Zelda was laughing and Liz blinked hard in her confusion. What had she said that was funny?

'I know what you meant. We all need to start over at some point in our lives, Liz. I've done it and I'm sure that Mia has too.'

Mia was nodding.

'Well, thank you for giving me this chance. I'm very grateful.'

'And I'm grateful to you for seeing potential in this cottage. Maybe one day I'll be able to find the courage to tell you why the cottage means so much to me.' Zelda said with a wry smile.

'I'd like that,' Liz said as curiosity filled her. The thought that Zelda had some secrets in her past intrigued her and she hoped that she would feel brave enough to share.

'Right, come on then.' Zelda opened the door and they all filed outside. 'I don't know about you two but I'm parched.'

Liz locked the door, checked it twice, then the three women walked up to Zelda's house together. Life could change so quickly – as Liz had found out recently – and she was glad to find that she didn't feel afraid. In fact, she could feel a flicker of excitement about what might lie ahead in this next chapter of her life.

Chapter 19

'Well, that's that then,' Liz said with a groan, then pushed the laptop away from her on the table and stretched her arms above her head. Her neck felt stiff, her shoulders tight and she had a sour taste in her mouth.

'You've done really well,' Nina said. 'Are you feeling OK?'

Liz pressed her lips together and inhaled slowly through her nose. 'I think so. I mean, I thought I'd feel a lot worse.'

She'd been dreading doing this but had known that it needed to be done. The time she'd spent with Zelda and Mia yesterday had fortified her and she'd returned to Nina's determined to get organised. She'd started cancelling things then and had finished it off today. Each cancellation took her further away from her previous life, closed the door a bit more, until everything was cancelled, deposits were lost and all that remained was to sell the house she had bought with Rhodri and to divide the furniture and contents. Not that she wanted the furniture. In fact, she would prefer Rhodri to take it all. There were a few things in Zelda's cottage that she could use, like the sofas and bed frame, and she'd need to get some new bits and bobs, but Mia had mentioned The Lumber Shed and how the owner, Connor Jones, would likely do her a good deal. Zelda had added that she had plenty of furniture up at the big house that wasn't used so Liz could take her pick and move it down to the cottage. It wouldn't be hers, of course, in the way that the furniture she and Rhodri had bought had been, but perhaps she could persuade Rhodri to buy her share of it out so she'd have some money put aside for the future. For the future when she *did* buy a house of her own, that was, she thought positively.

Nina handed Liz a mug of tea then sat opposite her at the kitchen table. Cora had gone to a friend's for a playdate and Demi hadn't got home yet, so the house was calm and quiet.

'Are you sure you want to rent that old cottage from Zelda?' Nina asked.

Liz had told her about it that morning after they'd walked Cora to school.

'It's perfect for me,' she replied.

'Well, as much as I love the thought of having you nearby, and I really, really do, it's a big move to make. You'll be leaving your whole life behind in Maidstone.'

'A job I no longer enjoy. An ex-fiancé. A neighbour who stole my fiancé. Well, not that you can steal a person but he seduced him. Unless it was the other way around and Rhodri seduced him.' She shook her head. 'Not that it matters either way. I loved our house and the area but, in all honesty, there's nothing to keep me there. Seeing you and the children again made me realise how much I've missed out on. All those years of Demi and Cora growing up, I wasn't around to see them and . . . and I don't want to miss another second of it.'

'You sound pretty sure to me so all I can say is . . . YAAAAAYYYYY!' Nina clapped her hands then waved her arms in the air, making Liz laugh. 'At last! I can have my baby sister close and spend plenty of quality time with you.' She got up and came around the table then wrapped her arms around Liz and hugged her tight. Liz relaxed into her sister's embrace and sent out a silent thank you to the universe, because even though she had lost Rhodri, she'd got her sister back.

'The cottage needs cleaning and decorating – it'll keep me busy and I feel quite excited about the prospect of a fresh start.'

'If you quit your job, though, what will you do for work?' Nina asked as she sat back down.

'I've been thinking about that too and I'm not 100 per cent sure yet, but this could be my time to do something different.'

'Like what?'

'Oh, I don't know . . . Life modelling?' Liz shrugged.

'What? Stand naked in front of a bunch of strangers so they can paint your bits?'

'They don't paint your bits! They paint *pictures* of your bits and the rest of your body.'

'Oooh, I don't know about that.' Nina grimaced. 'I wouldn't be comfortable getting my kit off in front of a room full of strangers. You never know who's going to take a few sneaky pics on their mobile phone.'

Liz sipped her tea. 'No, I don't think I'd be comfortable with that, actually. I could, I guess, become a bus driver.'

'I think you'd need to pass a test for that, wouldn't you? And remember how anxious you got before your last driving test.'

'Mmm.' Liz sighed. 'Perhaps not that, then.'

'You could get a teaching post at a local school? Then you wouldn't need to retrain.'

'But I don't know if I want that or if I'm ready for it. It's hard settling into a new school and tiring and I'm not sure I have the energy for it.'

They fell silent for a few minutes.

'I know!' Nina said excitedly. 'I have the perfect interim job while you decide what to do.'

'What is it?'

'Cora's school are going to be advertising for two higher-level teaching assistants for September and for a school librarian. The head teacher told me recently because she wondered if I'd be interested in applying for one of the roles. I'm not, because I'm happy as I am, but what about you?'

'Well, I do have to give my notice in at school and don't feel ready to start anything just yet, so September would be a good time for me to begin a new job.'

'They won't formally advertise for a few weeks and you certainly have the skillset.'

'I've never worked at a primary school before.'

'I'm sure you'd adapt easily. And it would take the pressure off for a while, plus you'd be doing something new but not too different from what you know.'

'It does sound appealing . . . and if it doesn't start until September it would give me time to sort the cottage and to settle in.'

'Exactly!'

'Thanks, Nina. Of course, I might not get one of the jobs because I might not be what they're looking for, but it does give me something to think about.'

'I'm so happy that you're going to be here. The girls will be delighted too.'

The sound of the front door slamming made them both jump.

Nina's eyes widened slightly and she rose from her seat as she called, 'Demi? That you, love?'

Feet raced up the stairs and a door slammed overhead.

'Oh dear,' Nina said. 'Must have been a bad day. I'd better go and speak to her.'

'Of course.'

Nina left the kitchen and Liz sat quietly, wondering what was wrong with Demi. Her niece had loving parents, a beautiful home and lots to be happy about but Liz knew that being a teenager was hard. Demi could be struggling with any one of a number of things.

'NO! Get out of my room!' The shout echoed around the house and was followed by a murmuring as Nina tried to speak to her daughter. Then feet padded down the stairs and Nina entered the kitchen, her face pale, her eyes wet.

'Nina, what's wrong?' Liz got up and went to her sister and enveloped her in a hug.

'I don't know what to do. I try so hard to be a good mum but everything I do is wrong, as far as Demi's concerned.'

'You're a wonderful mum and you're doing a brilliant job – it just sounds like Demi's going through a rough patch.'

'She hates me.'

'She doesn't hate you, but she's using you as the object for her anger right now. Teenagers can't shout and scream at their friends because they'll lose them and lose face. However, as her mum you're her safe place and you won't walk away from her. You love her and care for her and so, deep down, she knows that you'll be there no matter what.'

'I don't know about that.' Nina half-laughed, half-sobbed. 'If she keeps shouting at me like that I might just walk away.'

Liz pushed Nina's hair behind her ears. 'No, you won't. You're devoted to your girls.'

Nina nodded. 'It's true. It just hurts that she's so angry with me and I hate feeling that I can't help her. A few years ago I was the centre of her world and could do no wrong and now she can't bear to be near me.'

'It will change and she'll come back to you again. Just keep doing what you're doing and let her know you love her. This will pass.'

'I hope so because it's breaking my heart.'

Liz hugged Nina while her sister cried then she handed her a piece of kitchen roll.

'Would it be worth me trying to speak to her? I'm used to dealing with groups of grumpy teens so I might be able to get through to her. Plus, I'm not her mum, so that might help. And if she's rude to me, it won't hurt me like it does you.'

'Would you mind?'

'Not at all.'

'Thank you.'

Liz kissed Nina's cheek then made her way upstairs, hoping she would be able to make a difference in some way, however small. She'd been concerned about Demi's erratic behaviour and apparent bursts of anger since her arrival, so if she could break through the tough façade Demi seemed to have built around herself, it might well make a difference that would help not just Demi but her whole family too. She didn't want to interfere and make things worse but she also couldn't sit back and do nothing when her sister and niece both seemed so upset.

Chapter 20

Zelda paused outside the front door of a small stone cottage in the village. She licked her lips. Swallowed. Took a deep breath.

'It's all right, Zelda.' Mia offered a reassuring smile. 'We can do this.'

Zelda sighed and pushed a hand through her fluffy hair. She looked at the flower beds of the front garden and admired the rainbow of tulips, the bright yellow of daffodils and the wooden bird feeder that looked as though it was made of reclaimed wood. She suspected the latter item had probably come from Connor Jones' workshop.

'The thing is, Mia, I really am furious about this letter.' She held up the offending article, grimacing to illustrate her point. 'But despite my outrage when I received it and my desire to sort this Leopold out, I have spent my whole life avoiding conflict and it's hard to change the habits of a lifetime.'

'This is true,' Mia said. 'However, you're not actively seeking conflict, more aspiring to find a resolution. As am I. Neither of us wants to have an argument today. Neither of us wants to upset anyone or to be upset. But, if we don't speak to this man and tell him how we feel, then he'll never know. Perhaps he's used to having things his own way and rarely considers the feelings of others?'

'Like one of those psychopaths on the TV?' Zelda knitted her brows. 'Or is it sociopaths?'

A smile played on Mia's lips. 'Have you been watching true crime documentaries?'

Zelda chuckled. 'I stumbled across one recently and couldn't turn the TV off, even though it was quite simply terrifying.'

'I like them too. The human mind is fascinating.'

'It truly is.' Zelda had thought a lot over the years about why she'd behaved as she did and why Mother had acted in the way she had and knew she'd never have a full answer. It was easy to make assumptions but without all the facts and without having Mother there to ask about it all, she'd never know the truth. It was a very different time back then, when Zelda was growing up, and her mother had been from a different generation, had different values and priorities. Zelda had loved her and felt obliged to listen to her, even though it had contributed to the breaking of her own heart.

'He seems to like gardening.' Mia looked around at the flowers. 'Unless he has someone coming in to do it for him.'

'Some do these days. I've seen the vans around for the local businesses . . . What're they called? Lawn Mates? Dirty Hoe Landscaping? The Lawn Ranger? Used to just be the wealthy and those who didn't like getting their hands dirty who had gardeners – like Mother – but now lots of people do because they're too busy to do it themselves or not able to.' Zelda shrugged. 'I've always liked working the land. Gardening is good for the soil.' She paused and watched Mia's face as her lips turned upwards at the corners. 'I'm kidding with you. Good for the soul, but also good for the soil. Oh, anyway, I'm procrastinating, dear, so let's get this done, shall we?'

'OK. Here's the plan: you ring the doorbell and I'll kick him in the shins then push him over. You tie his hands then we can drag him through to the lounge and torture him until he agrees to let us keep our plots.'

Zelda's jaw dropped, then she caught the glint of mischief in Mia's eyes. 'Ha! You nearly had me there, Mia. However, this is not a true crime documentary and so we need to perhaps be a bit more diplomatic than that.'

Mia nudged Zelda gently, still grinning. 'Shall we?' She nodded at the door.

Zelda pushed the doorbell and they waited as the sound rang through the cottage. She noticed that although the garden was well kept, the frosted glass of the front door was dirty and the paint was peeling off at the corners.

A shout came from inside, then a figure appeared in the hallway. It paused, appeared to wave its hands in the air, then the door opened inwards.

'Hello?' A man stared out at them. A wiry man of about five foot three with thinning hair and a small jaw. He was wearing a faded black T-shirt with a white stain down the front and another on the shoulder and what looked like pyjama shorts.

'Can I help you?' He glanced behind him as if concerned, then back at Zelda and Mia.

'Are you Leopold Biggins?'

His eyebrows rose up his high, shiny forehead. 'I am. And who are you?'

'I'm Zelda Grey and this is Mia Holmes.'

For a moment his expression remained blank then something else filled his eyes.

'You know who we are, don't you?' Zelda pressed him.

'I . . .' He rubbed at his face then dragged his hand down to his non-chin. 'I'm sorry. I'm extremely tired and I just . . .' He looked behind him again and tilted his head as if listening for something. 'I'm dealing with something here.'

'Is everything all right?' Zelda asked.

He rubbed at his face again and his hand made a scratching sound on his patchy stubble. 'Not really.' He seemed to sag. 'I haven't slept properly in days. No, make that weeks. It could be years for all I remember. I—'

A high-pitched wailing from inside made him freeze mid-sentence and panic darkened his eyes. 'Oh God, not again!'

'Mr Biggins,' Mia said, holding up a hand, 'is there anything we can help you with? Do you have a baby in there?'

Zelda turned to Mia. Of course! That's what the noise was. A baby was crying.

'Could you? It's just . . . my wife and I . . . we're exhausted and . . . but I can't exactly bring you inside because we don't know you and my wife will go mad and—'

'Leo!' A woman appeared behind Leopold, holding a tiny baby against her chest. She was wearing a stained white towelling dressing gown and odd socks and her greasy brown hair was pulled into a bun on top of her head that wobbled as she shook her head. 'Be quiet or you'll wake the others again.'

Fear etched itself on Leopold's face. 'Oh God, please no.'

'Wake *the others*?' Mia prompted.

'The triplets. Well, two of them.'

'Triplets?' Zelda gasped. 'You have triplets?'

The woman and Leopold nodded, eyes wide, shadows like dark smudges beneath them.

'This is my wife, Jemima.'

The woman gave a small wave without fully removing her hand from the baby and Zelda saw the chipped varnish on her fingernails. 'Hello.'

'I'm Zelda Grey and this is Mia Holmes.'

'Hello.' Jemima waved again as if in a daze. 'Leo! Have you offered them a cup of tea?'

'Tea?' He frowned as if he didn't know what tea was.

'Yes, you idiot. That's what we do when people visit, remember?'

The baby whimpered and Jemima started rocking from side to side while looking as if she might start to cry herself.

'Why *are* you here?' He turned his cloudy eyes back to Zelda and Mia.

'We didn't tell you,' Zelda replied. 'But it's to do with the allotments.'

'Oh. Yes. Right.' He sighed and musty breath washed over Zelda, making her cough. This man needed to drink some water and brush his teeth.

'Offer them tea, Leo.' Jemima nudged him with an elbow then she smiled at Zelda and Mia. 'I don't suppose you have children, do you?' She squinted at them. 'Or grandchildren even?'

'I have three sons.' Mia held out her hands.

'Oh, thank God! Please come in.' Jemima nodded her head in the direction of a doorway behind her to encourage Zelda and Mia inside. 'I need some advice.'

Zelda and Mia followed Jemima through the hall and a doorway that led into a large open-plan kitchen-diner-lounge. It was surprising, Zelda thought, that there could be so much space in what appeared to be a very small cottage from the exterior. But when she looked more closely it seemed that the cottage had been extended out the back to create a lovely light space.

'See.' Jemima bobbed her head at three Moses baskets set side by side in the corner near an L-shaped sofa.

'How old are they?' Mia asked as they approached the baskets.

'Five weeks. They were born at thirty-six weeks and kept in hospital for the first three weeks for monitoring and feeding. I had some difficulties with my milk flow and then it took a while to get used to feeding three babies but we seemed to get into a routine – although I do feel as if I'm constantly feeding them – and then, yesterday, just when I thought things were going well, they didn't sleep for more than an hour at a time. And just as one fell asleep, the other woke and it's been like a carousel. I'm utterly exhausted.' Jemima looked close to tears.

'Me too,' Leopold had appeared behind them. 'It's dreadful being so sleep-deprived.'

'At least your nipples don't feel as though someone has rubbed them with sandpaper and your belly isn't throbbing because of the caesarean scar!' Jemima snapped at her husband. 'And you *did* sleep last night, even if it was just for two hours.'

Zelda looked from Jemima to Leopold and then to Mia. This young couple were exhausted and irritable and, it seemed, anxious. Her eyes strayed to the kitchen units where dirty dishes, mugs, pizza boxes, cartons and green food waste bags covered every surface. On the floor in front of the washing machine were piles of dirty clothes and in a basket near the doorway was what appeared to be wet washing. Jemima and Leopold both looked as though they needed a shower and a long nap.

Zelda had come here wanting to ask Leopold to back off with his demands for her to surrender her allotment plot but now she was overwhelmed by compassion. She had never known what it was like to be a parent but looking at these two, it was clearly no bed of roses. Although, as she peered into the Moses baskets, her heart fluttered. The babies were tiny, perfect human beings. Currently, two of them were sleeping and the third one lay in Jemima's arms, blinking large grey eyes at her mother, her rosebud mouth opening and closing as if in awe. Something inside Zelda contracted and she placed a hand to her chest as if to steady herself. At moments like this, she felt that tug inside that unsettled her. It was a sensation of deep sadness, of regret for chances not taken, for a life she could have had.

Just then, the tiny baby girl let out a squawk and Leopold and Jemima started as if they'd received electric shocks. They looked at each other, then at the baby, then back at each other.

'Here we go again!' Jemima carried the baby to the sofa, where she arranged a V-shaped pillow in front of her before placing the baby on it.

'Leopold?' Mia laid a hand on his arm. 'I know you don't know us but you do know *of* us. You know we live in the village and have allotment plots and that we both know your uncle. So look, this might seem a bit strange, but is there anything we could help you with today? I've been a mum to three young boys and I know how hard it is when babies are tiny. I had mine one at a time and that was challenging enough, but to have three at once must be overwhelming. Could Zelda and I maybe ... I don't know ...' She gave a nonchalant shrug. 'Help clean up a bit? Pop some of that washing on the line to dry?'

Leopold gazed at them as if trying to decide if it was safe to let them stay. He didn't know them personally, Mia was right, but he did know where they lived and that they were both

221

long-term residents of Little Bramble. Zelda wouldn't have blamed him if he'd asked them to go but she hoped, for their sakes, that he would be happy for them to stay. She hated to see people struggling and it was clear that Leopold and Jemima were not sailing through early parenthood without a hitch.

A wailing from one of the baskets made his mind up for him. He leant over and picked up a baby whose small face was puckered up and red as a squashed tomato. He held it to his chest and started to rock automatically, as if he did this in his sleep, which he probably did, Zelda thought.

'Please! Oh yes please – I'd be so grateful.' He looked down at the baby. 'Ssshhh. Shhhh now.' The baby's limbs flailed, and Zelda watched as it writhed in his arms. 'Oh God, what's wrong, little one?'

'May I?' Mia asked.

Leopold looked at his wife and she nodded so he handed the crying baby to Mia.

'When was she last fed?'

'That's Roland.'

'Sorry.' Mia adjusted the baby in her arms. 'Hello, little Roland.'

Roland screamed and balled up his fists then pulled his knees up to his chest.

'What's wrong with him?' Zelda asked.

'Could be a touch of colic,' Mia replied.

The third baby started to whimper then and Leopold looked at Zelda but she averted her gaze. As much as she could admire babies, her knowledge of them was very basic indeed. Leopold seemed to resign himself and he lifted the baby from the basket and carried it over to Jemima, who sighed as she opened the other side of her dressing gown.

Zelda looked back at Mia, who was holding the baby with ease and confidence, her face calm, her voice soft and low as she spoke to the tiny person. She lifted Roland and placed him against her shoulder then began rubbing his back in a circular motion while gently bobbing up and down. He continued to wail but it didn't deter Mia and Zelda was filled with admiration for her friend.

'I'll make a start on this lot.' Zelda gestured at the worktops covered with debris, dishes and mugs. 'See if we can't get this sorted out.'

Mia winked at her and Zelda pushed up her sleeves then got to work. They might not have come here for this but they'd found a young couple in need of help and support and if there was anything Zelda could offer, it was exactly that.

Mia looked around the kitchen area and smiled. They'd done a great job of cleaning and tidying. Worktops sparkled, the sink shone and there wasn't a pizza box in sight. Her eyes dropped to her chest, where Roland's downy head rested. Before she'd started helping Zelda, she'd spotted a baby sling on the sofa and so she'd popped Roland in it, settled him down and got to work. Having had three babies of her own, even if it had been a long time since they were this small, she'd known that the beat of her heart and the rocking of her body as she moved would soothe him. It had worked with her three boys but she knew that it was different for Jemima and Leopold because they had three babies at once to care for. There was no perfect way to be a parent; it was about managing to keep babies clean, fed and rested while doing the same with yourself. It sounded simple enough but often it was the parents who suffered – and though she wouldn't say as much to Roland's parents, she believed that she and Zelda had arrived in the nick of time. Now they had a clean house, Leopold had been able to go upstairs to take a shower and two of the babies had been fed.

'Jemima,' she said as she crossed to the sofa, 'would you like to swap one?'

The younger woman looked up and yawned. 'Excuse me, I'm so tired.'

'Of course you are, so don't apologise.' Mia loosened the sling, tucked Roland in the crook of one arm and accepted the baby from Jemima. 'And who do I have here?'

'That's Henrietta.' Jemima held out an arm for Roland then settled him on the pillow.

'I'll see if I can get some wind up for her then pop her in the basket.' Mia gazed at the tiny face. 'She's beautiful.'

Jemima smiled then winced.

'You OK?' Mia asked.

'It stings as they latch on sometimes. I seem to have plenty of milk but I still find it uncomfortable.'

'It can take some getting used to.' Mia perched on the sofa next to Jemima and placed the baby against her shoulder then started to rub her back. 'You're doing a brilliant job, though.'

Jemima smiled shyly. 'Thank you.'

Henrietta suddenly let out a loud burp, making the women giggle.

'Who was that?' Zelda asked from the kitchen, where she was rinsing out a cloth.

'Henrietta.' Mia stood up again and carried the baby to the Moses basket then laid her inside. 'Would you like me to burp the other little girl now?'

'Yes please. This is Paige.' Jemima handed Paige to Mia then adjusted Roland on the V pillow.

Mia rocked Paige against her shoulder as she waited for her to burp and watched Zelda unloading the washing machine. They'd been busy since they'd arrived but it had been enjoyable. It wasn't every day that Mia got to hold babies and she felt a bit bad because Zelda hadn't cuddled one yet.

'Zelda, why don't I peg those on the line and you can hold Paige for a bit?'

Zelda placed the basket on the table. 'Uhhh . . .'

'Come and sit down and have a cuddle. She's been fed and is sleeping now.'

Zelda twisted her mouth up and wrinkled her nose. 'Uhhh . . .'

'Come on. It's all right, she won't bite.'

'OK, then.' Zelda crossed the room and sat next to Jemima. She tugged at her right earlobe then chewed her bottom lip. She seemed nervous.

'Here you go.' Mia gently placed Paige in Zelda's arms then tucked a cushion under her elbow to support the baby's head. 'Perfect.'

Zelda smiled up at her but the smile didn't reach her eyes. In fact, she looked rather sad and Mia wasn't sure why but it wasn't the right time to ask.

'Enjoy your cuddle and I'll get that washing on the line.'

Zelda looked down at the baby in her arms and sighed. Paige was perfect with her soft, fluffy hair and fair eyelashes that fluttered against her cheeks. Her mouth was small and pink, her skin pale, her eyelids almost translucent.

Her vision blurred and she gritted her teeth together. Holding babies wasn't something she did very often. In fact, the last time she'd held a baby had been years ago at a village Christmas show when a woman had asked her to hold her little one while she drank her hot chocolate. It had only been for a few minutes and Zelda had been distracted by everything going on around her.

Now though, here like this, there were no distractions. Next to her, Jemima had her head back against the cushions as she fed Roland, her eyes closed. It felt as if Zelda was alone with Paige and it was strange. She blinked the tears away and watched the baby's chest rise and fall, her mouth pucker as she dreamt. It was a precious moment – but a painful one. How could she still feel so much pain after such a long time? Would the grief for her own loss never leave her?

She leant forwards and sniffed the baby's head and her heart squeezed. As she sat up straight again, she let the tears fall slowly behind her glasses. Sometimes, things rose to the surface even when you tried to stop them, even when you thought you'd tucked them away years ago. Something could trigger an emotion and it would burst forth like a geyser, no matter what you tried to do to stop it. This was quite clearly one of those moments and so Zelda ran with it, only dabbing at her eyes when the tears had stopped.

Mia returned to the kitchen to find Leopold with damp hair and wearing clean clothes, looking much fresher than when they'd arrived. He flashed her a genuinely warm smile.

'Thanks so much for this.'

'You're very welcome. I'm just glad we could help,' Mia said.

'Me too,' Zelda joined in. She looked more relaxed than when Mia had left her with the baby but her eyes did look a bit red. Holding a baby could soften the toughest of hearts, Mia knew, but she wondered if there was more to it than that with her friend. And from what she'd learnt about Zelda, she certainly wasn't tough.

'Are you hungry?' Mia asked.

Leopold nodded. 'Always. And Jemima is ravenous all the time at the moment. Feeding the babies burns a lot of calories.'

'How about I put something together for you both then Zelda and I can leave you in peace?'

'Can't you stay?' Jemima asked with a grin. 'It's been amazing having you here. We don't have any relatives nearby. My parents live in Florida although they wouldn't be much help if they lived closer anyway. The midwives have been brilliant but they're so busy and can't stay with us for long and sometimes Leo and I just feel out of our depth.'

'Sweetheart, most new parents do so don't beat yourselves up.' Mia looked at Roland, who was lying on the pillow with his mouth open. 'I think he's done so do you want me to take him so you can go and shower?'

'I'll take him.' Leopold stepped in. 'Unless you'd like to have him while I make something to eat?'

'No, it's fine. You burp him and I'll do some food.'

An hour later, all three babies were in their baskets, Mia had set the table and Jemima and Leopold were tucking into scrambled eggs, beans and toast. There hadn't been much in the cupboards so she'd made them a simple meal but it was a nutritious one and she'd made a mental note to batch bake some healthy dinners then drop them in for the couple to place in their freezer. Things would get easier for them as the babies grew, but Mia knew how difficult the first few weeks could be and how much difference some help and support could make.

'Ready, Zelda?' Mia said.

'Ready.'

'Uhhh, before you go . . .' Leopold stood up, dabbing at his mouth with a napkin. 'What was it you wanted to say about the allotments?'

Mia met Zelda's eyes then turned back to Leopold. 'It can wait.'

'No, no. Please tell me. If I can sort it out for you then I will.'

'Well, we'd both like to keep our plots. For the foreseeable future that is, anyway. Zelda has owned hers since the allotments were created. Her father donated the land for the whole thing, you see.'

'I didn't know that.' Leopold looked crestfallen. 'I'm so sorry.'

Zelda waved a hand. 'It's fine. But don't think that just because someone gets old that they're of no use anymore. I'm still fit and healthy and I like my plot. It gives me somewhere to go and something to do.'

'Of course.' Leopold nodded, his cheeks flushed. 'I'll see to it that no one troubles you about it again.'

'And as for me . . .' Mia swallowed. 'The plot was in my late husband's name but – but if it's OK, I'd like to take it on. I know that there's a waiting list and that others would like plots but you see . . . Gideon only passed away recently and we spent time at the allotment together. It's important for me because it's a connection to him and – and so I would like to keep it. Please.'

Leopold was nodding vigorously. 'Absolutely. I understand, Mia. Please don't worry about it. I know I wrote to you both but I wasn't aware of the circumstances and the last thing I want to do is to upset either of you.' He rubbed at his temples. 'Please accept my apologies. It was wrong of me to try to take the plots away from you when I hadn't even looked into your circumstances.'

'You should be ashamed of yourself, Leo,' Jemima said through a mouthful of toast. Her clean, damp hair was pinned up with a clip and she looked better for her shower, just as Leopold did. 'Imagine if someone tried to do something like that to one of us or to our children one day.'

He hung his head. 'I really am sorry. And I'm so very grateful for your help today. We've been muddling along but it's so hard and you won't believe how wonderful it felt to have you come in and take over. The relief I felt at your competence in dealing with the babies and the house was just immense.'

'I know what it feels like,' Mia said. 'I've been there. A long time ago but it's not something you forget in a hurry. I'm just glad we could help.'

'I'll see you out,' Leopold said.

'No need. Eat your food then try and have a nap, the pair of you. It's not always easy to sleep while the baby – or babies – sleep, but it's worth a try. You'd be surprised how much even just twenty minutes of sleep will help.'

'Thank you.' Jemima smiled. 'You're both angels.'

'See you again?' Mia said.

'We'd be delighted if you came again soon,' Leopold said. 'Especially as my paternity leave is over and I have to get back to work. I took some holiday time too because we weren't sure when the triplets would get out of hospital but I have to go back next week and I'm worried about Jemima being alone.'

'No problem at all. I'll be in touch.' Mia took one final look at the contented sleeping babies then walked out into the hallway with Zelda.

As they stepped out of the front door and Zelda closed it behind her, their eyes met and Mia raised her hand. Zelda looked at it curiously so Mia took Zelda's hand and tapped its palm to hers. 'High five, Zelda.'

Zelda chuckled. 'High five.'

'We did a good job of that.'

'Indeed we did. I feel rather elated now.'

'Me too. It's good to help others.'

'It is. Plus, we got our way with the allotment plots.'

'We did. What is it that they say? Oh, I know – teamwork makes the dream work.'

'And we're a good team.' Zelda bobbed her head.

'Shall we set up a babycare and cleaning company?' Mia teased.

'Definitely. With some baking thrown in. And let's get Liz on board too.'

They linked arms and were still laughing when they reached Mia's car on the road outside.

Chapter 21

Liz let herself into Nina's home and called out, 'Hello! Only me!' as she always did when she arrived. Even though Nina and her family had made Liz feel very welcome, she still didn't want to take anything for granted. She was aware that Demi might be home because she hadn't gone out with Nina but suspected that the teenager might still be in bed.

There was no answer, so she removed her trainers and placed them on the rack by the door then walked through to the kitchen. The scent of coffee and toast hung in the air but the kitchen was clean and tidy, as it always was. Nina, Kane and Cora had gone out to a garden centre – a very pleasant Saturday morning pastime, Liz thought. She'd been invited but declined because she planned to attend tai chi with Mia and Zelda then have breakfast in the village. Tai chi had gone well and Liz had enjoyed the release it provided, followed by a delicious breakfast at the café with her friends. They filled her in on their meeting with Leopold Biggins earlier that week and Liz had been pleasantly surprised to hear that it went well. Apparently, Mia and Zelda had found Leopold and his wife struggling to cope with their young triplets and given them a hand; in return, Leopold had promised to sort out the allotment issue for them.

A noise from overhead made her look up. Sounded like Demi was here. Liz got herself a glass of water and drank it down then placed the glass in the dishwasher and headed upstairs. On the landing, she saw that her bedroom door was open and frowned. She was sure she'd closed it before she left but perhaps she was mistaken. A flash of movement caught her eye and she paused and listened. Was there someone in there?

She crept the rest of the way across the landing and peered into the room. And what she saw made her heart thud. Demi had Liz's suitcase open on the floor and was rifling through it. Liz had unpacked her clothes and placed them in drawers and on hangers in the wardrobe but what she hadn't unpacked she'd left in the suitcase, not wanting to put certain things away because she knew, deep down, that she shouldn't have brought them with her. Although, having said that, she couldn't have left them in the house she shared with Rhodri because if she had then he might have found them and that would have been awful.

Torn between wanting to run from the house, jump in her car and drive away and feeling the need to reprimand Demi for going through her things, she stood frozen in the doorway. As if sensing that she was being watched, Demi looked up.

'Oh!' Her face went bright pink right up to the roots of her brown hair. 'Uhhh . . .'

'Demi, wh-what are you doing?'

Demi stood up and Liz saw the small white cardigan in her hand. The pair of white booties in the other.

'Why do you have these?' Demi asked.

'Why are you going through my things?' Liz was aware of her heart racing, her legs trembling. The things she would not want anyone to see more than anything else she possessed were on display. Her teenaged niece had found them and now her secrets were exposed.

'Why do you have these?' Demi held up the items. 'And the rest of them? Are you pregnant?'

'What? No!' Liz clenched and unclenched her hands. 'I-I . . . bought them a while ago. I was . . .' How on earth did you explain something like this to a child? To someone who couldn't possibly understand what it felt like to grow up in a house where you felt lost? A house where your mum was gone, your dad was absent and your sister was trying her best to raise you? A house where you longed for stability, for a mum who'd make you a healthy dinner then help you with your homework while your dad made you hot chocolate. Liz had known that such parents existed because some of her school friends had them. Some of them had two parents together, had stability, and even some of them who lived with one parent often had that parent around most of the time. Liz and Nina's dad hadn't been there very often and when he had been, he'd been detached, distant, and they hadn't wanted to trouble him in case he disappeared again. Demi had two parents, a sister, a lovely home and all the love and stability she could possibly want. So how, then, could Liz explain this to her?

'*Were* you pregnant?' Demi asked, her eyes going automatically to Liz's middle.

'No.' Liz sank onto the bed and folded her hands in her lap. There was no point lying and she didn't have the energy to invent something anyway. Honesty would have to do. 'I was hoping to be. After I got married. I . . . bought those things because I wanted to be a mum.'

'Like my mum?'

'Yes. She's very lucky to have you and Cora.'

To Liz's horror, Demi started to cry.

'What is it?' She got up and went to her niece, wrapped an arm around her shoulders, surprised to find that Demi was almost as tall as her. It seemed that the girl must have been hunching over quite a bit to hide her height.

Demi shook her head and the tears turned into sobs. She dropped the baby clothes into the case then turned to Liz and embraced her.

'Shhhh.' Liz rubbed Demi's back. 'It's OK, sweetheart. I'm OK.' She added the last, but she was unsure if Demi was overwhelmed by sympathy for childless Liz or if it was something else. Considering how Demi had behaved recently, Liz suspected it was the latter. She held the girl and rocked her gently, stroked her hair and made soothing noises.

When Demi's crying subsided, Liz pulled a tissue from the box on the bedside table and handed it to her then they sat on the edge of the bed.

'I'm so sorry,' Demi said.

'What for?'

'That you didn't get to have a baby or get married.'

'You don't need to be sorry about that. It's probably for the best, seeing as how my ex-fiancé has since admitted he prefers men.' The previous day, Rhodri had phoned to tell her that the estate agent had a client who'd been looking for a house in their area and that she was interested in seeing the property. The estate agent had strongly hinted that the client would put in an offer if she liked what she saw and Liz's stomach had plummeted to her feet but then she'd realised that this was, in light of the circumstances, the best thing all round. And when Rhodri had gone on to say that he'd been doing some soul-searching and released that he was actually gay and not bisexual as he'd initially believed, Liz had sat quietly and listened. Her initial feeling had been to shout and rage at him, to cry and say horrible things to him, but something had told her not to react, to let him have his say and then to digest it. She was glad she had because after the conversation had finished, she felt that she understood herself and Rhodri a bit better. When they'd got together, they'd both been searching for something and thought they'd found it in each other. What they really should have been looking for was themselves. They were both lost and being in a relationship together had not been the solution, just a temporary reprieve from the loneliness. But things hadn't been right and, sooner or later, it was inevitable that they would come to an end.

'I am sorry, though.' Demi looked up at Liz with her pretty hazel eyes. She might be sixteen but she looked younger without the heavy makeup she often plastered on in the mornings before she left the house. Now, not long out of bed, her eyebrows were natural, her eyes unadorned by black pencil, her freckles visible. When she wasn't stomping around, slamming doors or scowling, she seemed innocent, still a child. 'I'm sorry you've been hurt.'

Liz smiled. 'But I'm OK. I didn't think I would be and although I'm still sad at times, I feel better than I did just a few weeks ago. I'm not saying that it's all gone away or that I expect it to just disappear suddenly, because grief isn't like that, but I'll get there.'

'Will you stay here now?' Demi asked.

'Well, not in this house because you and your mum and dad and Cora need your space but I might stay in the village.'

'Where?'

'I have a friend who had a cottage she can rent to me.'

'Wow! That's exciting.'

Liz nodded. 'It's up by the allotments.'

Demi wrinkled her nose. 'That old cottage with the dirty curtains?'

Liz laughed in spite of herself. 'Yes. That's the one.'

'Why would you want to live there?'

'It's actually very nice inside and with a lick of paint and some new . . . uh . . . curtains, it could be a nice place to live.'

Demi nodded. 'I suppose so.' Her eyes wandered to the suitcase again. 'Will you keep those?'

'The baby clothes?' Liz asked the question just to make herself say it out loud. 'I don't think so.'

'But what if you have a baby?'

'What if I don't?'

'True. So what will you do with them?'

'I think they need to go to someone who could benefit from them.'

'That would be kind of you.'

'There's no point in them sitting in a suitcase.'

'You're very brave, Aunt Liz.'

'I try to be but I'm not always. Sometimes I'm terrified.'

'Bravery is about feeling scared but doing something anyway.' Demi smiled.

'When did you get so wise?'

'It's something I read on Instagram.'

'I like that. I'll keep it in mind.' They sat quietly for a moment then Liz asked, 'Demi, why were you looking in my suitcase?'

'Oh . . . I . . .' Demi's eyes slid away and a blush crept into her cheeks. 'I . . . I was looking for something?'

'What?'

What could possibly be in Liz's suitcase that Demi might want?

'Money,' Demi whispered.

'Money?'

Demi gave a tiny nod. 'I'm so sorry. I'm very embarrassed.'

Liz took Demi's hand. 'Why do you need money?'

'To get my . . . uh . . . my belly button pierced.'

Liz's eyes widened but she knew better than to jump in with a judgemental comment.

'You'd like your belly button pierced?'

'Yes.' Demi chewed at a fingernail.

'Why don't you just ask your parents?'

'They give me an allowance but it's not enough to get it done.'

'I wouldn't have thought it was that expensive.'

'Uh, it can be. At a proper salon.'

'Well, I'm sure you could speak to your mum or dad about it.'

'I can't.' Demi sucked in a deep breath. 'It wasn't for that, actually. Promise you won't say anything?'

'Demi, I can't promise that. I'm sorry, but if it's something worrying then I can't swear that I won't need to speak to your mum or dad about it. If something went wrong and I could have prevented it, imagine how awful I'd feel.'

'OK, then, it was to . . . get my tongue done.'

'Pierced?' Liz had seen pupils in school who'd had their tongues pierced and while she knew some people liked it, to her it seemed extreme. Each to his or her own, of course, but she wouldn't fancy it. Seeing how those pupils had constantly toyed with the studs in their tongues, tapping them against their teeth, had been enough. She could barely stand having a filling done at the dentist.

'No. Split.'

'*Split?*' Liz couldn't keep the surprise out of her voice now. 'But why?'

'It's cool.'

'Cool? Having your tongue cut in half?'

'Yes.' Demi nodded but there was uncertainty in her eyes.

'Wait a minute. Is that even legal in the UK?'

'I'm not sure.'

Liz had a feeling she'd read somewhere that it had been made illegal for anyone other than a plastic surgeon to do it a few years back but she'd need to check. Besides which, she suspected that it could lead to illness and tooth damage if something went wrong.

'And how much would this procedure cost?'

'A couple of thousand.'

'Wow! And you thought I might have that kind of money in my suitcase?'

Demi started to smile. 'I don't know. I don't think I really believed you'd have money in there. Who carries cash these days, right? That's what Dad always says anyway. Everything is paid by card or phone now. I was really just being nosey.'

'I guess so.' Liz squeezed Demi's hand gently. 'But . . . regarding the tongue splitting. I know that right now it might seem like the thing you want to do but it's rather drastic and I doubt it's reversible. It's probably one of those things that you should think about for a while.'

'For how long?'

'About a hundred years, I'd say.'

Demi laughed. 'I don't know if I do want it done. It's just that some of my friends are so cool and I just feel so—'

'Awkward?'

'Yes. How'd you know?'

'Look at me.'

'You're gorgeous.'

'I'm tall. I have lots of freckles. I like my hair now but I didn't when I was younger. It takes time to feel comfortable with yourself and I certainly think I'll always be a work in progress. Some things I've dealt with and some things I haven't – and I'm talking internally here as well as physically – but all I can do is keep trying. You're young, Demi, and beautiful inside and out. You have so much ahead of you and I think that if you want to do something extreme like tongue splitting, then perhaps wait a few years and see how you feel. You might change your mind or you might become even more convinced that it's what you want. At least then you can be certain.'

'That's true. I really am pretty sure that I just got caught up in wanting to be cool like them so they'd like me better.'

'You shouldn't ever have to change yourself to make others like you. If you feel that way, find some friends who do like you for who you are. Find your tribe.'

'Point taken. It's hard being a teenager.'

'It's hard being any age.' Liz laughed. 'Ask my friend, Zelda.'

'That old woman who lives in the big house?'

'That's the one. Although I think old is a word I wouldn't associate with Zelda. She's very sparkly.'

'Sparkly?'

'Yes. She has this special something that makes me want to spend more time with her.'

'Really?'

'Yes, really. You should come and chat to her. She's been around a long time and has a lot of stories.'

'I'd like that.'

'Being unique is wonderful and I'd hate for you to feel that you need to be the same as everyone else. This is something I'm still learning to do.' Liz winked at Demi. 'But we can try together. If you want.'

'I'm really glad you came to stay. Sometimes I feel so lost and so angry and I know I take it out on Mum but since you've been here, she seems calmer.'

'Your mum always seems calm to me.'

'She's not. She can go off on one, but I think you being around is good for her.'

A lump rose in Liz's throat. 'I'm glad,' she said softly. 'It's nice to feel useful. And wanted.'

Demi moved closer and wrapped her arms around Liz, who tried very hard not to cry. For a long time she'd felt that she wasn't wanted, had suspected that Rhodri didn't want her the way she'd longed for him to, the way she should be wanted. But now, things could be different. Now, she was with family and friends. Now, she was learning to accept herself for who she was and she knew she should heed her own advice.

'If you'd like some help with decorating your cottage, I'm good with a paintbrush.' Demi peered up at her.

'Is that right? It would be nice to have some help. Tell you what, why don't we go downstairs and make a snack and some drinks then have a browse at paint colours? You can give me some help choosing paint, curtains and so on. What do you think?' Liz held her breath. It might sound like hell to a teenager but Demi's eyes had lit up.

'I'd love to. I've always liked looking at house stuff. I love imagining what my house will be like one day, what sofas I'll have and what cushions and bedding.'

'Excellent, because I'm rubbish at all that.' Liz hid her smile at the fib that had rolled off her tongue. She loved choosing furniture and décor but right now she wanted Demi to feel important and cherished, that her opinion was worthwhile. 'And if you do help me with the painting, I'll pay you back with pizza.'

'We could have regular pizza nights if you live so close!'

'That's an amazing idea. I love pizza. Come on, let's go and get my laptop turned on and you can tell me all about your favourite pizza toppings.'

'Oh! I almost forgot. If you do want to give the baby clothes away, there's a swap shop coming up at the village hall next week.'

'A swap shop?'

'Yes. You take things there that you no longer want or need and swap them for something you do. Or just give them away if the other person has nothing you want.'

'What a brilliant idea. I might find some things there for the cottage.'

'You might.'

As they rose to leave the room, Liz looked back at the suitcase. The tiny clothes and booties she'd bought were from a previous life, one that had sometimes felt out of her control, however hard she'd tried to shape it. Giving them away to someone who needed them would be a positive step. She was lucky enough to have a fresh start and she was going to make the most of it and live her life her way from now on.

Chapter 22

'Are you sure about this now, Mum?' Joel asked when they reached the village hall. Another week had passed. Mia had spent more time with Zelda and Liz and found that being with them helped in many ways. They were good company and she always looked forwards to spending time with them. A few days ago, Mia had spoken to them about needing to take Gideon's things to a charity shop and Liz had told her about the swap shop this weekend. Mia had seen the fliers around the village and wasn't sure if it was the right way to go, but then she'd spoken to Joel and he'd said it was a good way to pass things on and environmentally friendly too.

'I'm sure, my darling. I mean, I could hold on to Gideon's clothes and belongings for ever but if I do that, then who does it help? I've kept a few bits, like his favourite shirt, one of his ties and his old gardening jumper, but keeping the rest is silly when they could be used by someone else.' She didn't add that the last thing she wanted was for Joel and his brothers to have to clear everything out when she too one day passed away.

The more she could part with now, the better it would be for everyone as far as she was concerned.

'You're being very brave.' Joel wrapped an arm around her shoulders and gave her a squeeze. 'I think Gideon would be pleased that his clothes will get another lease of life.'

'I hope so. In fact, I know so. Gideon was a generous philanthropist.'

They went inside, carrying the black bags of Gideon's things. It was already busy but Joel pointed at a free table on the far side of the hall so they made their way over. Mia had been to tai chi that morning with Liz and Zelda so she knew they were coming too. Liz said she had some things to swap and Zelda said she'd have a dig around at home and see what she could find.

'Let's get set up then we can have a look around.' Joel placed the bags under the table then started to unpack them.

Mia watched for a moment as Gideon's clothes, shoes, hats, cufflinks and more appeared in front of her. It was like a systematic dismantling of his life, bit by bit, piece by piece. She rubbed at her arms as if suddenly chilled, even though the hall was warm with afternoon sunlight and with the body heat of all the people in there.

Joel looked up at Mia from where he was crouching and a tiny line appeared between his brows. 'You're finding this hard, aren't you?'

She sighed. 'I am, but I need to do this. I knew it wouldn't be easy but I need to try to create a new life for myself now. However much I want him back, it's not going to happen and so I have to try to find my new direction alone.'

'It doesn't have to be alone, Mum,' he said as he stood up and touched her arm. 'You could still find someone else. I know you won't want to yet, not for some time, but one day you might fall in love again.'

Mia gave a wry laugh. 'Oh, I don't know, Joel. I'll be sixty in four years and I've already been married twice. Surely that's enough for one lifetime?'

'You're still very young, Mum, and have plenty of life in you yet.' He winked to show he was teasing her. 'Just see how things go and don't close yourself off to the idea, that's all I'm saying. Obviously you can't imagine being with another man at the moment, but one day, you might.'

She smiled sadly. 'Who knows, right?'

'Exactly.'

'And how about you?' She widened her eyes. 'When are you going to give love a chance?'

Joel laughed. 'Touché, right!'

'Well . . . you're a handsome young man and you have a lot to offer a woman.'

'Hi, there.' Joel's gaze had moved over Mia's shoulder and his cheeks turned slightly pink. Mia turned around to see who'd affected him like that.

'Hello.' Liz grinned at her.

'Hey, Liz.'

'I've just got here but there aren't many tables left.' Liz grimaced.

'We can make room for you here.' Joel demonstrated by shifting some of Gideon's clothes to one side.

'Are you sure?' Liz asked.

'Absolutely.' Joel's cheeks turned a shade darker and Mia watched him with interest. Did he have a soft spot for her friend? It was risky with Liz so fresh out of a relationship, but she also knew from what Liz had told her that things with Rhodri hadn't been right for a long time, if ever. Liz had been hurt but she was taking control of her life again, even giving serious consideration to living in Little Bramble, so she was clearly keen to move on with her life. If she and Joel did find each other attractive, then it wouldn't be the worst thing in the world, now, would it?

Zelda carried her box into the village hall and looked around. It was busy, busier than she'd expected. In her youth, people had been more inclined to mend and exchange things but then had come the days of more and cheaper goods, with easier ways to buy them and then a phase where, if something broke, people threw it away and bought another. However, more recently, society seemed to realise that this couldn't go on indefinitely and things were changing. The sight of the hall filled with people browsing tables of other people's things made her smile. It was an excellent way of giving new life to the things you didn't want. What was the saying? One man's trash is another man's treasure? She chuckled to herself.

'Zelda!' Across the hall, Liz was waving at her. She responded then weaved her way through the crowd to her friend's table.

'Gosh, what a lot of stuff you've brought,' Zelda said as she perused the table that seemed to be covered with men's and baby clothes. She knew Mia was bringing some of Gideon's things here today but wasn't sure where the baby clothes had come from.

As if reading her expression, Liz came close to her and whispered in her ear. 'I brought the baby things. I went through a phase of being unable to resist purchasing them for my . . . uh . . . future offspring.'

Zelda met Liz's gaze and her heart squeezed. 'Oh dear heart, I'm sorry.'

'It's OK.' Liz shrugged. 'It was just a dream. It didn't happen and there's no point holding on to them now.'

'But Liz, you're young and you'll fall in love again.' Zelda knew this wasn't necessarily true but it was one of those things people said to offer comfort. After all, hadn't someone said it to her once, a long time ago?

'Well, maybe . . . but if I do and if we are lucky enough to have children then we'll buy our baby clothes together. I bought these alone, kept them hidden from Rhodri and so I never saw his reaction to them. If I had, I might've understood sooner that it could never work between us and maybe that's why I hid them . . . Anyway, what have you brought?'

Zelda placed her box on the table where Joel had cleared a space for her. 'Eggs. A vase. Some scarves.'

'How lovely.' Liz smiled as she helped Zelda to arrange the scarves on the table. 'Are these silk?'

'Yes.'

'And you've certainly brought plenty of eggs.'

'The girls are happy and they're laying well.' Zelda would never eat all the eggs they laid and even though she'd given Mia plenty for baking, and Liz some for her sister's family, there were still lots left over.

'Excellent.' Liz sniffed the air. 'Ooh, I can smell coffee. Anyone fancy one?'

'That's an excellent idea,' Joel replied. 'I'll give you a hand.'

'Oh . . . OK.' Liz looked up at Joel from under her lashes and Zelda glanced at Mia but her friend was busy helping a man try on a waistcoat. Zelda was no relationship expert but watching the interaction between Joel and Liz, she thought she could see a definite spark.

Liz and Joel crossed the hall where just that morning Liz had been moving through the tai chi routine that was becoming familiar. She loved Kyle's classes and how energetic and relaxed she felt after them; also, through attending the classes she was getting to know some of the other villagers.

'Is your mum OK?' she asked Kyle as they stepped to one side to let a woman carrying a rug pass.

'I think so,' he said. 'It's not easy for her, but it's something she needs to do.'

'She's a wonderful person.'

'I think so.' He gestured at the space in the crowd so Liz went through it, conscious of him close behind her. 'She's an amazing mum.'

'You're very lucky.'

'I am. She's been so supportive of everything my brothers and I have done, even after losing my dad and then Gideon.'

They reached the hallway and found a queue for the kitchen area so they took their place in line. The aroma of coffee was stronger out here and Liz could also smell baking.

'What about you?' Joel asked.

'What about me, what?'

'Are you OK? With bringing the baby clothes here? I don't know your story but I'm guessing you bought them for a reason.'

'Oh, I didn't lose a baby. I . . .' She rubbed at her cheeks. 'It's a bit embarrassing, actually. I was engaged and now I'm not anymore. But during our time together I bought some baby things because it was the next stage in my plan.'

'Your plan?'

She nodded, torn between the urge to confess and wanting the ground to swallow her whole along with her embarrassment. But going forwards, she'd decided that it was best to be open and transparent about her feelings. She'd buried her true wants and desires for a long time and it hadn't worked out for her, so doing something different was worth a try.

Besides which, Joel was Mia's son and if he was anything like his mother then Liz knew he wouldn't be at all judgemental.

'You had a life plan?' His warm brown eyes were fixed on her face.

'Yes. I didn't have a great childhood and so I always wanted to create the kind of family I never had.'

'I'm sorry to hear that. I know I'm lucky.'

'With your mum, yes, but you lost your dad so you've suffered the pain of loss.'

'I was very young.'

She nodded. 'I lost my mum. She died when I was ten and my dad didn't cope very well, so he . . .' She exhaled slowly. It wasn't easy saying it out loud.

'He was absent?' Joel asked gently.

'Yes. Very much so. Nina did what she could to look after me and she was amazing but she was a child too. We weren't abused or anything as awful as that . . . Dad didn't hurt us and he wasn't cruel to us, but we were, I guess, neglected.'

'Neglect can have long-term repercussions on a person.'

'Tell me about it! It's probably why I jumped into a relationship with Rhodri even though I've finally admitted to myself that I suspected from the start that he was wrong for me.' Liz swallowed her surprise at how easy she'd just found it telling Joel about Rhodri.

'And why you wanted to create a stable family environment of your own. It's perfectly understandable. As human beings we crave stability and security, love and acceptance.'

Liz watched him as he spoke and couldn't help admiring his handsome face, thick dark hair and how he held himself with a quiet confidence. She could imagine that when he arrived in an ambulance, he'd be able to put patients at ease and soothe them with his calm manner and kind eyes. He had a lot of his mum about him, as well as qualities that were all his own. And best of all, he seemed to understand her. Rather than judge her for buying baby clothes and wanting a stable relationship and home, he got it.

Without realising, they'd reached the front of the queue. They ordered some coffees and, at Joel's suggestion, added some cakes and then returned to the main hall. Joel carried the tray of coffees and cakes and Liz led the way. He'd insisted on carrying the tray and she'd found it endearing. She liked the way he treated her. It wasn't some chauvinistic action, more one of thoughtfulness and generosity. Joel was, it seemed, a very nice man, and that thought made Liz smile.

The afternoon at the village hall passed in a blur and before Mia knew it, most of Gideon's things had gone. She had wondered if she'd find it strange seeing other men from the village wearing her husband's clothes, but the chances of her recognising them were, she realised, slim, because lots of men shopped at M&S, Primark and John Lewis and so it would be impossible to tell if the items had been Gideon's or not. Plus, some of the men who'd taken them were unfamiliar, so likely not from the village anyway. It seemed that the swap shop, arranged by the village committee, had attracted visitors from nearby towns and villages too.

Of course, the swap shop was meant to involve an exchange of some sort, and the men who'd taken Gideon's belongings had pointed at where their tables were so Mia could see if she wanted something in return. But simply seeing the table empty was quite cathartic and she realised that she didn't want to take anything home. Not today, anyway. Today was about making room in her home and taking another step in letting go. Things were just things and Gideon would always have a place in her heart.

She'd watched Joel and Liz interacting through the afternoon, seen the way that they looked at each other and her initial suspicion that there was a mutual attraction between them had grown like a plant in the sunshine. She did have concerns that it might be too soon for Liz to get involved with Joel, but then, she also knew that life was short and happiness had to be grabbed hold of when it came along. Perhaps nothing would come of this attraction anyway; perhaps Liz and Joel would – if Liz stayed in the village – become good friends and nothing more. Or perhaps they would fall madly in love and live happily ever after. As much as Mia would always be there for her sons, she was aware that they were all adults, capable of making their own decisions and that while she could offer advice or guidance, ultimately their life choices were theirs and theirs alone to make. Plus, she liked Liz. A lot. And she wanted to see her happy as well as Joel.

'What will be will be,' she whispered to herself.

'Your Joel seems quite taken with Liz,' Zelda said, gazing across the hall. Liz and Joel had gone to a table where a couple had some antique lamps. It seemed that Liz had swapped one for a baby outfit.

'Indeed it does.' She laughed softly. 'Some things are just meant to be, I guess.'

Zelda turned to her and smiled. 'That's true. Such as when lovely people appear at my doorstep with cake and friendship.'

'And don't judge a widow who occasionally pours tea onto her husbands' graves. And who offer their friend a cottage to rent.'

'Do you think she'll stay once she's got over what happened with Rhodri?' Zelda asked.

'I hope so. Perhaps Joel will be an added incentive for her to stay in the village.'

'That would be nice.'

'It would.' Mia nodded, her smile growing as Liz and Joel returned to them. Liz was holding a lamp with a glass shade and, as she got closer, Mia saw that it was covered with plants and dragonflies. 'What a beautiful lamp.'

'I know. I can't believe they were prepared to swap it for a few Babygros.'

'That would look lovely in the cottage,' Zelda said, casting a wink at Mia. 'Oh, and my solicitor has got the tenancy agreement ready to sign so let's do that on Monday and get on with whatever work needs to be done in the cottage as soon as possible.'

'Brilliant!' Liz grinned broadly at Mia and Zelda. 'So I guess I really am going to be sticking around for a while, then.'

'Hopefully permanently,' Mia and Zelda said together.

'Hopefully,' Joel said shyly.

'Excuse me?'

Liz turned around and, behind her, Mia saw Leopold and Jemima. He was pushing a twin buggy and Jemima had the third baby strapped to her chest in the sling.

'Yes?' Liz said.

'I was wondering if I could take a closer look at the baby clothes. With these three, we're getting through an alarming amount of outfits every day.'

'Of course.' Liz stepped aside. 'Help yourselves.'

Jemima and Leopold admired everything Liz had brought and said they had some things across the hall at their table if Liz would like to take a look. Mia had wanted to walk around the table and hug her when she'd seen how Liz had looked at the three tiny babies. It was the look of a woman accepting that she might never have the very things she'd thought she always wanted. And yet . . . there was something else there and Mia wondered if Liz actually was ready to surrender her dreams of motherhood just yet.

Before she got around the table, however, she saw that Joel had read the situation and was already offering support to Liz. As they walked over to Leopold and Jemima's table, Joel's hand rested gently in the small of Liz's back and Mia felt herself relax. Her son was a good man and he'd make sure Liz was all right, whatever direction their friendship took.

Chapter 23

The following Wednesday Liz entered the cottage alone for the first time. Zelda had spoken to some local tradespeople and all the necessary checks and work would be carried out the next week, followed by the council health and safety inspections. It turned out that Leopold Biggins had some contacts at the council and he'd been able to secure a favour so the cottage could be seen at the earliest date possible in order for Liz to move in sooner rather than later. Zelda had said that she'd accept Liz decorating the cottage in lieu of a deposit, which suited her just fine, but she suspected Zelda simply didn't care about an actual deposit. In fact, she seemed delighted that Liz wanted to rent the cottage.

Liz had also spoken to Rhodri about the furniture and furnishings at their house and he'd agreed to buy her out of most of it. They'd also received an asking price offer on the house from the interested buyer and were waiting for the survey to be carried out in order for the sale to proceed. Suddenly, things seemed to be happening at a fast pace, but Liz knew that was a good thing. Now that decisions had been made, there was no point in delaying. She'd also sent an email to her head teacher and the board of governors, stating that she had decided to resign from her teaching post. After another conversation with her GP, she'd decided to resign immediately so the school could advertise her position in time to get a replacement for the autumn term. She knew that they could have insisted that she return to work out her notice, but, surprisingly, Mr Brownlow had been very accommodating and told her they were happy to accept her resignation from the end of the Easter term, which meant that she was, as of now, unemployed. There were rules, of course, about when a teacher had to resign in order to avoid working another term, but different circumstances could allow for some flexibility, and because Liz didn't feel up to returning to her post, and possibly because Mr Brownlow realised that pushing her to return could be detrimental for her and the pupils, allowances had been made and Liz was free.

Free! At last!

She closed the cottage door behind her and stood in the silent, dusty hallway. There was a lot of work to do here but it would be physical, would get her heart beating and keep her busy and it had a purpose because this cottage was to be her home.

She went to the kitchen and placed the bag of cleaning products on the worktop along with the mop, bucket and rubber gloves. She tucked her AirPods into her ears, scrolled to her favourite playlist on her phone then rolled up her sleeves. It was time to get to work . . .

Zelda stood watching the chickens roaming around in her back garden. They were busy things, pecking at the grass and the earth, clucking as they bobbed their heads and occasionally flapped their wings. The cockerel stood proudly at the end of the grass watching his mates while simultaneously keeping an eye out for danger.

Liz had popped by to get the keys for the cottage first thing and Zelda was excited to know that she was making a start there. Yes, they had a few legal things to take care of but her family solicitor was excellent and Leopold had been brilliant at getting his contacts at the council to speed things up. Hopefully, within two weeks, Liz would be able to move into the cottage and get on with her fresh start.

Zelda winced and rubbed at her chest. Damned indigestion. She'd been feeling it a bit this week. Over the years, her body had changed in many ways and one of them had been her tolerance for certain foods. Of course, she had eaten more cake recently because of Mia's generosity, but surely it was all right to have some treats once in a while? As if in response, her heart fluttered wildly and she grabbed the door frame to steady herself. She'd been very lucky to get through her life without any health issues but at eighty-two, she knew she should be prepared to expect some decline in her fitness. Now that she thought about it, though, she had been feeling quite tired this past week, more tired than usual. She'd considered not attending tai chi on Saturday but then gone because didn't they say that exercise made you feel better because it energised you?

She checked her watch and saw that it was almost noon. She could make a cup of tea and have a little sit down, possibly a short nap. Then she'd head down to see how Liz was getting on. Yes, a short nap would be just the thing, she felt sure.

Liz raised her head and listened. She'd been scrubbing the bathroom while singing to Ed Sheeran, but through her AirPods she was sure she'd heard a knocking. She removed the AirPods and went to the top of the stairs.

There it was again! Someone was at the door.

She trotted down the stairs and opened the door.

'Hello!' Mia smiled at her.

'Hi, Mia.'

'I thought you might like some help,' Mia said. 'And some cake.' She held up a tin.

'I *was* fancying a tea break.' Liz laughed. 'Perfect timing.'

'I hope it's OK but I brought Joel as well. He has a day off so he said he'd be happy to come with me and help out.'

'Lovely,' Liz said as her stomach flipped. 'Where is he?' she asked, peering behind Mia while patting down her hair.

'Just getting some things from the car. We were clearing out the garage and found a load of paint that Gideon bought last year. Before . . . Well, anyway, we were going to redecorate and then – then we didn't, and I forgot it was there. The tins haven't even been opened. It's only white paint but I thought I'd bring it and see if you wanted it. If not, no problem at all.'

'That's amazing. Thanks so much. I had a look for some ideas for paint and furnishings with my niece recently but I kept coming back to neutral walls.'

'Hi,' Joel said as he appeared behind Mia.

'Hi,' Liz replied, feeling suddenly shy. She hadn't seen Joel since the swap shop when they'd talked a lot and she'd felt so very comfortable with him, and she'd tried to push away thoughts about him when they tried to creep in, but seeing him now made her realise how much she liked him. However, she gave herself an inward shake; she was a thirty-five-year-old woman and not a teenager. She was fresh out of a relationship and not in a good place to allow herself to feel attracted to someone else – however lovely he might be. 'Come in, please, both of you.'

She led the way through to the kitchen and Joel set the tins of paint on the table while Mia placed the cake tin and a bag on the worktop.

'Shall I make some tea?'

'That'll be lovely.' Mia smiled.

'Would you like me to put these tins anywhere?' Joel asked while the kettle boiled.

'To be honest, Joel, I need to finish cleaning first. There's so much dust everywhere,' Liz replied, touching a hand to her hair again. She'd piled it on top of her head in a messy bun, but now she was feeling self-conscious as she realised how sweaty and dusty she was. Joel must think she looked a terrible mess.

'Well, we can help you with that.' Joel removed his shirt, revealing a fitted grey T-shirt that showed off a very toned physique that made Liz's heart beat faster. 'I'm quite nifty with a mop.'

'Brilliant.' Liz turned away quickly and dropped teabags into mugs, hoping Joel hadn't seen her wandering eyes or the blush that had crept into her cheeks.

'So that's the bedrooms and I think that hatch there must lead up to the attic.' Liz pointed at the ceiling.

'I'd say so,' Joel said as he looked up at it. 'Want to take a look?'

Liz turned to Mia, who shrugged. 'Could do, Liz. See if there's storage space up there.'

'OK, then.' Liz nodded. 'I don't have a ladder, though.'

'I have one in the car,' Joel said. 'It's a small one but enough to get me to the hatch.'

Five minutes later, Joel was balanced on the top step of the ladder, arms above his head as he pushed open the hatch. He reached up and, in what Mia thought was a rather athletic manner, hoisted himself up into the attic.

'Be careful!' she said, her maternal instinct kicking in.

'Don't worry, Mum, I'm fine.' He grinned down at her. 'Can you pass the torch?'

'Here you go.' She handed him the torch he'd brought with him and the space above their heads glowed when he switched it on.

'What can you see?' Liz asked.

'Lots of cobwebs. What seems to be a water tank. Hold on . . .' Joel's voice got quieter as he made his way across the attic. Mia hoped he wouldn't put a foot through a board or bang his head on a low beam.

'Rather him than me,' Liz said to Mia with a grimace. 'I'm not a big spider fan.'

Mia chuckled. 'Not many people are.' She'd observed Liz and Joel as they'd walked around the house, seen how they looked at each other. At the swap shop, she'd been almost sure there was something brewing between them but today she was certain of it. Whether it would come to anything was yet to be seen, but Liz was such a lovely young woman and Joel was, well, he was Joel and in Mia's eyes he couldn't do much wrong.

'I've found something up here but I don't think I should open it. Shall I bring it down?' Joel said when he'd returned to the hatch.

'What is it?' Liz asked.

'A chest of some sort. Looks like it's been here for a long time, judging from the amount of dust on it. Also, there's a lock; the lid won't open and I'm not sure if it's rusty or locked.'

'Hand it down and let's take a look,' Liz said. 'It could belong to Zelda or to one of the people who stayed here over the years.'

Joel leant over and with both hands lowered a small chest down. Liz and Mia took one end each and carried it across the landing away from the ladder. Mia wiped her dusty hands on her jeans then went back to steady the ladder as Joel came down.

'Anything else up there?' she asked.

He shook his head. 'Enough space for storage but we probably should place some boards down if Liz wants to put anything heavy up there.'

The three of them went to the chest and gazed at it.

'You want to try the lock or take it up to Zelda?' Joel looked at Liz.

'We should probably take it to Zelda.' Liz chewed at her lip.

'I agree,' Mia said. 'It might be something private.'

'Shall we go now?' Liz asked. 'I know we haven't finished here but I don't think I can carry on with that sitting there like an unsolved mystery. It'll drive me mad.'

'Good plan,' Mia replied.

Joel crouched down and picked the chest up then carried it downstairs effortlessly while Mia and Liz followed him. When she'd come to the cottage today, Mia had thought she'd be helping clean and possibly paint but she hadn't expected to be involved in the discovery of what could be treasure. Or could, much more likely, she suspected, be something from Zelda's past that had sat there for years undisturbed.

They would, she reasoned, hopefully soon find out.

Chapter 24

Zelda opened the door and was surprised to find Liz, Mia and Joel there.

'Hi, Zelda,' Liz said.

'Hello, my dears. Is everything OK?' Still feeling a bit unsteady, Zelda had dozed off on the sofa for about an hour and not long woken up. She felt a bit better but not her normal self at all and the last thing she wanted to do was to worry her friends.

'We were tidying the cottage and Joel went up into the attic and found this,' Liz said as she pointed at the chest Joel was holding. 'We thought we should bring it over to you in case it's something you want.'

Zelda eyed the chest warily as her heart started to race. She pressed a hand to her throat, sucked in a shaky breath.

'Zelda? Are you OK?' Mia stepped forwards and peered at her. 'Do you need some water?'

Zelda waved a shaky hand and shook her head. 'I'm fine. Come in.'

She led the way through the hall and instead of going to the kitchen, she made for the drawing room to the left of the staircase. She pushed open the heavy door to the bright and airy room. It was a space she rarely occupied because it seemed ridiculously large for one small person and it could get cold in the winter months, but on a glorious spring day like this it was warm and golden with sunlight.

'Ooh! This is a lovely room,' Mia said, gazing around.

'I seldom use it. Seems a waste, really. But I feel a bit lost in here when it's just me.' Zelda gestured at the large sofas with a rectangular coffee table between them. 'Take a seat. Joel, you can place the chest on the table.'

'No problem,' Joel replied as he set the chest down.

'Would you like tea?' Zelda asked.

'I'm good, thanks.' Liz shook her head. 'Anyone else want one, though? I'll make it.'

No one did, so they all sat down and Zelda perched in the corner of one sofa, her hands resting lightly in her lap.

'It's been a very long time since I saw this chest and, to be honest, it's been tucked away in the cottage attic for so long that I'd almost forgotten it was there.'

'Would you like us to put it back?' Mia asked. 'If you don't want to see it, touch it or think about it? I know that sometimes it's easier to hide things away.'

'Literally and metaphorically,' Zelda said, giving a wry laugh.

'Yes indeed,' Mia said with a nod.

'I think now that the chest is here in front of me, I should face up to things.'

'What things, Zelda?' Liz asked. 'It's all very mysterious.'

'Things I have tried to put behind me for most of my life, dear,' Zelda replied. 'But as with everything, we often have to face our secrets at some point and this is as good a time as any. At least I have company.'

'We're here for you,' Mia said.

'Uhhh . . . Would you like me to go?' Joel asked. 'I don't want to be in the way. I feel like I'm here by mistake and—'

'It's fine, Joel. Unless you'd like to go?' Zelda smiled at the handsome young man. 'It's no big secret that I have to share. Just a story about a woman and something that happened in her youth.'

Joel glanced at Mia then at Liz and seemed to make up his mind. 'I'll stay then, if that's OK.'

Zelda nodded, then took a deep breath and began speaking.

'In the summer of 1962, our gardener retired and his nephew took over. He'd come to the village to stay with family and he started work here in the July. At first, I barely noticed him. I was used to there being a gardener around, and while always polite towards them, I hadn't been raised to interact with them for any significant amount of time. Christopher – that was his name – was different, though. One day, while I was reading in the garden, I looked up to find him smiling at me.' Zelda pressed a hand to her cheek at the memory. 'He was very handsome, with wavy dark hair, the brightest blue eyes I have ever seen and he was tall and broad-shouldered. He had this mischievous smile that was simply infectious . . .'

She looked at her audience, found them rapt, so carried on.

'I've never told anyone about this before and it's quite strange. But also quite pleasant. You see, I had a very sheltered upbringing. Mother was strict and had her set views about how a young lady should behave. Father was often away on business and so I spent a lot of time alone. I read a lot of books and daydreamed about a life away from the village – but I wasn't raised to be brave enough to leave on my own. Over the summer, I found myself searching for Christopher, bumping into him accidentally on purpose, wearing my prettiest dresses and practising what I would say to him. All of this was done when Mother was out or when I knew she was napping. She suffered from terrible migraines and often spent the afternoons in bed with the curtains drawn. It meant that Christopher and I had time to get to know each other. And during that time, my dears, I fell in love . . .'

Liz watched Zelda's face as she spoke. It was as though the elderly lady had left the room and entered a different dimension. Her eyes were alight and a smile played on her lips as she spoke about Christopher. Liz found herself leaning forwards to listen, eager to hear more.

'I knew it was wrong and that Mother and Father would disapprove, but I couldn't help myself. Christopher was unlike anyone I'd ever met before. Of course, I'd encountered young men from the village at church and village events, but never one like Christopher. He was kind and attentive, had stories that made me smile. He brought me things like flowers and chocolates, unusual stones he'd found while working and he told me about his childhood in Wales. His father had been a miner and his mother had died when he was born, so when his father had been injured in a mining accident, Christopher had cared for him. He hadn't gone down the mines as many young men from his village had because his father hadn't wanted that for him. He'd worked at the local shop while looking after his father but then, when his father passed away, his uncle and aunt had invited him to live with them. And so he came to Little Bramble. He was a working man, didn't have a penny to his name other than his wages, and so he felt he didn't have anything to offer me, a young lady from a wealthy family. And yet to me, the financial side of things didn't matter at all. Christopher said that he would work hard and save and, when he'd saved enough, he'd ask for my hand in marriage.' Zelda paused, sighed, and a frown wrinkled her brow.

Liz found herself blinking back tears. This was a love story, a tale of two young people who wanted to be together more than anything else.

'What happened?' Mia asked and Liz noticed her friend dabbing at her eyes with the back of her hand.

'We were young.' Zelda gave a small shrug. 'We were passionate and, as happens with those in love, we became . . . intimate. Soon we were snatching moments together, making love off in the woods, under the stars when I sneaked out at night . . . and at the cottage, which was vacant at that point.

It was a magical time and I'd never felt so alive. Christopher's kisses . . . his sweet caresses . . . I fell deeply in love with him.'

Liz blinked hard. Love had made Zelda feel alive. When Liz had been with Rhodri, she'd never felt that strength of emotion. Something had been missing.

'Autumn arrived and I was . . . late.'

'As in your period was late?' Mia asked, forthright as ever.

'Yes.' Zelda pressed her lips into a thin line. 'I told Christopher and he said we had to marry right away. He wouldn't desert me. He said he'd speak to my father and mother and we could get their blessing to marry. He promised . . .'

Zelda rubbed at her cheeks and Liz shuffled closer to her on the sofa, wanting to offer comfort to her friend, although she was worried she'd burst into tears soon.

Zelda leant forwards and touched a hand to the chest. 'This holds letters he wrote to me, my wedding dress and a shawl I crocheted for the baby.'

'Oh my goodness.' Mia had tears running down her cheeks. 'Things didn't work out, though?'

Zelda gave an almost imperceptible shake of her head.

'Mother saw us talking in the garden and it was obvious that we had feelings for each other. She was furious. She told me that I was to have nothing more to do with him. In fact, she banned me from seeing him. For the first time in my life, I disobeyed her. I went to him and told him and he said he'd take me away and marry me and we could start a new life together. But then . . . then, that weekend, he was walking home in the dark and a car ploughed into him. It wasn't someone from the village – no cars here were damaged and they would have been – so it must have been an out-of-towner and the driver d-didn't stop. Christopher was found in a ditch. He was . . . gone.' Zelda covered her mouth with both hands, her arthritic knuckles white, her eyes staring into space as if she was back there in 1962.

'Zelda, I'm so, so sorry.' Liz reached for Zelda's left hand and took it and Mia did the same with the other. They held on tight as she finished her story.

'I wasn't even able to attend the funeral. Mother wouldn't let me and I was too distraught to put up a fight.'

Silence fell in the room as the enormity of Zelda's loss washed over them all.

'Where's he buried?' Mia asked eventually.

'In the village churchyard, at the rear of the church. I visit him when I can bear it. Which isn't often.'

'And the baby?' Liz asked, swallowing hard.

'I lost the baby too. It could have been the shock or that it just wasn't meant to be. I never told anyone about the pregnancy other than Christopher. I kept it secret. It was very early days, over almost as soon as it had begun.'

'Zelda, this is terribly sad.' Liz squeezed Zelda's hand. 'You've been through so much.'

Zelda raised shining eyes to meet Liz's gaze. 'The same as some, less than others. Being human comes with pain and suffering. It also, however, comes with love. I lost Christopher and our child within days of each other. Over the years I have wondered if I had the power to go back and change things, to not fall in love with him, if I would.'

They sat silently, not wanting to pressure Zelda for her response to this hypothetical. Finally, she said, 'And I wouldn't. I wouldn't change a single thing because I loved Christopher and he loved me. I was twenty-one but I knew what I felt and I still have no doubt in my mind that he was the one for me. The only one. And so, I'll say this to you now – the three of you – if you have a chance, then take it. You won't regret the chances you take.'

Liz gasped. 'That's something I've been wondering about recently. I've taken some chances in my life but not others and I often think about what might have happened if I had.' Her eyes strayed to Joel and she found him gazing at her in a way that made her heart squeeze. He had tears in his eyes too and again it made her think about what a sensitive and compassionate man he must be.

'Christopher and I didn't have much time together but I've often imagined what it would have been like if he'd lived. It comforts me to think that in another life, on another plane, we're now grandparents and have lived a full and happy life together.'

Liz felt her lip wobble and then the tears started to flow. She leant forwards and hugged Zelda and Mia joined in, three women who'd been through their own pain, losses and struggles but who were still standing, still present, strong and resilient.

'Thank you, my darlings,' Zelda said after a while, accepting a box of tissues from Joel that she then handed to Liz and Mia.

'What for?' Liz and Mia asked in tandem.

'For being here. For allowing me to tell my story. The story that's been all bottled up for over sixty years – and while it was hard to say the words, I feel light, that a weight has lifted from my shoulders. At times, I've wondered if it actually happened, if Christopher was real, if the baby inhabited my womb at all. But it did; and somehow, saying it out loud is incredibly cathartic. Painful, yes. But cathartic.'

'You're very strong, Zelda,' Mia said. 'You've kept going all this time with that grief in your heart.'

'Grief, yes, but also so much love. I have held Christopher close, our baby close, and they have kept me going. And now I am lucky enough to have two wonderful women as friends. I am grateful that you came into my life. More grateful than I can ever convey.'

They hugged again and Liz felt simultaneously heartbroken and uplifted. Human beings could experience tragedy and loss that could almost destroy them and yet they could keep on going. Friends might not be able to take pain away but they could make the burden of it a little bit lighter just by being there.

Mia walked down to her car with Joel and Liz. The three of them had been silenced as if by a spell. And in a way they had;

Zelda's story had cast a spell upon them all. She hadn't actually opened the chest, saying that seeing the dress and shawl again might be a step too far, but it was something she said she'd do if and when she felt ready for it.

Zelda had lived with her loss for over sixty years. Before they left, she had reassured them that she had enjoyed her life and made the most of it in many ways but it was clear that she'd missed out on what could have been a wonderful life had things worked out with Christopher. Of course, that might not have been the case because there were no guarantees, but her love for Christopher was evident when she spoke about him.

'I feel bereft,' Liz said when they stopped at Mia's car. 'Not for me but for Zelda. What a tragic story.'

'It is,' Joel said, leaning his back against Mia's car. 'But it's also one of hope. Zelda clearly loved Christopher and I'd say she still does. She said she never felt the need to find another man and that no one would ever compare to him so I guess she meant that what she had with Christopher was enough for one lifetime.'

Liz nodded sadly. 'But she could have found someone else if she'd opened herself up to it.'

'She could,' Joel agreed.

'There's a message there for us all, I think,' Mia said, smiling at them. 'Tragedy touches us all in some way or another but life goes on. Zelda has been happy over the years and she seems brighter now than when I first went to her house. I think that telling her story also helped her. Imagine keeping that a secret for so long? It could break a person holding all that in.'

'She's an incredible person.' Liz pulled a tissue from her sleeve and dabbed at her eyes.

'What do you want to do now, Liz?' Mia asked. 'We can come and help you finish cleaning if you'd like.'

'I reckon we could even make a start on painting,' Joel said, rubbing at the back of his neck. It was a gesture that Mia recognised; he was feeling shy about asking but hopeful.

'That would be amazing, thank you.' Liz twirled a lock of her lovely hair and, as she looked up at Joel, Mia noticed the faint blush rising into her cheeks.

'No time like the present, then.' Joel grinned. 'Let's go!'

They headed down to the cottage and Mia couldn't help wondering if her son and Liz were about to begin a story of their own.

Chapter 25

It had been a busy week for Mia and Liz. The work on the cottage had been carried out and the council inspector had been and approved it. They'd made progress with the painting and, with Joel's decorator friend's help, along with assistance from Nina and Demi, the cottage was all ready for Liz to move in. Preparing it had become a family affair and Mia had thoroughly enjoyed getting stuck in. That was something worth celebrating, Mia thought, so she was planning on baking a celebratory cake. Joel had said he'd pick up some champagne for Monday when Liz officially moved in and Nina had said she'd be there with her family too.

'Hello there, Mia. How are you?' Mia turned to find Marcellus David next to her in the baking section of the village shop.

'I'm good, thank you. Are you?'

'Very well indeed, thanks.' He pushed back his cap and scratched his head. 'Are you making a birthday cake for the lovely Zelda by any chance?'

'For Zelda?'

'Yes. It's her birthday tomorrow. Didn't you know?' He shook his head when she said no. 'Typical Zelda, wouldn't want any fuss.'

'Well then, I must make her a cake.' Mia added another bag of flour to her basket. 'Marcellus, how do you know it's her birthday?'

'I deliver her post, of course. She has a couple of birthday cards arrive at the same time every year from childhood friends who left the village many years ago, and I've been delivering her post for a very long time.'

'Of course. Right, well she's going to be eighty-three so I think we should do something special.'

'What's this?' It was Kyle. 'Something special for whom?' He waggled his eyebrows.

'Marcellus just told me that tomorrow is Zelda's birthday so I thought we could do something nice for her. Show her how special she is.'

'What a fabulous idea!' Kyle clapped his hands. 'We have tai chi in the morning so we could surprise her with a cake there.'

'We could.' Mia tapped her mouth. 'Or we could get her to tai chi and while she's distracted, we could set something up at the allotments.'

'I love a good party and that's a brilliant plan! But she'll expect you and Mia to be at the village hall with her. And me, of course, seeing as I'm the teacher.' He laughed. 'However,

I can speak to my business partner Hazel as well as Mum and Sam and I'm sure they'll be happy to help.'

'Kyle, you are a star!' Kyle's mum and her husband, Sam Wilson, the local vet, were lovely people and Hazel Campbell was Kyle's partner in Country Charm Weddings, so she'd certainly know how to plan a party.

'I try.' Kyle patted his hair. 'I have your number so I'll be in touch once I've spoken to everyone.'

'Brilliant.'

Mia threw a few more bags of flour into her basket along with some icing sugar and some sugar paste flowers. It looked as if she had a busy day of baking ahead of her.

Liz parked outside the cottage and got out of the car. She'd driven up because she was bringing some of her belongings from Nina's. Nina, Demi and Cora were with her so they all trooped into the cottage.

'Wow! It looks amazing in here.' Nina looked around. 'We did a good job.'

Liz smiled. 'We did. Thank you so much for helping.'

'I didn't help,' Cora said, pouting.

'But you did,' Liz said, resting a hand on her niece's shoulder. 'You helped your daddy make us dinner while we were all here painting.'

'That's true.' Cora shrugged. 'Daddy said we had to keep the workforce fed.'

'Daddy was right.' Nina winked at Liz. 'OK, where are you going to put things?'

They spent some time deciding where to put the dragon-fly lamp Liz had got at the swap shop and arranging throws and rugs around the lounge then putting cutlery and crockery that she'd ordered online into kitchen drawers and cupboards. Upstairs, they made the bed in the master bedroom, hung curtains and put towels in the bathroom. Soon, the cottage felt like a home and Liz found that she was looking forward to moving in.

She stood at the bedroom window overlooking the garden and savoured the view. Spring was in full swing now and the garden was a riot of colour with flowers in the borders and blossom on the trees. Joel had even insisted on tidying the garden while he was there and Mia had arrived with some pots containing hostas, hebes and heucheras. The garden looked beautiful now, so Liz could imagine how wonderful it would be in summer once the honeysuckle on the trellis attached to the wall bloomed.

A lot had happened in the eight weeks since she'd arrived, broken and grieving. In that time she had healed her relationship with her sister, made new friends and found a new home. She had been able to start to let go of her former life and, while she wasn't fully there yet, being in Little Bramble had helped enormously with moving on. Perhaps it was being in a different location, perhaps it was keeping busy, perhaps it was knowing that Rhodri had never really been the one – but mostly, perhaps it was being surrounded by family and friends. By friends who she felt were becoming an extended family. Here, she was surrounded by people who liked her, who had time for her and who wanted to spend time with her. That was hugely different to her life in Maidstone, where she'd spent so much time treading on eggshells, trying to build a life that, now she could look at it from a different perspective, was in reality very empty.

'What are you thinking?' Nina wrapped an arm around her shoulders, rested her head against Liz's and gazed out of the window with her.

'Oh, you know . . . How glad I am that I came to stay.'

'You have no idea how happy I am and the girls are that you're here. And Kane, of course, because he's always known how much I miss you.'

They stood there for a while, closer than they'd ever been, while downstairs the girls giggled as they got up to mischief and Liz's heart swelled with joy.

Mia knocked on the cottage door then stepped back to admire the new curtains at the windows as well as how clean the glass was and how much better the frames looked since they'd been painted. The front garden was clear of debris and Liz had set a pot either side of the front door containing bay trees and solar lights.

The door opened and Cora grinned at her. 'Hello.'

'Hello, sweetheart. Is your aunty here?'

'Yes. Please come in.'

In the hallway Cora went to the bottom of the stairs. 'Aunty Liz! Mia's here to see you. And I think she brought cakes.' Cora's eyes locked on the tin in Mia's hands.

'I did. Would you like to take this to the kitchen?'

'Can I open it?' Cora asked.

'Cora! Don't be so cheeky.' Demi was in the lounge doorway, shaking her head.

'But I can smell them already and I'm soooo hungry!' Cora poked out her tongue at Demi then ran to the kitchen with the tin with Demi chasing after her.

'Hi, Mia.' Liz descended the stairs followed by Nina. 'You OK?'

'Great, thanks. I brought some cakes and some news.'

'Oh?'

'Apparently it's Zelda's birthday tomorrow.'

'Oh, she didn't let on.'

'I know. Marcellus told me. Anyway, I saw Kyle in the village and he said he'll help us to plan a surprise party at the allotment.'

'That's a brilliant idea.'

'We'll take Zelda to tai chi as normal and Kyle, Hazel and some others will get everything ready at the allotment.'

'How exciting!' Liz's face lit up. 'What do you need me to do?'

'Well, I've already started baking but I thought we could get some bunting and make some sandwiches and drinks and so on. Kyle did say he'd enlist some help but I don't want to leave it all to them.'

'Is Joel going to come?' Liz asked, lowering her gaze to her hands, where she worried at a cuticle.

'I'm sure he will.' Mia couldn't help smiling.

'Great!' Liz said. 'The more the merrier. Shall we have a cuppa and get planning?'

'Sounds perfect.'

Mia followed Liz to the kitchen, excitement fluttering in her belly at the thought of how surprised Zelda would be.

Chapter 26

'I really enjoyed that,' Zelda said as she left the village hall and stepped out into the spring sunshine. It was a beautiful April morning with a blue sky and not a cloud in sight. Colourful flowers bloomed in pots and window boxes and in the borders around the village green.

Tai chi, along with sharing her story with her friends, had made her feel lighter. After a lifetime of keeping everything to herself, talking about Christopher and their child had been a release and she was glad that Liz and Joel had found the chest in the attic, glad it had been them and not someone else. She still hadn't opened it, didn't feel the need to, because she knew what was inside and was content to place the chest at the foot of her bed. When her time came, she had decided, she'd wear the dress and have the shawl buried with her. It seemed a fitting way to end the story.

But for now she was feeling good. She'd had a few wobbles over the past few weeks with some breathlessness and chest pain but she'd given herself a shake and made an effort to get on with things. After all, she had goats and chickens relying on her so she had to keep going. However, though she wouldn't admit to it out loud, she was glad that Liz was moving into the cottage on Monday. Knowing that her friend was nearby was comforting. Not that Zelda intended on being a nuisance, but if anything happened to her then Liz would be able to see to the goats and chickens until alternative provision was made for them.

'It's so invigorating, isn't it?' Liz said as she stretched, tall as a tree.

'I feel fabulous.' Mia smiled.

'Breakfast on me?' Zelda asked, keen to follow their usual routine.

Mia and Liz shared a glance that unsettled Zelda slightly. Was she taking their time and company for granted? The last thing she wanted to do was to get on their nerves.

'Sure, why not?' Liz checked her smart watch. 'Plenty of time yet.'

'Time before what?' Zelda asked.

Liz went red. 'Oh . . . uh . . .'

'Before lunch,' Mia jumped in. 'We were thinking that we could go out for lunch today too.'

'Oh, that would be nice.' Zelda patted her belly, thinking it was a wonderful coincidence that they'd be going out on her birthday. She'd stopped celebrating birthdays a long time ago but it would be nice to do something to mark the occasion, even if she didn't tell her friends about the significance of the date. 'It's a good job I've done some exercise this morning, then. You two will make me fat.'

The three of them laughed as they made their way over to the café, arms linked, sunshine on their faces.

Mia's phone buzzed on the table so she turned it over and checked the screen. A message from Joel with a thumbs up. She met Liz's eyes across the table and Liz gave a brief nod. It was all systems go up at the allotment.

'Well, I'm full. Either of you want anything else?' she asked.

'I'm good.' Liz shook her head.

'Me too. Better not eat more if we're going out for lunch later,' Zelda said. 'Where were you thinking of going? Just so I know what to wear.'

'Ooh . . .' Mia frowned. 'We could just drive and find a nice pub somewhere.'

'Sounds wonderful.' Zelda nodded. 'And it can be my treat.'

'You've already treated us to breakfast so it'll be our treat.' Mia winked at Liz and when she looked back at Zelda, the older woman was frowning as if she wondered what was going on.

During the drive from the village to the allotment, Mia and Liz chatted about people they'd seen that morning, the weather, what Mia was aiming to grow on Gideon's (and now her) allotment and the cottage. They seemed more energetic than usual, almost frenetic, as if they were anticipating something exciting. Zelda might have kept to herself over recent years, but she was quite intuitive about people and she suspected that something was going on. However, she hadn't told them it was her birthday and they had no way of finding out so it must be something else.

But what?

Mia parked the car outside Zelda's gate and they got out. Zelda stretched her legs, keen to keep her limbs warmed up after the morning's exercise. She had a bit of a headache but suspected that if she drank some more water she'd be fine.

'Right, Zelda . . .' Mia smiled at her. 'We have a surprise for you. I would suggest blindfolding you but I'd worry about you tripping on something or falling and perhaps it's better if you see things as we approach anyway.'

'What on earth are you talking about, Mia?' Zelda chuckled.

'Turn around.' Mia pointed behind Zelda.

She turned slowly, her heart fluttering as she tried to prepare herself for whatever was happening. It wouldn't be anything bad, though, she felt sure of it, but she had no idea at all what . . .

'Oh!' she gasped. 'A party?'

'Yes.' Liz came and took her arm. 'For you.'

Mia came to her other side.

'For me?'

'Yes,' Mia and Liz said in unison.

'But why?' Zelda looked from Mia to Liz and back again.

'Because it's your birthday.' Mia gave Zelda's arm a squeeze. 'Come on, let's get over there.'

As they walked towards the allotments, Zelda tried to understand what was happening. It seemed that there was a party being held there. She could see people she knew from the village, including Marcellus, Joel, Kyle, Clare, Sam, Hazel, Jemima and Leopold to name a few. There were others too, although she couldn't recall all of their names at once. She knew most of the people who lived in the village but not well, although over recent weeks she had got to know some of them better when she attended tai chi or visited the village shop and the café. Being friends with Mia and Liz had brought her back into the community, integrated her in the village she'd lived in for eighty-two – no, eighty-three – years.

Bunting fluttered in the breeze, balloons bobbed against the blue of the sky like buoys on the sea and music and voices filled the air. Aromas of hot dogs, burgers and onions drifted towards her, making her mouth water even though she'd not long had breakfast. A large banner was tied between two trees and on it was written: HAPPY BIRTHDAY, ZELDA!!!

'This is really for me?' she asked when they reached the allotments and Kyle stepped forward and handed her a glass of champagne.

'Yes!' Kyle flashed her a winning smile. 'Happy birthday, darling!'

He leant forwards and kissed her cheeks in turn.

'Goodness!' She laughed. 'Thank you, Kyle.'

'Come and see everyone,' Kyle said, 'They've been waiting for you.' He led the way towards the plots.

'I've never had a party,' Zelda said softly.

'What, never?' Liz asked.

'Mother and Father weren't big believers in celebrating birthdays and since Mother passed away, I've spent my birthdays alone.'

'Oh, Zelda.' Mia shook her head. 'I'm so sorry. I should have made the effort to get to know you sooner.'

'No, dear. You had a family and a busy life. Don't you dare blame yourself for that. I've been absolutely fine. In all honesty, I didn't want to celebrate each passing year anyway because it took me further from my Christopher. I was ageing but he never would. However, dear Mia, I think we came into each other's lives at the right time. I was at my lowest point and feeling like there was no point to anything anymore. But you . . .'

'Zelda . . .' Mia wiped at her eyes. 'I can't bear to think of you feeling that way. And I was . . . I was so low too.'

'Me too.' Liz sniffed.

The three of them looked at each other, then burst into laughter while tears ran down their faces; then they hugged, three women who'd been through pain and loss, who'd been scarred by life and grief. Three women who were still standing, resilient and now hopeful once more.

'Come on, let's go and dance,' Liz said eventually, handing them tissues. 'We don't want to waste the afternoon crying, do we?'

'No, we don't,' Zelda said.

Zelda followed her friends over to the gathering, pausing to look back at the big house, and for a brief moment she thought she could see a handsome young man with dark hair and broad shoulders standing in the garden waving at her with one hand, his other arm cradling a baby. He was gone as quickly as he'd appeared, so she didn't know if it was real or a figment of her imagination, but it didn't matter because she knew she'd always hold Christopher and their child safe in her heart.

'I need a drink!' Liz laughed as Joel tried to twirl her round again. He was a bundle of energy and had been dancing with her for ages. Unlike some men, he was happy to dance, sing on the karaoke (Hazel had arranged for a portable karaoke machine to be brought to the allotments) and to make a fool of himself. He was warm and funny, kind and generous. When the supply of beer had run low, he'd walked back down to the village with Connor Jones – who'd come with his partner, Emma, and her dad, Greg – and they'd returned with beers, cider and more champagne. Maybe it was the sunshine and fresh air, the dancing and karaoke, maybe it was the champagne she'd drunk or the punch that Marcellus had brought, but Liz was feeling a bit giddy. In a good way, though, because her heart was full of love and laughter.

'I'll get you one. Another champagne?' Joel asked.

'Water would be fine, thanks. I'm thirsty now,' she said, knowing that rehydrating would be a good plan.

'Coming right up,' Joel said and he went over to the trestle table that had been set up for drinks.

'Hello, little sister!' Nina grabbed her and kissed her cheek. 'How's it going?'

'Nina – are you tipsy?'

Nina squinted at her. 'I might be a little bit!' She giggled. 'It's not every day that I have drinks at the allotment. This is brilliant. We should do this regularly.'

Liz looked around. People were standing and chatting, sitting on deckchairs, dancing and singing. Children chased one another around, trailing balloons behind them and dogs barked in excitement. The sky was a beautiful shade of pink now, laced with peachy hues and the air smelt of barbecued food, cut grass and spring flowers.

'I think so. Now that I'm a resident of Little Bramble, we could arrange something once a month or something similar. It's such a wonderful location and the community is simply fabulous.'

'But even in a village like this, people can get left at the periphery,' Nina said, looking across at Zelda. 'I can't believe I didn't think to check on her before now.'

'You have a young family, Nina, and you didn't know her that well. Besides which, some people like their own space. You can't force yourself onto people just because they live alone. It's something that depends entirely upon the individual.'

'People need people, honey, whatever they say.'

'Perhaps.' Liz nodded. 'I certainly do. And I'm glad Zelda has company now. She said earlier that she thought she was done with the world and then Mia and I came into her life. It's amazing the difference that people can make to others.'

'It's true, Liz.'

'And it's the same for me. I feel that I've been . . . renewed. That might sound dramatic but I feel like a different person.'

'It's not dramatic. I know what you mean. Something was missing from my life too. It was you.' Nina hugged Liz and nearly knocked her over. Liz staggered under her sister's weight, then they both started to giggle.

'Careful, Nina!'

'Is my wife being too demonstrative?' Kane had appeared at Liz's side and he reached out and took Nina's arm. She flung it around his shoulders and planted a kiss on his lips.

'Love ya, hubster.'

Kane laughed. 'Hubster?'

'Yeah. You're a wonderful hubster.'

'Thanks.'

Nina wrapped her arms around him and nestled her head in his neck and he winked at Liz over Nina's head and mouthed *She's had a few too many*. Liz nodded in response.

'Come and dance with me, Kane, my hot hubster.'

'I think perhaps we need to head home, wifey.'

'Just one dance? Pleeeeeease.'

'OK. Just one.' Kane allowed himself to be dragged over to where people were dancing and soon he was slow dancing with Nina to Marcellus' rendition of 'I Can't Help Falling in Love With You'.

'Here you go.' Joel was back with her water. Liz accepted it gratefully and took a long drink.

'Thanks. I needed that.'

'Nina's having fun.' Joel bobbed his head at Nina and Kane, who'd been joined by Demi and Cora now and the four of them danced together holding hands.

'They all are.'

'You have a lovely family,' he said.

'I'm very lucky. I can't believe I've missed so much time with them.'

'I don't think there's any point regretting things,' he said. 'I'm more of an everything happens for a reason kind of guy.'

'Is that right?' She looked up into his eyes and her breath caught. There was something about him that made her want to gaze at him all day.

'Liz?'

She turned to find Mia approaching them. 'Yes?'

'I think it might be time for the cake.'

'Of course. I'll go and get it.' They'd had the cake that Mia had made brought up to the cottage while they were at tai chi so they could keep it fresh until they were ready.

'I'll come with you,' Joel said. 'You know . . . in case you need help.'

'Thanks.' Liz blinked, willing the heat that was rising in her cheeks to subside. At this rate Mia would wonder what was going on with Liz and her son and the last thing Liz wanted was to worry Mia.

They strolled over to the cottage and once inside, Liz said, 'I'm just going to pop to the bathroom.'

'Sure. I'll go and get the candles and the matches ready.'

While he went to the kitchen, Liz padded up the stairs and into the bathroom. She ran the cold tap and splashed some water onto her face then looked at herself in the mirror above the sink. Her eyes were lit up as if something inside her was burning brightly. For so long her eyes had been dull and empty and no amount of mascara or eyeshadow had been able to bring them alive. But now, changes were happening to her and it was evident in her eyes, her smile, her energy. It wasn't just Joel – he was like the icing on the amazing birthday cake Mia had made, a delicious extra. She really liked him but she knew she needed to tread carefully because the last thing she wanted was to hurt anyone or to rush into something. She was simply enjoying the feelings she had when he was around and surely that was OK as long as she didn't act on them.

When she felt fresher, she went downstairs. The kitchen was bathed in the rosy hue of the sky outside and Joel was standing there, waiting for her.

He stepped forwards and gently cupped her cheeks. His eyes were like dark pools and she felt herself sinking into them.

'Joel . . . th-this probably isn't a good idea.'

He leant forwards and touched his lips to hers. It was a soft, sweet kiss and when he raised his head again, Liz was breathless.

Her heart and body shouted at her to grab hold of him and kiss him again but her mind stopped her and so, instead, she pressed her fingers to her mouth as if to hold the kiss there.

'I know what you've been through. I know you have things to work out. I know it's too soon for you, that you needed to settle into your new home and your new life here. But I wanted to do that . . . just so you know.'

'So I know what?' she asked as she lowered her hand. Her heart was racing faster than she'd ever felt before and her whole body trembled with desire and something else, something much deeper that promised a connection with this incredible man.

'So you know that I'm here. If you only ever want me as a friend, that's OK. But if, when you feel ready, you'd like to find out if there could be something more between us . . . then I'm here.'

'Oh.' It was all she could think of to say because her mind had gone completely blank.

'Oh?' He raised his dark brows and a smile played on his lips. 'Did I read this wrongly?'

'No! Not at all. I'm just . . . a bit overwhelmed.'

'Which is why it's too early. But maybe in six months or a year or even longer, it won't be too soon. So I wanted you to know that I'm here and that I like you.'

She reached out and took his hand. 'I like you too.'

'That's good enough for me. Shall we get this cake out to the birthday girl, then?'

'We better had,' she replied, thinking that if they stayed in her kitchen much longer she'd be unable to hold back and she might end up throwing caution to the wind.

She picked up the cake, noticing that Joel had already put the candles on it, and Joel grabbed the matches then they left the cottage and walked back to the party. When they reached the periphery of the allotments, Joel signalled to Hazel for the music to be turned off then he lit the candles and they started to sing.

'Happy Birthday to you! Happy birthday to you! Happy birthday, dear Zelda, happy birthday to you!'

Zelda gazed in awe at Liz as she carried a large rectangular cake towards her. The party had been wonderful and she'd had a fabulous afternoon, sipping bubbly and catching up with villagers she hadn't spoken to in ages. Liz and Mia had fluttered around, checking that her glass was filled, that she was comfortable on the deckchair, warm enough, hydrated enough and more. She had never felt so cared about, except for when Christopher had showered her with affection and love. She had no idea how she could ever repay her friends for their kindness but she would try to think of a way.

Liz set the cake down on a table and Kyle helped Zelda to her feet and she leant over and looked at the cake. It was beautiful, with white icing, tiny sugar flowers in pink and lilac, *Happy Birthday Zelda* in pink swirly letters and two candles shaped as numbers 8 and 3.

'It's wonderful, Mia,' she said. 'Thank you.'

'Blow out the candles and make a wish!' Mia said with a broad smile.

'OK, then.' Zelda took a deep breath and blew.

After Mia had seen Zelda safely to her house, she walked home with Joel. It had been a wonderful day and she was tired but happy. The air was balmy and fragrant with the scents of flowers and the sky had turned from pink to indigo, the stars appearing like tiny pinpricks of silver.

'That went well,' Joel said as they walked.

'It did and I think Zelda had a good time.'

'I'd say so. I don't think she drank much champagne but she had a smile on her face all afternoon and evening.'

'She's a special lady.'

'Just like you.' He nudged her as they walked.

'So, you and Liz seem to be getting on well.'

'She's another special lady.'

'She is. But, Joel . . .' Mia pressed her tongue to the roof of her mouth. She didn't want to interfere, Joel was a grown man and perfectly capable of taking care of himself, but she couldn't help worrying. 'You will take care, won't you?'

Joel stopped walking so Mia did too. They'd reached the edge of the village green and they gazed at the pots filled with tulips and daffodils, at the hanging baskets of primroses, anemones and crocuses.

'You don't need to worry, Mum.' He shook his head. 'I know what I'm doing.'

'I'm sure you do, Joel. It's just that Liz is . . . vulnerable. She's had a rough time and I don't think her fiancé treated her very well—'

'Ex.'

'Sorry?'

'Her *ex*-fiancé. They're not engaged anymore.'

'No. That's what I meant. But I can see that there's a spark between you two and there could be more. Just . . . don't rush anything. That's all I wanted to say. I love you so much and would hate to see you hurt.'

'Mum, I get it. I've already spoken to Liz about this.'

'You have?' Pride swelled in Mia's chest. Her son was so caring and sensitive. He didn't shy away from difficult conversations and he was also very wise.

'I have. We do like each other.' He smiled then nibbled at his bottom lip. 'But we know that Liz needs time to work out what she wants and to get over Rhodri. We're going to be friends and just see what happens.'

'Oh, my darling boy, I'm so happy to hear that. I think the world of Liz and of you and if . . . eventually . . . something happened between you, then that would be wonderful. She just needs some time to heal and to find herself again. I think she got lost in a life she thought she wanted. Perhaps, in some ways, it *was* the life she wanted but with the wrong man.'

'Will you stop worrying now?' Joel slowly raised his eyebrows and Mia squeezed his shoulder.

'I will, I promise. Actually, no, that's a fib. I'll always worry about you because I'm your mum and it comes with the territory. But I promise to trust you on this one with Liz.'

'And I promise to take my time.'

'You're an amazing man, Joel.'

'I have a good mother who raised me well.'

Mia blinked as her vision blurred. 'I hope I did a good job.'

'You did the best job. Now come on, let's get you home.'

'Are you coming in for a cuppa?'

'Try and stop me!'

He wrapped an arm around her shoulders and they walked back to Mia's together, smiling under a beautiful Little Bramble night sky.

Chapter 21

The day had arrived and Liz felt like a child on Christmas morning. She was moving into the cottage today and felt that her fresh start had arrived. She'd already taken most of her things to the cottage so it was a matter of grabbing her toiletries and heading up there.

She'd already walked Demi to the bus stop and Cora to school then strolled back with Nina. They'd had a late breakfast, just the two of them, and Liz was surprised to find that Nina had become quite emotional.

'You will be OK up there alone, won't you?' Nina asked once she'd made them another mug of tea.

'Of course I will. It's hardly miles away and I'm a big girl.'

'I know you're capable of looking after yourself but it's been so nice having you stay. I'm going to miss you.' Nina's eyes shone as she looked at Liz across the kitchen table.

'I'll miss you too but we can still see each other every day. You can come to the cottage and I can come here and we can meet in the village. It's not like I'm going back to Maidstone.'

'I'm so glad you're not. I think I coped before because I was used to not seeing you very often. We'd drifted apart, something that I'm mad at myself about, but I was also able to tell myself that you were fine, that you were living your best life. Only now that we've got to know each other again, it's different. I feel so close to you.'

'And I to you. I would miss you desperately if I went far away now, so don't worry. Everything's going to be all right.'

Nina nodded and took a shaky breath. 'I know.'

Once they'd drunk their tea, Liz took the mugs to the dishwasher and put them inside then climbed the stairs to the guest room that had been her home for the past eight weeks. She looked around to check she'd packed everything, picked up her washbag and closed the door behind her. So much had changed in her since she'd arrived in Little Bramble and she felt like a different person. She'd arrived broken and grieving – now she felt whole and hopeful.

'OK, then. If I've forgotten anything, I'll come pick it up later,' she said as Nina walked her to the door.

'I can pop it up to you.'

Liz laughed. 'I guess I'll see you later for afternoon tea, then?'

'Try and keep me away.' Nina smiled then pulled Liz into a tight hug. 'Love you, sis.'

'Love you too.'

Liz headed to her car then got in and started the engine, a smile firmly fixed on her lips, a wonderful sense of joy in her heart.

'Oooh!' Zelda rubbed at her chest as she trudged across the goats' field. She wasn't feeling good at all today. Perhaps she hadn't drunk enough. She'd make sure to have big glass of water when she got home. 'See you ladies later.' She shut the gate then turned to double-check it. All secure.

She took her time walking back to the house, looked across at the allotments. The party on Saturday had been fantastic and such an amazing surprise. She'd had so much fun and felt so special. Apart from Christopher, no one had ever made her feel like that and she was indebted to Mia and Liz for arranging it all, as well as to everyone who'd helped out and everyone who'd come. There had been dancing, karaoke, food and drink and it had made her feel proud to be a part of such a warm community. She had wondered what her parents would have thought about it, knowing how they'd been about socialising – her mother had hated it although her father had enjoyed the company of others – and she'd realised that she didn't care. For so long she'd lived in their shadows, still tied to their ways, especially Mother's, but it no longer mattered. They were gone and she was here. She had, however, felt that Christopher was close, that he'd have enjoyed the evening and joined in with everything.

What would he look like now? When she thought of him it was always as a young man but he'd be in his eighties now too, so he'd be changed. Just like her. Instead, he was forever young, forever blessed with the beauty of youth.

She reached the gate to her garden and placed a hand on it, pausing to try to catch her breath. Looking up, she saw him. Standing in the garden, one hand raised, the other arm cradling their baby.

'Christopher!' she whispered, as the ground moved beneath her.

Then everything went black.

Liz parked outside the cottage and got out of the car. It was only a short drive from the village and she was still feeling a bit emotional after seeing Nina getting upset. She would definitely make an effort to see her sister every day and to continue to work at their relationship.

She looked around her, taking in the green of the leaves on the trees, the bluebells that grew sporadically around the area along with various daffodils and listened to the sweet sound of birdsong. Living here would be good for her and she would continue to heal while being able to find out who she was now and to decide what she wanted to do with her life.

Her gaze fixed on something up near Zelda's house. She couldn't make out what it was but there seemed to be a mound of something outside the gate, as if someone had dropped a pile of clothes there. It took her a moment to work out what this could mean and then she started running.

When she reached the mound, she dropped to her knees and reached out a hand, fear rushing through her veins like ice.

'Zelda?' She touched a hand to the elderly woman's wrist. 'Zelda, are you OK?'

Zelda was quite clearly not OK; she was lying on the ground, her eyes closed and her skin the colour of ash.

'Zelda? It's Liz. Can you hear me?'

She pressed her fingers to Zelda's wrist and held her breath while pulling her phone from her pocket and swiping the screen with her other hand.

It was there. A pulse. Faint, but there.

'It's all right, Zelda, I'm going to call for help.'

She dialled 999, still holding on tight to her friend.

Liz carried two mugs of tea through to her lounge and handed one to Mia then she slumped onto the sofa near the window. She felt exhausted after the day's events, as though she'd been wrung out and hung up to dry.

'I can't believe this has happened,' she said for what was probably the hundredth time.

'I know, Liz. It's hard to accept it.' Mia nodded solemnly. 'Poor Zelda. I wonder if she's been having symptoms for a while and not telling anyone?'

'Joel said that some people do and some people don't even know they have a problem until they're tested. But she didn't say that she was feeling unwell.'

'Zelda's not one to complain.' Mia sighed.

'That's true.' Liz's throat tightened again. She'd cried most of the afternoon even though she told herself there was no point, that crying wouldn't change anything. But seeing her friend so pale and helpless had broken her heart. Zelda didn't deserve this; she was such a kind person and she should have many more years ahead of her.

The ambulance had arrived quickly but to Liz it had felt too long. The emergency call-taker on the phone had talked her through what to do for Zelda and Liz had tried her best to focus and not to break down. But once the ambulance had arrived and Joel got out, the tears started falling. Joel and his colleague had been brilliant, calm and professional, assessing Zelda then stabilising her before getting her into the ambulance. They'd allowed Liz to go in the ambulance with her and on the way to the hospital she had phoned Mia.

Zelda had been rushed away so Liz had found a chair in a corridor and waited until Mia arrived, then they'd sat together, waiting for news about their friend. Joel had come to update them then had to leave for another call, but Liz and Mia had stayed until they knew what was happening. Eventually, a nurse had come to find them and told them that Zelda had experienced a heart attack and would be kept in hospital for treatment so they should go home and get some rest.

And here they were, on what Liz had thought would be a happy first night in her new home. Instead she was worried sick about Zelda and what would become of her.

'She's in the right place, anyway,' Mia said. 'They can do wonders these days with medication.'

'Do you think she'll need surgery?' Liz cradled her mug between her hands, trying to find some comfort in the heat.

'Perhaps. But they might be able to treat her without it. We'll know more tomorrow, probably.'

'Of course.' Liz nodded. 'I just wish there was something more I could do.'

'It sounds to me that you arriving when you did saved her life.'

'It was terrible, seeing her like that.' Liz hung her head, only looking up when Mia came to her side and slid her arm around her shoulders.

'Just let it out, Liz. No point trying to hold it in. When Zelda comes home she's going to need us to be strong so it's probably best to cry it all out now.'

'You think she'll be able to come home?'

'I think that anyone who tries to stop her won't stand a chance. It might just take a few days or even weeks, but she'll come home. In the meantime, she'll need us to look after the goats and chickens.'

'Of course. I can do that.'

'*We* can do that. We're a team now, remember.'

Liz leant her head on Mia's shoulder and they stayed like that for a while as the light in the room changed and their mugs of tea went cold.

Zelda had to be OK, because Liz had only just found her and she couldn't bear the thought of losing one of her dearest friends.

Chapter 28

Over the next two weeks, along with Liz, Mia threw herself into working on the allotment both at her own plot and on Zelda's. She weeded, prepared soil, planted seed potatoes and other vegetables. She worked hard through the days so she fell exhausted into bed every night. It was, she knew, a way of keeping herself busy so she wouldn't worry constantly about Zelda. Some days she chatted to Liz as they worked, others they worked side by side in silence, the fresh air on their faces and the soil between their fingers the perfect therapy. Every morning and evening they saw to the goats and the chickens, becoming a team effortlessly as they cared for the animals, determined to keep everything ticking over for their friend. Mia had lost two husbands but never lost a friend and the fear of losing Zelda had surprised her with its intensity. She wanted Zelda to recover and to come home so she could enjoy more time with her goats and chickens, more time with her friends.

Mia looked in the mirror one evening after her shower and was surprised by what she saw. Her skin was tanned from the time outdoors, her body firmer than it had been, and when she jokingly flexed her arms, she could see that the skin there was toned with the outline of muscles beneath. She knew she'd been more active recently and it was starting to show on her body, but the best thing about it was that she felt stronger, both physically and mentally. Changes were happening and it confirmed for her that, whatever happened, life went on.

One of the conversations Mia and Liz had enjoyed was about Christmas and what they could plan together. Last Christmas, Mia had struggled because it was so soon after losing Gideon. Joel had been there between shifts and her older sons had visited with their families but her grief had hung above her like a dark cloud and she'd struggled to put on a brave face. This year, however, it could be different. It was only April but planning for the future helped her to feel hopeful and she could see that it did the same for Liz.

'Tea break?' Liz asked, her tone infused with hope.

'Lovely.' Mia sat back on her haunches and dusted the soil from her gardening gloves.

'All this veg that we're planting . . .' Liz said as she handed Mia a tin mug of tea. 'What will we do with it when it grows?'

'Eat it. Give some away. Make kimchi.' Mia shrugged and smiled.

'I was thinking that if there's surplus then we could arrange a kind of swap shop for veg.'

'That's a good idea. A food swap shop.'

'Exactly. And making things like pickles and kimchi is a great idea. It could become an annual thing, kind of like a harvest festival.'

'Sounds good to me. We could also have a stall at the summer fête and at the Christmas market.'

'The village has those?'

'Oh, yes. The summer fête is wonderful. You'll enjoy it.'

'And the Christmas market?'

'It's a December highlight.'

'I'll look forward to both.' Liz blew on her tea then took a sip.

Zelda sighed with relief as the consultant cardiologist, a young woman who she was convinced couldn't be more than twenty-one, but who must be to do the job she did, told her that she could go home. After two weeks of trying to sleep on a ward amidst the beeps of monitors, the snoring of other patients and swishing of scrubs as hospital staff did their rounds, Zelda longed for her own home, her own bed and for the fresh air and open space of the country village allotments more than anything.

She'd known something was very wrong when she'd collapsed outside her garden then woken in hospital – although she had hazy memories of someone holding her hand when she was on the ground outside and then of being transported in an ambulance – but being told she'd suffered a heart attack was terrifying. Apparently, one of the arteries to her heart had been blocked by a clot caused by coronary heart disease and this had caused the heart attack. However, the consultant had reassured her that the medicines they were giving her should help her to avoid another such attack although she would need to be monitored and make a few lifestyle changes. Zelda had promised to do whatever it took so she could go home and so, here she was, two weeks after collapsing, waiting for her lift.

'I really would like to sit outside in the fresh air,' Zelda said when Liz parked outside her gate.

Liz glanced at Mia as they got out of the car and Mia gave a small shrug.

'I don't want to be a nuisance, my darlings, I really don't.' Zelda accepted Liz's arm. 'It's just that I felt such stifling cabin fever spending two weeks in the hospital and I'm desperate to feel the sun on my face and the wind in my hair.'

'Whatever you want is fine with us,' Mia said, 'but I do wish you'd consider coming to stay at mine.'

'I'll be fine.' Zelda waved a hand.

'Well, in that case, Liz and I have a suggestion for you,' Mia said. 'We'd like to take turns to stay at your house for a few days. Just until we know you're all right.'

'We would,' Liz said, pressing her lips together as they waited for Zelda to reply. She'd discussed the idea with Mia because they were worried about Zelda being in that big house all alone. What if she suffered another heart attack or woke in need of help?

Zelda exhaled slowly then smiled at them. 'I'm so grateful to you both for everything. You saved my life, Liz, and you both gave up your time to visit me in hospital and now you've brought me home. The last thing I want is for you to feel you need to do more.'

'Zelda,' Mia said, taking Zelda's hand, 'we love you.'

'We know you'd do the same for us if one of us was ill. It's what friends do,' Liz said.

'Well . . . just for a day or two then.' Zelda nodded. 'But I won't be a nuisance and I will get back on my feet quickly.'

'We know that.' Mia laughed. 'Nothing keeps you down for long.'

'Are you sure you don't want to go inside first?' Liz asked as she gestured at the house.

'I've been inside for too long as it is. I'd love to sit outside and enjoy the morning.'

'Come on, then. I'll put your bag inside later on.' Liz and Mia walked slowly towards the allotments with Zelda between them. 'Shall we have a picnic too?'

'That would be lovely. Although the consultant said I'm not allowed to eat too many cakes. However, I'm sure a little of what I fancy will do me good.'

'I'm sure it will.' Mia chuckled. 'And I can always make some low-fat ones.'

'Part of the attack was my age, I'm sure,' Zelda said. 'You can't get to eighty-three without creaking a bit.'

'I creak enough at fifty-seven,' Mia said.

'So do I at thirty-five,' Liz added, and they all laughed.

Soon, they had Zelda settled in a deckchair with a blanket over her knees and a tin mug of tea in her hand. Mia had done a food shop that morning so Zelda would have all the essentials when she got home and she went up to the house to make some sandwiches while Liz stayed with Zelda. They chatted for a while about what Liz and Mia had planted and drank a flask of tea that Liz had taken in the car in case Zelda was desperate for a cuppa.

When she turned to Zelda to ask her how she was feeling, she saw that her friend had fallen asleep, so she gently removed the mug from her hand and tucked the blanket around her. Zelda needed to rest and recuperate and she would be able to do so with love and support from her friends. There was no way that she would ever feel alone again, not if Liz and Mia could help it.

Epilogue

August had arrived, bringing long sunny days and balmy evenings where the air was filled with the heady fragrance of roses and honeysuckle and sunsets where the sky was painted peach and lilac then faded to ebony pricked with tiny, shimmering diamonds. The chickens were wandering the garden, clucking away happily while their guardian cockerel watched over them.

Zelda had recovered well from her heart attack, but it had changed her. At the start of the year she'd been sad and low, wishing the days away because she felt that existing had become a burden, something to be endured. And then things had shifted. Mia and Liz had entered her life and brought joy and love, had wrapped her up in their friendship in a way that made her heart sing as she awoke each day. That was until her heart had decided to falter. Since the heart attack, though, she'd felt a renewed sense of enjoyment in life and appreciated every single day as if it could be her last, because, of course, she knew it could. Not that she was living under a shadow, though, because she certainly wasn't. Along with Mia and Liz, she'd been busy working the allotments, caring for the goats and chickens and taking some lovely day trips to local parks and gardens. She'd even been into London several times to have afternoon tea at The Ritz and to see musicals including *The Lion King*, *Grease* and *Mamma Mia!*. Every day was a gift and she was excited to see what it would bring.

Mia and Liz had suggested a village swap shop for allotment produce and so today they were holding one. However, rather than do it at the village hall, they'd decided to hold it at the allotment. The weather was glorious and it seemed a shame to hide away inside, plus they'd thought it would be a good way to promote the allotment to the rest of the village, especially to the younger generation. Being able to grow your own produce was a valuable skill as well as very rewarding and time outdoors with nature offered numerous benefits for both physical and mental health and so sharing this with younger people seemed to be an excellent plan. Zelda wasn't getting any younger, and while she didn't want to surrender her plot completely, she had come up with the idea of sharing it with the local primary school. Liz had applied for a job there as a higher-level teaching assistant and one of the things that had secured the job for her – apart from her years of teaching experience and winning personality – had been her offer of starting a gardening initiative for the pupils. The head teacher and governing body had loved the idea and it would start in September when Liz started her new job. Zelda was incredibly proud of Liz, who she'd seen transform from a sad, dejected individual into a strong, healthy woman with plans, hopes and dreams.

As for Mia, she was like the daughter Zelda never had and they often joked about this. Mia was warm and kind, funny and sincere and Zelda wondered how she'd ever coped without her. Even though Mia had been through so much in her life, she still had a ready smile and a generosity with her time and energy that Zelda admired. Over recent months, when Mia's other sons had visited with their families, she'd insisted on including Zelda in their activities and it had been lovely. Mia's eldest son had even pulled Zelda to one side and thanked her for being there for his mum, something that had surprised her. She hadn't thought she'd done anything for Mia but Dane, an editorial director at a publishing house in London, had told Zelda that his mum seemed happier since she'd become friendly with Zelda and Liz. He'd told her that the brothers had been concerned for Mia after Gideon's passing, but Mia being Mia, she'd insisted that she was fine and would just get on with things. However, her friendship with Zelda and Liz had helped her to keep going and the brothers were impressed at the positive impact it had on her.

'Are you ready?' Liz asked, breaking Zelda from her reverie.

'Oh . . . yes, dear. I'm ready.'

'You sure that sunhat is big enough?' Liz teased. She'd bought the hat for Zelda from one of those trendy websites the youngsters knew about. It was a large straw one with a big floppy brim and she'd said it was perfect to keep Zelda cool in the sunshine. Zelda loved how she could have a sneaky nap while wearing it and had done so several times at the allotment when she'd sat with Liz and Mia for a mug of tea or a glass of home-made lemonade.

'It's a fabulous hat,' Zelda replied with a smile.

'Come on then, let's get down there and make this event a success.'

Mia looked up from the stall where she was tweaking the baskets she'd filled with apples, pears, blueberries, potatoes, carrots and more, and smiled when she spotted Liz and Zelda approaching. Zelda looked so well now in her floppy sunhat and pretty floral sundress that they'd found in a wardrobe when they'd been helping Zelda to sort out her house. It was an ongoing process because Zelda had a lot of stuff, but the three women had enjoyed the process, keeping it for rainy days when they couldn't enjoy the outdoors together. Zelda's house had six bedrooms and an attic filled with chests and wardrobes bursting with vintage clothing and other treasures and, rather than leave them there unused, Mia and Liz had introduced Zelda to eBay and Etsy and she'd been having a great time listing things on the sites. At first, she'd been hesitant to use the internet, believing that screen time was wasteful and that it could destroy communication, but Mia and Liz had convinced her that it could have its uses and now Zelda agreed. She'd bought herself an iPad and aside from the websites she used, she also liked that she could video call her friends to speak to them if she was home alone and feeling a bit unsure. She'd also, hilariously, accidentally called them a few times and Mia and Liz had been treated to Zelda's renditions of songs from the musicals they'd seen as well as Zelda cursing at the goats for escaping and heading straight for the allotments, where they'd munched on one plotholder's prize-winning cabbages. He had not been amused and Zelda and Leopold had needed to gift him a lot of eggs and a good bottle of whisky to assuage his grumblings.

'Hello, ladies,' Mia said when Zelda and Liz reached the stall. 'We have a beautiful day for it.'

'Indeed we do.' Zelda came around the stall and appraised Mia's work. 'You've done well, growing all this. Our village will benefit from the fruits of your labours.'

'And yours, Zelda. You're not exactly workshy.'

'I suppose not.' Zelda grinned. 'But this wonderful idea came from you two and I couldn't be prouder.'

Mia and Liz beamed at each other, delighted by what they had achieved.

'Look, there's Joel!' Liz said waving. 'I'll just go and—'

'Go on, girl, what're you waiting for?' Zelda waved Liz away then winked at Mia. 'Summer loving and all that, right?'

'Absolutely.' Mia inclined her head then watched as Liz jogged over to Joel. He was wearing his paramedic uniform because he was attending the event to promote the local ambulance service as part of the initiative to encourage young people to consider pursuing a career in paramedicine.

When Liz reached Joel, they gazed at each other in the way they always did and Mia couldn't help smiling. In spite of their insistence that they were not going to get involved and that they were just friends, it was clear for anyone to see that something deep and meaningful was developing between them. It had, after all, been six months since Liz arrived in Little Bramble and she had a feeling that, sooner or later, Joel and Liz would have to admit their feelings to each other and to everyone else.

'The heart wants what it wants,' she said softly.

'I couldn't agree more,' Zelda replied, her hearing incredibly good for someone her age, Mia thought. 'Now let's see what else we can put on the table, shall we? I'm sure Liz had some Mirabelle plums to swap too, didn't she?'

'It looks good. You, Mum and Zelda should be proud of what you've achieved,' Joel said as he gazed at the allotment swap shop.

Liz nodded. 'We're delighted that so many people got involved and with the local response. Who'd have thought that village allotments could bring a community together like this?'

'I'm very impressed at your plans for the school involvement too. It's a fantastic idea and will benefit the children of Little Bramble for years to come.'

'I hope so.' Liz thought of the plan she'd taken to her interview at the primary school with details of how she'd like to start an educational initiative that would help get children engaged with growing their own fruit and veg, as well engaging with the community by taking what they grew to people in need of it. 'Sharing is caring and all that.'

'You have such a generous heart, Liz.' Joel's voice was gruff and the look in his eyes made her stomach flip. Over recent months they had done as they'd said they would and taken things slowly. They'd become friends, got to know each other and given each other space. Joel shared Liz's love of history and they'd visited some historical sites together, shared some of their favourite historical novels and discussed Liz's dream to one day write non-fiction historical books. Joel had been very encouraging and Liz felt that her dream could become a reality sooner rather than later. They were also running together, something that Liz thoroughly enjoyed, and they planned on training to run a charity race the following spring.

The better Liz got to know him, the more she liked him and she found herself longing for the next time she'd see him. And now, as she admired how handsome he was in his paramedic uniform, she realised that she wanted to be with him more than she'd ever wanted to be with anyone.

'Hey,' he said, a smile playing on his lips. 'Why're you looking at me like that?'

'Like what?' she asked, colour rushing to her cheeks.

'Like . . . well . . . you know.' Now it was his time to blush.

'Would you like to come for dinner this evening?' she asked, deciding that it was time to admit how she felt. To herself and to Joel.

'I would love to join you for dinner.' The warmth in his brown eyes made her heart swell.

'Would you like to . . . bring your toothbrush?' She widened her eyes and pressed her fingernails into her palms. What would she do if he said no?

'My toothbrush?' His brow wrinkled. 'Do you mean in case I . . .'

'. . . want to stay the night,' she finished the sentence when he left it hanging in the air.

Joel tilted his head and rubbed at the back of his neck. Liz's heart was racing as she scanned his face for clues as to what he was feeling.

'Are you sure,' he asked, 'that you're ready for that?' The concern for her that was evident in his eyes made her want him to say yes even more.

'I'm sure,' she said.

And then, in a way she had dreamt of him doing for a long time, he stepped forwards and cupped her face. 'Liz . . . I would love to spend the night with you.'

As he bent his head and kissed her, she slid her arms around his neck and gave herself up to their connection.

When they finally broke apart, Joel took her hand. 'I'm glad you came to Little Bramble.'

'Me too.'

Her mind strayed back to that poster she'd seen on the reprographics room wall all those months ago:

IN THE END, WE ONLY REGRET THE CHANCES WE *DIDN'T* TAKE

Liz had taken a chance, coming here. She'd taken a chance on staying. And she was about to take a chance on loving Joel. But as she gazed at his lovely face, then around them at their friends and family at the allotments, she knew without a doubt it was a chance she was willing to take.

Acknowledgements

My thanks go to:

My husband and children, for your love, support and encouragement. You and the dogs are my everything. Thanks to our little bulldog girl, Zelda, for the name – it seemed a perfect fit for the feisty, resilient and colourful character!

My wonderful agent, Amanda Preston, and all at LBA.

The amazing team at Bonnier Books UK – with special thanks to my fabulous editor, Salma Begum, my lovely editor Claire Johnson-Creek and to Kati Nicholl for the copyedits!

My dear friends – in no particular order – Sarah, Dawn, Deb, Ann, Sam, Clare, Yvonne, Emma, Kelly and Caryn for always being there.

Huge thanks to Yvonne, Valerie and Julie for the inspiration behind this story of female friendship and resilience. Life brings many challenges, but friendship and love can help us to keep going.

My very supportive author and blogger friends. You are all amazing and I love being a part of the writing community.

All the readers who take the time to read, write reviews and share the book love.

The wonderful charities Greyhound Rescue Wales and Hope Rescue for the incredible work you do every single day.

Our wonderful paramedics and everyone in our NHS for being there for us and giving so much despite the daily challenges. Thank you for everything you do!

**Don't miss Cathy Lake's perfect feel-good
summer read . . .**

Emma Patrick's life is spiralling out of control. On the cusp
of her fiftieth birthday, she realises that she's been so focused
on work that she's lost any real connection to people.

When Emma's ageing father needs her help, she decides to go
back home to the countryside to spend some time with him.
But returning to Little Bramble after years away is filled
with complications and people she'd rather avoid.

To her surprise, as Emma settles in, she finds herself loving
village life. When the opportunity to get involved in the
running of the summer fête comes her way, soon she's
embracing jam making, cake baking and bunting.
And with romance brewing, Emma begins to doubt the
glamorous city life that she worked so hard to build . . .

Available now